Caligula

Also by Allan Massie

Allan Massie

Caligula

SCEPTRE

Copyright © 2003 Allan Massie

First published in Great Britain in 2003 by Hodder and Stoughton
A division of Hodder Headline

The right of Allan Massie to be identified as the Author
of the Work has been asserted by him in accordance with the
Copyright, Designs and Patents Act 1988.

A Sceptre Book

1 3 5 7 9 10 8 6 4 2

A CIP catalogue record for this title is
available from the British Library

ISBN 0 340 82313 5

Typeset in Sabon by Palimpsest Book Production Limited,
Polmont, Stirlingshire

Printed and bound in Great Britain by
Mackays of Chatham plc, Chatham, Kent

Hodder and Stoughton
A division of Hodder Headline
338 Euston Road
London NW1 3BH

For Alison, as ever

The Julio-Claudians

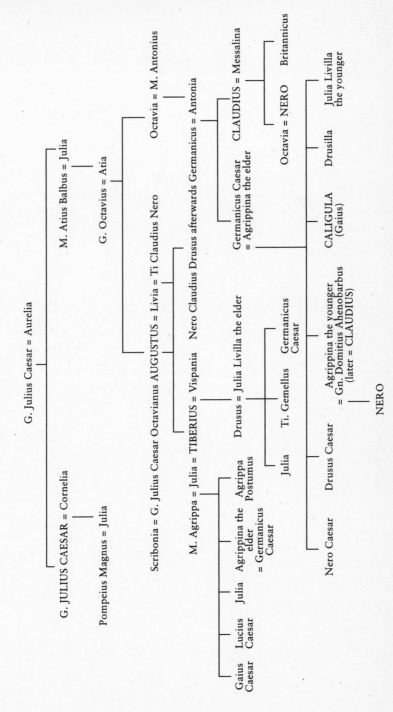

Part I

I

It is more than a suggestion. It is a command, and one that I dare not disobey. How happily I would do so, how happily rest in my retirement, withdrawn from tumult, here where there is no sound but that of the cicadas among the olive trees; where my gaze is held by the distant uncaring sea; where I know for the moment only an azure calm, that seems to stream down from on high. How happily I repose on these odorous heights, oblivious of duty, military glory, politics, listening only for that siren's call which the old Emperor himself longed to hear in the hope that it would soothe his tormented spirit.

And now this command, tersely delivered, that I should write the biography of the late, and by few lamented, Emperor Gaius. Why does she want it? Why is it needed? For what malign purpose?

Of course you may say, as my boy Agathon gravely suggested, that the request is an honour, and that she demands it as an act of family piety. No doubt this is so, up to a point. She is not lacking in family piety. I know that, to my cost. And perhaps she retains some affection for me, inasmuch as she is capable of feeling that for anyone but her so charming, as I am assured, son. But why Gaius? Why seek to rehabilitate him – for that must be her purpose. Would it not be better to commission another – yet another – biography of her hero-father, the sublime Germanicus?

I put this to Agathon, not that he understands, or indeed cares, for he has a blithe lack of curiosity about the past. Why should he? He lives entirely in the present and is careful only of my comfort in so far as that ensures his. As for me, I take pleasure in him, but do not love him. I have loved no one since Caesonia was torn from me, and indeed I wonder if I truly loved her, or whether she merely – merely! – intoxicated and enslaved me. Perhaps I was never capable of love, in the best and fullest sense of the word, but only of lust. That certainly, often. How Agrippina and I tore at each other in the year of our affair! Now even that has passed. I do no more than toy with Agathon, this curly-headed Greek boy of eighteen with his grave face, lustrous eyes, fringed by long girlish lashes, and smooth limbs. When I first saw him lines of Horace I have long loved came to my mind – 'If you were to place him in a group of girls, the most discerning strangers could scarce tell the difference' – and so I bought him. That was three years ago. He is now fond of me in his way, I think, mildly fond, and I am at ease with him.

These reflections distract me, which is why I indulge in them.

'No one,' Agrippina writes, 'knew Gaius better than you, for so long. No one remained as loyal. Be now, I pray you, as loyal to his memory, poor Gaius.'

'Poor Gaius' – a note of tenderness that is uncharacteristic.

I shall submit, because I have no choice.

And it will be occupation. It may be also that it will bring me to an understanding of the shipwreck I have made of my own life and of the iniquities of our times. But if this is the case, if I write all that I know, and dare to recall, that will not serve Agrippina's purpose. Therefore I shall write first for myself – and for posterity – before preparing a doctored or sanitised version for the Empress.

II

Is there anything in life, even first love, more exhilarating than your first military posting? It is the moment when you become, in your own eyes, a man. It is the moment for which, as a Roman nobleman, you have been reared. My heart sang throughout the long journey from Rome to the Rhine. Nothing – nor cold nor wet nor bad inns nor the insolence of a magistrate encountered at Lugdunum – could depress my spirits. I was eighteen, rich enough, handsome enough, with ancestors enough to make my name respected, and I was on my way to serve as a legate on the staff of the Emperor's grandson Germanicus Caesar, already spoken of as the most audacious general of the day, the darling of the soldiers, surely himself emperor-in-waiting. I was certain I could win glory at his side. My uncle, who had arranged the posting, was equally certain that it would put me firmly on the first rung of the ladder of preferment.

Actually, though we talked of Germanicus familiarly as the grandson of the Emperor, or Princeps, as Augustus still preferred to be called, this wasn't quite accurate.

Though I write this for myself and not, as the later version will be, for Agrippina, nevertheless it now occurs to me that my own grandchildren, or even their children, may wish some day to read this full and unexpurgated version, if only to learn what manner of man I was, and also perhaps to learn the true, rather than the approved, history of my time.

So, for their benefit, I should perhaps lay out the relationships in what we had already come to call, shame-facedly, the imperial family.

At the time of which I write Augustus was still alive, and his authority was unquestioned. He was very old, in his seventies, but, though he suffered from rheumatism in cold weather, and though his health had been poor in his youth, remained vigorous and alert. I knew him, my grandfather having been his friend when they were both young. As a small boy I often met him walking on the Palatine, and he would pat my cheek or pinch my ear and say, 'I do hope you're not going to grow up to be as naughty as your grandpa.' Then he would chuckle and give me a sweet or a dried apricot.

That is by the way. Augustus was married three times, but had only one child, Julia. Her mother Scribonia was a cousin of my grandfather. So Julia was a sort of cousin of mine too. However, since I was the child of my father's old age, my mother being his fourth wife, I was actually younger than any of Julia's five children.

She herself was married three times, first to Augustus' nephew Marcellus, then to Marcus Agrippa, his close colleague, a man of humble birth but great ability, finally, and disastrously, to the Emperor's stepson Tiberius.

Agrippa was the father of all her children. There were two daughters, Agrippina and Julia. (Agrippina is called 'the elder' to distinguish her from her daughter of the same name who has commissioned this history.) You will learn more of this Agrippina soon, but the younger Julia plays no part in my account.

There were also three boys: Gaius, Lucius and Agrippa, called Postumus because he was born after his father's death. Augustus adored the first two and would have made them his heirs, but death cheated his purpose. The young Agrippa was an idiot, given to violence, and had to be confined; he was later disposed of.

When Augustus divorced Scribonia because she nagged him, he married Livia. They remained together for more than forty years. My mother used to mutter that he was 'too frightened to divorce her', but that was only when Livia had irritated her. In other moods she called them 'the perfect married couple'. They may have been. Who knows the truth of any marriage?

Livia had two sons by her previous husband: Tiberius and Drusus. I shall say more about Tiberius in time, much more. Drusus was dead before my story starts, but his son was my commander Germanicus Caesar, whose wife was Augustus' granddaughter Agrippina. So in a sense it is accurate enough to call Germanicus the Emperor's grandson, since he was the son of his stepson and the husband of his granddaughter.

There was another connection. His mother was Antonia, who was the daughter of Mark Antony, first Augustus's colleague and then his rival, and Octavia, Augustus's much loved sister. Later of course Antony deserted Octavia when he was seduced by the Egyptian queen Cleopatra; but Octavia and Antonia were always regarded as members of the imperial family, and Augustus was delighted that Antonia should marry his stepson Drusus. It was a happy marriage and Germanicus always spoke well of both his parents. Admittedly his father, as I have already remarked, was dead by the time I knew Germanicus, and men find it easier to speak well of dead fathers than of living ones. The same goes, in reverse, for sons who predecease their fathers. Tiresome often in life, they are made perfect by an untimely death.

It is fair however to say that Germanicus' story might have been different had his father lived. So indeed might Rome's.

To resume: I travelled north in high expectancy. I was received in a manner fitting to my birth, but also as a friend.

Germanicus clapped me on the back, hugged me, and kissed me on both cheeks.

'We don't stand on formality here,' he said. 'My wife and I regard all you young legates as members of the family.'

I was enraptured by the warmth of his greeting. No doubt I blushed with pride and pleasure. (I blushed easily in my virtuous youth.) It is of course natural for a young officer to delight in receiving a warm welcome from his commander, but there was more to it than that. Germanicus had been my hero, even my idol and inspiration, since I was a small boy and watched him excelling in the Troy game, which Augustus loved to watch young aristocrats playing.

There are many statues of Germanicus in Rome and other cities of the Empire, but none that I have seen does justice to him. They show that he was handsome – the handsomest man of his time, as was agreed; but they cannot catch his charm or the vivacity of his manner. No sculptor – not even the most masterly of the Greeks, Phidias – could make manifest in marble the combination of strength and delicacy that he possessed. None could convey the readiness of his smile, and, of course, statues being dumb, they cannot give you any sense of his voice – a voice that was both light and firm and which rendered the harshest Latin mellifluous as Greek.

'But of course,' he said, 'I was forgetting, you are indeed family. Agrippina has been eagerly awaiting your arrival.'

It was, as I soon understood, characteristic of Germanicus to introduce Agrippina so quickly into his conversation. He truly adored her, and she him. There has never been a more harmonious marriage; they had eyes only for each other. I believe that from the day of his marriage Germanicus never looked at another woman. As for Agrippina she was as virtuous as she was strong-willed. No wonder they had nine children. Three unfortunately died in infancy, to their great grief. One of these, called confusingly Gaius like their youngest, is said to have been adored by all. Certainly when he died his great-grandmother Livia dedicated a statue of him dressed as a Cupid to Capitoline Venus, and I have heard that Augustus used to keep a replica of this statue in his bedroom and would kiss it whenever he entered the chamber. It's pleasant to recall such tender affection, given the ravages that the imperial family would inflict on itself.

Germanicus now led me to Agrippina, talking all the while

about my journey and never failing to greet the legionaries we encountered with a smile and a friendly word.

The children were at supper. Agrippina always saw to this meal herself rather than leaving it, as is usual, to her slaves. She used to say that her children were her jewels and that nothing pleased her more than to look after them. No doubt this was true, but I believe that the explanation for her unusual conduct is to be found in her own childhood. Her mother Julia was notoriously promiscuous – you may know that her father Augustus eventually had her exiled and held under house arrest on account of her flagrant and very public immorality. This being her nature, she neglected her own children who would have grown up anyhow if it hadn't been for the love that Augustus and, more reluctantly, Livia, lavished on them. Agrippina often told me that, despite this, her own childhood had been miserable; she particularly resented her grim and taciturn stepfather Tiberius, Livia's son, the future Emperor. Though she rarely spoke of Julia, she had also been disgusted by her behaviour. So she was determined that her own children should know nothing but love and security. She may have overdone it. The two elder boys, Nero and Drusus, loved her so passionately that their first fear was to offend her. Though they lived to be adults, neither grew up. As for Gaius . . . well, more of that later.

I had my first sight of him now. He was stamping about the floor dressed in the miniature uniform of a private soldier and waving a wooden sword with which he from time to time smote one of his brothers on the back. When he did so his sister Drusilla scooped him up and covered his face with kisses. Then she offered his face to Germanicus to kiss, while the little boy, who was not quite three, struggled and protested that he was a soldier and not to be kissed. Everyone laughed and there were cries of 'little pet' and 'lambkin' and such like. Germanicus took the boy and placed him astride his shoulders and said, 'Now you're the general of the army, the commander-in-chief.'

At which Gaius crowed in triumph. Meanwhile young Nero, though only seven, greeted me with grave courtesy and hoped I had had a good journey.

Later that evening after dinner, which was attended by the other young legates, I was asked by Agrippina to remain behind, 'to talk family matters'. This was merely an excuse. What she really wanted was information about the state of things in Rome, and by things she meant of course politics.

At first this surprised me. The only women I knew well were my mother and my aunts, and they never talked about politics. In retrospect I can't blame them. One aunt's husband, the austere but brutal T Quinctius Crispinus, had been one of those accused of committing adultery with the Emperor's daughter, Julia, dismissed from the Senate and exiled. My own father had suffered likewise, for the same reason, at the same time, unjustly, my mother averred. No matter: the ladies knew well the danger and the horror of political involvement in the New Rome where, already in the reign of Augustus, benign 'Father of his Country', people were learning to be secretive even within the family circle, and to eschew speaking their mind to even those whom they thought to be their close friends. So my mother and her sisters occupied themselves only with domestic matters, and talked nothing but trivialities.

Accordingly, when Agrippina began to question me closely, I was at first reserved. When, soon, she spoke her own opinions, or what might be her own opinions if they were not uttered merely to test me, I was suspicious, then alarmed, and only after some time, entranced. She seemed to me wonderfully fearless. I was honoured that she should trust me, and regretted only that, on account of my habitual shyness and reserve, even with those of my own age and rank, I must appear to her ignorant and clownish; a sore disappointment.

Augustus was dying. Everyone, she said, knew that, and many were afraid, some hopeful. He had been there, it seemed, forever. You had to be a man of sixty to remember Actium and the Civil Wars which had ended with the death of Antony. Yet Rome was still nominally a Republic. Augustus himself in the monumental record of his reign, the *Res gestae*, had boasted that he had restored the Republic and claimed that while only equal to his fellow magistrates in power, he excelled them only in authority; a fine distinction which deceived nobody. Yet undoubtedly some now looked for the restoration of the true Republic, my own uncles and cousins among them. Vain hope.

Agrippina knew better. She knew that we – my family and those like us – were only noble. She and her family were imperial.

'My stepfather Tiberius,' she said, 'pretends to be a Republican of the old school. He is forever grumbling about what he called "these imperial assumptions which are an insult to the nobility". He's very mindful that he is a Claudian, member of a family which can boast of consuls for centuries, while in his cups, where he is often to be found, he will mutter that Augustus' father was a small-town moneylender, while my father Marcus Vipsanius Agrippa was a nobody, nothing known of his father or family. Well, that's as may be, but he was a great man and a great general. As for Tiberius, he's an old humbug, you know. When Augustus dies he'll protest that he's unworthy of the succession, and wishes the Senate to resume its old pre-eminence, and then – just you watch – he'll assume all Augustus' powers, protesting that they've been forced on him.'

I was charmed by her frankness, charmed into rashness.

'Is there nobody else?' I said. 'Your brother Agrippa Postumus?'

'Poor Postumus,' she sighed. 'Nobody likes him. He'd be his own worst enemy, if it wasn't for Tiberius. And Livia of course. We mustn't forget the old she-devil. She hates him. She hates me too. I'm lucky she adores Germanicus. Well, everybody must. Except Tiberius of course. He's jealous as can be.'

She was right about Tiberius and right too about her brother. He survived the new reign for only a few days. Some say he was put to death by posthumous (rich irony) order of Augustus; some that Livia was responsible, others Tiberius. Nobody knows and it doesn't matter.

III

Germanicus was of a sunny disposition; the world grew bright in his presence. It is no wonder his troops loved him. Admittedly, he had his critics. One of his senior legates, A Caecina Severus, was heard to grumble that popularity was not the test of a commander, and was anyway easily attained if you did not subject the men to regular and rigorous drill.

At the same time Germanicus was ambitious for glory, and his ambition was thwarted. These were the years after the disaster in the Teutoburg Wood in which, through rashness and carelessness, Quintilius Varus in command of three legions allowed himself to be surprised and surrounded by the Germans, and all were annihilated. This disaster provoked a change in imperial policy. Forgotten was the divine promise of 'unlimited Empire' which Virgil recorded. Instead Augustus ordered that the frontier was to be fixed on the Rhine and that no attempt be made to subdue Germany. At first Tiberius, as the senior commander of the armies, opposed and resented this restriction on aggressive war. Later he persuaded himself of its wisdom.

Germanicus was not likewise convinced. He was young and ardent. He sought glory which was apparently to be denied him. It was not long before Agrippina, forgetting that the policy had been determined by her grandfather Augustus himself, insinuated that it testified to Tiberius' jealousy of Germanicus, and his fear that Germanicus winning glory and Empire would be seen by all as a more suitable Emperor.

At the time, being young and eager for warlike action myself, I did not question this interpretation. Now I am not so sure. Agrippina was certain that Tiberius was deeply jealous of Germanicus, who was of course his own nephew, and feared him on account of his popularity with the armies and the People. Perhaps he did, though it is possible to argue to the contrary. Be that as it may, the decision to abandon the attempt to conquer Germany was surely wise. Caesar took ten years to subdue Gaul, and that conquest was to be threatened by frequent rebellions, before the Gauls saw the advantages of Empire. The Germans are braver and harder warriors than the Gauls, and are moreover devoted to the idea of Liberty. The effort to subject them would have been dangerous, perhaps even beyond the means of Rome. And I do not believe that the freedom-loving Germans would ever have submitted in their hearts to our rule.

Nevertheless Agrippina fed her husband with her suspicions, and clouded even his sunny nature. He began to wonder if Tiberius was determined not only to deny him glory, but even to destroy him.

Now I see Agrippina as his evil genius. But then . . . then I adored her. I do not mean that I desired her. My adoration of her was part of my adoration of Germanicus. They were in my mind inextricably joined together in perfect harmony. Welcoming me into their innermost circle, at first only, I suppose, on account of my birth, subsequently because they perceived my merits and formed an affection for me, they gave me what I had never enjoyed: a warm and loving family life. Indeed, if I was in love, it was truly with the whole family of Germanicus and Agrippina.

I had no brothers or sisters. Now I found myself adopted as an elder brother by six adorable children.

Adorable? Yes, I stick to the word. Of course it would not be many more years before strait-laced Roman matrons – like my aunts – would be severely critical of them, and of the upbringing Agrippina had given them. And indeed, in one respect, by the standards of the world, this was rightly deplored. They were so natural. None of them knew what it was to be a hypocrite, something that, in the corruption of our times, the children of the great are taught to practise as soon as they can speak. In time, as I shall show, Gaius too learned this lesson, so necessary now that the essential Republican virtue, freedom of speech, has been outlawed, now that books are burned by official command, to destroy liberty and suppress criticism. This is the world we are condemned to inhabit, and in which the wise man can strive only to practise moderation, steering a path, safe from intrigue and peril, between obstinate denial and disgusting subservience.

But these children knew none of this. They laughed when they were happy, cried when they were hurt, gave way to ill-temper when they were crossed; in short, behaved as nature intended and had made them.

It is true that Nero, the eldest boy, was reserved, shy, ever mild in demeanour, so much so that you might have taken him, even at his tender years, for a cautious politician. But this too was his nature. It dismayed and pained him if he thought he had given offence, and he was even then careful to avoid the appearance of doing so. He was a child of warm affections, graceful, charming, tender-hearted. He loved Agrippina passionately, was dazzled by his father, and so anxious to please him that he did not know how to address him. Easily alarmed, ill at ease with the rough humour of the legions, he attached himself to me so completely that it is not too much to say that he had fallen in love. Agrippina was delighted. 'You have given him the self-confidence which was the only virtue he lacked,' she said, after I had been a few weeks in the camp.

Little Gaius was the soldiers' pet. They loved to see him swagger about the camp in his uniform of a tiny legionary, waving his toy sword and shouting out commands learned from the centurions. I can even recall him drilling a small detachment of them who pretended to understand his disjointed and often contradictory commands. Of course he was too young to understand the meaning of the words he shouted; he had picked them up by imitation, as a cage-bird may mimic the speech of its owner. As the baby of the family he was, I suppose, over-indulged, even spoiled, not only by the soldiers, who gave him his nickname Caligula, or Bootikins, but also by his three sisters. Agrippina sometimes reproved the other children, though only mildly, but never little Gaius. Perhaps she would have been inclined to be more strict, even severe, with her brood, but Germanicus would say, 'Let them be; we mustn't bruise their spirit.' Then he would look melancholy, and sigh: 'The world will do that soon enough.' Once, I remember, little Gaius lifted a hammer over a fine piece of pottery, preparing to smash it. 'Must you?' Germanicus said. The boy nodded and beamed his ready smile. 'Well,' said his father, 'if you must, you must'; and the hammer was brought down and the fine Attic piece reduced to smithereens.

Have I ever been as happy as in these summer months in the camp on the banks of the Rhine?

IV

Augustus died, and became a god. Some pious idiot, or sycophant, assured the Senate he had seen his soul ascending in
flames to the heavens. Germanicus plunged into deep mourning.
Agrippina was rash enough to say, if only in private, that the old
man had done the State a disservice by not hanging on for a few
more years. She was sure that, had he done so, he would have
named Germanicus, and not Tiberius, as his successor.

News of the death provoked unrest in the armies. The
legions stationed in Pannonia mutinied, demanding higher
pay, fixed terms of service, and timely discharge with generous
pensions. The demands were reasonable, the timing and the
method employed to secure them dangerous.

Word of the mutiny came to the armies on the Rhine.
Mutiny is like plague, the infection easily caught. Almost
before we were aware of what was afoot, the soldiers flared
up in frenzy. It was a contagious madness.

Germanicus acted swiftly. No one could question his courage. He called the men together and addressed them. Where,
he asked, was their pride, where their military restraint, where
their discipline?

His speech, however, encouraged them to voice their demands
still more fiercely. The fiercest outcries came from the veterans, weary of service and eager for the retirement that was
denied them.

But there was no hostility to Germanicus himself. Indeed
some cursed Tiberius, known for his harsh discipline. Others
went further, calling for Germanicus to seize the Empire. If he
did so, they would follow him devotedly.

The idea horrified him, or seemed to. He tried to leave the stage from which he had spoken – the tribunal. They opposed his withdrawal. Some drew their swords and waved them threateningly. But he cried out, 'I would rather die than break my oath of allegiance.' Whereupon he drew his own sword and made as if to stab himself, but was prevented by those around him who seized his arm. Then a certain Calusidius, a known troublemaker and one of the ringleaders of the mutiny, offered his own sword to his commander.

'Try this one,' he said, 'it's sharper.'

Then, amid mocking laughter and with much confusion, we managed to withdraw.

In our private quarters, secure under loyal guards, Germanicus shook, though whether with anger or fear I could not say. He was flushed and certainly nervous, as who wouldn't be? Mutiny is a reversal of all that is normal. Once it is unleashed all rules of life are broken, natural superiority is set at naught, fear governs all. I learned then how much depends on the habit of command and obedience. When that is broken, all is discord.

Besides, it is likely that Germanicus had a double reason for his fear. The news that the mutinous soldiers had in effect offered to make him Emperor in place of Tiberius, if he would only consent to their demands, was sure to be carried to Rome; and there suspicion would fester in Tiberius' dark mind. That Germanicus had rejected the invitation would count for little. Tiberius would remember only that the legions were ready to dispose of him and acclaim his nephew; henceforth a rival to be feared.

At Germanicus' request, while he composed himself, I made my way to inform Agrippina of what had happened. She was already alarmed, and no wonder: the sound of mutiny echoed round the camp like the rumble of a thunderstorm. The children sensed the danger. The smell of fear is like rank sweat, disgusting, inescapable. Young Nero, more alert to realities than his siblings, trembled and wept. He clung to me begging me to stop them from cutting his throat. Only little Gaius Caligula was unaffected; he stood on a table and crowed, waving his wooden sword.

When I told Agrippina of how the mutineers had clamoured to hail Germanicus as Emperor, she sat rigid as a statue. For a long time, as it seemed, she said nothing.

Then, 'If he had not declined . . .' she said, and fell silent again.

'There are times,' she said at last, 'when the course of danger is the only road to safety . . .'

I dared not reply, either to calm or foster temptation. Instead I busied myself comforting and reassuring young Nero.

Night closed in. The sound of singing, drunken singing, came from without. Some of the mutineers had broken into the quartermaster's store and looted it.

At last Germanicus joined us. He too had been drinking. His face was flushed, and the wine had excited rather than calmed his mind. He could not conceal his apprehension. Accustomed to easy popularity, never having had his authority questioned, untried in a crisis, he was at a loss now, when brought against brutish realities. He picked up the children, one by one, and kissed them, feverishly, as if he might never do so again, or see them for a long time. To be fair, it was evident that his first fears were for Agrippina and the young ones. But there was fear for himself also. I saw that, and my admiration fell away. He was caught between the desire to assert himself and his fear which impelled him to seek some means of appeasing the mutineers. Yet, though I could not admire him at that moment, his very weakness made him more attractive. He mopped the sweat from his temples and talked too much in his agitation. I cannot remember what he said. There was no matter in his words.

One of my colleagues, a young knight, Marcus Friso, drew me aside.

'Our commander is an actor in a play he doesn't understand,' he said.

What was I to make of this confidence? Was he tempting me into disloyalty? I shrugged him off, and made no reply. But I knew he spoke the truth.

This Friso, as I later learned, was Tiberius' man in the camp, sent there to spy on Germanicus. So I was wise to distrust him. But I did so because he smelled wrong. I have an unusually acute sense of smell (which is why I detest cities). My nose is, as it were, an organ of judgement, and Friso smelled of rotten apples, corruption.

There was a stand-off lasting two days. Germanicus consulted senior centurions who had remained loyal. Some advised harsh measures. 'Take,' they said, 'Calusidius and a couple of ringleaders and cut their throats. The men will then return to duty.' But Germanicus shrank from this advice.

He resolved to send Agrippina and the children away to a place of safety under heavily armed escort. She was loth to consent. She spoke out angrily, reminding him that she was the granddaughter of Augustus and the daughter of Agrippa, matchless in war. She would not run away, but would be worthy of her blood, no matter how high the danger. She spoke bravely, perhaps to shame her husband. But, with a great show of force, he insisted.

All this was done before us, members of his staff. It is possible that the exchanges between them went otherwise when they were closeted together, with no audience. That is certainly my opinion now.

Agrippina yielded. I was given command of the escort. Agrippina and the children mounted a covered wagon. I surrounded it with cavalry, Gallic auxiliaries, and two maniples of loyal legionaries. So, slowly, we made our way towards the gate of the camp, while Agrippina and her ladies, and the children too, sent up wails of lamentation.

The mutineers had posted guards at the gate. I advanced,

alone, assuming an appearance of calm. One seized my horse's bridle. Another extended his sword towards me. I looked him in the eye. I smelled fear on him too. So far, the mutineers had abstained from irrevocable, unpardonable violence, unlike, as we subsequently discovered, their fellows among the Pannonian legions where one general, Gnaeus Cornelius Lentulus, had been stoned and saved from death by a detachment of the Praetorian Guard. So I commanded the men who had stopped me to step aside.

'I am carrying,' I said, 'the Lady Agrippina and her children to safety, as instructed by your commander, Germanicus himself.'

This disturbed them. They began to argue among themselves, while we waited, and the gate remained barred against us.

'Germanicus,' I said, now raising my voice so that it carried to the groups of disaffected legionaries who were standing by in attitudes that suggested both truculence and uncertainty, 'Germanicus,' I repeated, 'can no longer trust his wife and children to the care and protection of Roman soldiers, but has commanded me to escort them to the camp of our allies, the Treviri' – and I indicated the mounted auxiliaries who belonged to that tribe, and who certainly at that moment looked fierce enough.

My words disconcerted them. They began to waver. At that moment Agrippina thrust her head out of the wagon, and imperiously demanded that we be allowed to pass. Little Gaius Caligula's head appeared over her shoulder; he opened his mouth and began to bawl.

'Caligula,' one soldier cried out, 'is he to be taken from us? Can we not be trusted to care for our little darling?'

'No,' I said. 'Germanicus fears for his safety, and must do so as long as you behave like ravening wolves and not like Roman soldiers. How can he trust Caligula, his dearest child, to men who have forgotten their duty of obedience?'

Then all was confusion. Some cried out that the gate should be opened, others that Caligula should not be allowed to leave the camp where everyone loved him. Some swore that if he remained with them, not a hair of his head should he harmed. And others now cursed the agitators who had led them astray and protested their undying loyalty.

So, gradually, the mutiny subsided. And that is how the infant Caligula made the restoration of order possible and saved the honour of the army.

What followed was less impressive, was indeed, as I now realise, shameful.

The repentant legionaries took the law into their own hands. They themselves arrested the leading rebels, whom they had followed ardently a few hours previously. The men with swords at the ready formed themselves into a circle. The prisoners were paraded on a platform. The question was put and, if the answer was 'guilty', the wretched victim was thrown to the ground and killed. It seemed as if the men revelled in the massacre, as if this slaughter purged them of the guilt which they themselves had incurred by the act of mutiny.

Germanicus made no effort to intervene. So order was restored and he escaped the odium which naturally attaches itself to the commander who inflicts harsh punishment, however well-merited that punishment is. The men acted as both judges and executioners, and then swore that they would follow Germanicus wherever he led them. When he heard this, Germanicus wept, and allowed himself to be embraced by soldiers whose hands left bloody stains on his neck and shoulders.

Meanwhile, in Pannonia, the Emperor's son, Drusus, subdued the mutiny by more orthodox methods.

I was young then, young enough to think things are as they seem. Our deliverance appeared a miracle. The mutineers had not felt the disgrace inherent in the repudiation of just authority, but when they saw themselves abandoned by Agrippina and her children because they could no longer be entrusted with them, their hearts were touched, generous sentiments prevailed, natural affections were revived, and they knew shame. So indeed it was, or seemed. Now, cynical on account of all I have since experienced, I ask what was theatre, what reality?

V

I remained for two years with the army on the Rhine. My experience then is not part of Caligula's story. How could it be? In truth, since I was now commanding troops in the field, and no longer attached to Germanicus' personal staff, I saw little of Agrippina and the children. Yet I cannot pass over these seasons without comment.

Tiberius, as I have said, had chosen to accept Augustus' decision, formed after the disaster forever associated with the name of Varus, that the limits of Empire had been reached; that there was nothing to be gained by attempting to push its frontier beyond the Rhine and up to the River Elbe. As long as the Germans on the north side of the Rhine remained quiescent, and did not threaten Gaul, the German nations should remain free. At most, Tiberius would sanction only punitive expeditions, brief and disciplinary.

This decision irked Germanicus. He thought it pusillanimous. He persuaded himself, or was persuaded by Agrippina, that the policy had been adopted to deny him glory. He said, 'If the Empire does not continue to expand, then it must decay. Such is the law of Nature.'

His words suggested that the argument, unvoiced but deeply felt, between him and Tiberius was purely political, a matter of what was best for Rome. Yet it was precisely because we no longer inhabited the Republic, but instead lived in the intense shadowy suspicion that is inherent in despotism, that the argument could never be brought into the open, debated in that Forum in which free men thresh out policies.

So Germanicus was compelled to dissemble. Apparently

obedient to the Emperor's command, apparently accepting the restrictions it enjoined, he nevertheless went his own way. Each winter was passed in rigorous training and the preparation for a summer campaign across the Rhine, and each spring this was launched. We marched into Germany, engaged the tribes, won victories, took prisoners, and taught the enemy, as we supposed, fear and respect. Yet, at the end of summer, we withdrew, harassed by raiding parties as we did so, right to the very brink of the river, and returned to our camp, with no enduring advantage having been gained. More than once we came close to disaster, averted as much by fortune as by skill and courage.

Everything hitherto had inclined me to be of Germanicus' opinion, and not only because he inspired both affection and admiration in me. Even now it seems natural that I should have thought as I did. I was young, and youth is ardent and adventurous. There was no one who loomed larger in my imagination than Caesar himself; his *History of the Gallic Wars* was my inspiration. It seemed to me that we in our generation should seek to emulate his ambition and audacity. He had conquered Gaul; why should we hesitate to subdue the Germans, no more formidable an enemy than those whom Caesar had brought within the Empire?

Moreover I had listened to Agrippina, and felt her seductive power. Why should I doubt what she was certain of: that Tiberius' prohibitions were inspired by fear and envy of his glorious nephew?

VI

My term of service at an end, I was recalled to Rome, wiser, as I think, and chastened. For a little I threw myself, with all the ardour that I had brought to war, into the delights of the city. I frequented the baths and theatres. I was in demand for dinner-parties. There was attached to me something of the glamour that, in the eyes of so many, belonged to Germanicus. If at any such gathering I found one who doubted or questioned his achievements on the Rhine, I spoke out eloquently in denial. My account of how we had come upon the scene of Varus' disaster and of the horrors we had known made me a sort of lion. I was asked time and again to repeat it. Those of my generation who had not yet known war – some of them thankfully – looked on me with a mixture of awe and jealousy. It is not surprising that I very quickly acquired a mistress, the wife of a senator; she was ten years my senior, and I was by no means her first illicit lover. My name and my beauty might by themselves have been insufficient to attract her; she was drawn by something grim, distrustful, even dangerous in my manner. She was a woman who had long surrendered all claim to virtue. She now longed to be treated harshly, even to be punished. I did not fail to satisfy her desire, and despised myself for the pleasure this gave me.

When I had been in Rome some weeks I was summoned to an audience with the Emperor. (I call him that, though Tiberius disdained, or affected to disdain, the title, even to resent it, as Augustus had done, and preferred still to be known merely as the Princeps, or First Citizen, of the sham Republic.)

Tiberius was now in his late fifties, still tall and broad-shouldered, but stooped and slow-moving. His character, if you credit the pseudo-science of physiognomy, could be read in his face: the eyes clouded, the thin-lipped mouth down-turned, the jaw strong. He was formidable. It was said – though on what evidence I am ignorant – that the loquacious Augustus used to leave off chattering and fall silent when his stepson entered the room. And others put it about that the old Emperor had once remarked, 'Poor Rome, to be chewed by these heavy jaws.' But that is the sort of thing people say.

Now he looked on me for a long time without speaking, then ordered a slave to pour wine, then told me to be seated. When we were alone, he continued for some minutes in silence. I felt his gaze fixed upon me, and dared not meet his eyes.

At last he said, 'Your father served with me in Illyricum, a good soldier, whom I respected.'

This was encouraging. I had not expected him to speak of my father, who had died in exile after being accused of adultery with Tiberius' wife, Julia. I bowed my head in acknowledgement.

'He was a good Republican,' Tiberius said, 'as we should all wish to be.'

He took a deep swallow of his wine, and sighed.

'But the Republic is now impossible. We have reared a generation fit only for slavery. They speak even of "the imperial family". I detest the expression, but there it is. People use it, and what can I do?'

No reply, evidently, was required.

'You're a handsome young man, which, as I remember, is more than could have been said of your father . . .'

He looked me up and down, as if I was a slave for sale in the market.

He said, 'I fought a dozen campaigns, fifty battles, against the Germans, advanced three, four weeks' march into their forests, brought my men out again, never lost an eagle. Did you know that? Nothing enduring was gained, ever. Did you know that too? My nephew Germanicus – your friend, I hope, and by the command of the late Augustus also my adopted son and heir – is young, ardent, beloved, they tell me, by his men, as I never have been – though they dare not add that. Does he believe he can succeed where I failed, where my father-in-law Agrippa also failed?'

I hesitated. He did not seem to be watching me. Yet I felt under observation. The room, deep in the palace, was very still. It looked out into a little courtyard, and onto a statue of the winged Mercury, god of, among others, liars, which rose over a fountain's dancing water.

'I am not in his confidence, Princeps,' I replied. 'But his expeditions have been undertaken to deter the tribes and remind them of Rome's power.'

'Just so. As it should be. You reassure me. Give yourself some more wine, there's no need to summon the slave. And fill my cup too.'

As I did so, he stretched forward and gripped my thigh, digging his nails in.

'Agrippina does not love me,' he said. 'You needn't trouble to deny that. She blames me for her mother's misfortune, as if I, or anyone, could have controlled Julia. A wise man once said to me that eventually we all become prisoners of our own character. He said it with reference to Augustus, whom he knew very well and had loved all his life. He was not a man I either liked or respected, but he spoke the truth. I realised it even then when he was telling me how Augustus, for his own purposes which he equated with the good of Rome, would compel me to divorce my wife Vipsania and marry Julia, to serve as the guardian of her children. Now,' he relaxed his grip on my leg, 'I apply his words to Julia also, and to myself. And perhaps to Agrippina. It may be that she is compelled by her nature and experience to fear me, resent me, hate me. The question is,' his fingers now lay lightly, even tenderly, on my skin, 'has she infected Germanicus with her distrust, her fear? I wish him nothing but well, believe me. Think before you answer.'

I remained silent, a long time, unable to judge how best to respond to this invitation to betray Agrippina, who had shown me nothing but kindness. I glanced away, towards Mercury the deceiver. I looked back at the Emperor, whose jaws were slowly moving. It was cool in the chamber, but I began to sweat.

The Emperor smiled. Can you smile bitterly?

'That same man,' he said, 'then described to me the world he had helped Augustus make. We restored the Republic, he said, and, as I recall, laughed at the thought, and made a despotism, a world fit, he said, for power, ruled by power, a world in which all gentle virtues had been made obsolete, a world in which one commanded and others served, a world in which a cruel frost gripped men's hearts and generous sentiments were annulled by the habit of fearful subjection. You see, after so many years, I remember his words perfectly. You may say they are engraved on my memory, like an epitaph. In the days of the Republic men like you and me, from families such as ours, competed openly for office and for glory. Now competition has been replaced by conspiracy, and so we live in the shadows of suspicion. I have no wish to think Agrippina my enemy, still less to regard Germanicus, the son of my brother Drusus whom I loved deeply and have never ceased to mourn, as a rival. Do you understand me?'

He left it there, gave me leave to depart, which I did gratefully, and found I was trembling. For the first time I knew the meaning of Empire, was gripped by its cold constriction. Tiberius seemed to me both terrible and pitiable, for, if he exerted an awful power, he was equally its prisoner.

But I was not yet permitted to escape. A soldier, one of the Praetorian Guard, stopped me, and told me that his commander required my presence. So I was brought before Sejanus.

His name then meant little to me. I had heard it some months before when he had made, at the Emperor's command, a tour of inspection of the northern frontier. I had not met him then, absent on patrol. But I had heard, since my return to Rome, men speak of him as the Emperor's particular favourite.

I found a tall handsome man with a mane of tawny hair and a frank open smile.

'I can offer you,' he said, 'better wine than the Emperor drinks, the real Falernian. I don't know how you would describe the stuff I'm sure he gave you, but I can tell you it's the ordinary legionary's poison. He got a taste for it on his first campaigns and, since he despises connoisseurship as a mark of effeminacy, which he detests above everything, he's stuck with it. There are some men whose sexual tastes run to a bit of rough, if you'll pardon the expression, and the Emperor's taste in wine is the equivalent, as you might say.'

He laughed. It was a rich, warm, companionable laugh.

'I can say that,' he continued, handing me wine which was certainly, as he had promised, much finer stuff that the red rot-gut Tiberius had provided, 'because I'm devoted to him, body and soul. That's not surprising or even greatly to my credit, because he made me, I'd be nothing without him. Though my father L Seius Strabo was Praetorian Prefect before me, and subsequently Proconsul in Egypt, he was one of Augustus' new men. Our family is nothing to boast of, not like yours. We come from a small municipality in Etruria and, though my father made a good marriage and my mother therefore provided me with consular relatives, I'm quite ready to admit that without Tiberius' favour I wouldn't be where I am today and in most people's eyes wouldn't amount to anything. You see, I'm being perfectly frank with you.'

There was no reply to make to that, so I said nothing, and only smiled, politely, I hoped.

'The Emperor's had good reports of you,' he said. 'Don't think, I beg you, that in telling you this I'm in any way seeking to patronise you. And in any case he's well disposed towards you, on account of your father.'

'I see you are in his confidence,' I replied.

He threw himself on a couch, and in that relaxed posture seemed full of animal energy, kept on a tight rein.

'But I'm told you're a favourite yourself, of Agrippina.'

'If you say so.'

'And, to be frank again, that worries me. See, I'm going to be open with you. When I made that tour I came upon certain things, heard others, that disturbed me. There was a mood in the army I didn't like. You'll correct me if I'm wrong, but it seemed as if they were nerving themselves for something big and dangerous – and I don't mean necessarily a German war, though that would be dangerous enough, and folly too. Then again, I was told – and I hope mistakenly – that after the suppression of the mutiny, in which I gather you played a fine part, when Germanicus was away on campaign, Agrippina acted as commander-in-chief herself. Is that true? I hope it isn't.'

'You forget,' I said, 'I was with Germanicus myself.'

'Point taken. Then again – you understand I'm merely putting to you what was put to me – I was told that the letter of congratulation which the Emperor sent the army was never read to them, but that instead she personally thanked the men for what they had done, on behalf of the Roman state and Germanicus. You see what I'm getting at. If the reports I've had have any substance, it's as if she is setting up Germanicus as a rival to the Emperor, and we can't have that. We've had enough of that sort of thing – it leads to civil war. And I'm told she takes her youngest brat – what do they call him? Caligula, isn't it? – with her whenever she visits the troops because he's their little darling, their peculiar pet. Again it sounds as if she is trying to secure an especial personal devotion, to her, her family, and Germanicus. What do you say?'

VII

These interviews with Tiberius and Sejanus foreshadowed what was to come. They should have left me perturbed. If they didn't, it was doubtless on account of the vanity of youth. I had made, it seemed, a good impression on the Emperor and his closest confidant. Sejanus indeed showed himself eager to further our acquaintance. He sought me out at the baths, invited me to dinners, then to a hunting party at his estate in the hills above Tibur, and kept me there for some days after his other guests had returned to Rome. In short he set himself to seduce me. Our intimacy was remarked. A kind friend let me know that I was held to be Sejanus' catamite. Such friends are ever to be found. But the rumour was false. Sejanus had no more interest in my body than I in his. He was in any case mad for women, as I was myself. (And indeed he supplied me with an athletic Greek girl.) The seduction he attempted was intellectual, at least in part. He let me feel his power, and its attraction. He had the Emperor's ear, and his absolute trust; and so enticed me with the promise that I too could flourish in the sunlight of imperial favour.

How should I not be tempted? The Empire might extend from the Rhine to the deserts of Africa, from the western sea to the frontier of Parthia, but power was concentrated. The Republic, in which free men contended for distinction, had become a court, in which no man could rise by merit alone, but rather by favour and patronage. Sejanus opened its gate for me.

I see now what I did not understand then, when all seemed natural to me: that earthly fame, which like all men of virtue

I sought, is but a breath of wind that blows now from one quarter and now from another, changing its name because it changes direction. Sejanus was thoroughly of our time, not therefore to be condemned. He competed for mastery and so for fame, in the court, not in the Forum.

Germanicus was recalled from Germany. Tiberius received him with as much warmth as he could muster. He lavished honours on him. An arch by the temple of Saturn was dedicated to his achievement in recapturing the eagles lost by Varus. He was awarded a triumph. To the Emperor's displeasure Agrippina insisted on sitting by her husband in his chariot, surrounded by their children, her jewels. Little Gaius crowed lustily and threw flowers at the crowd. Like the soldiers, they took him to their heart and called him 'darling'. No one could doubt that Germanicus and his family excelled Tiberius in popularity. Nevertheless the Emperor, long schooled in dissimulation, gave no sign of envy. It was, seemingly, to Sejanus alone that he confessed his displeasure and his fears; and Sejanus reported them to me.

He said, 'You are a friend of Agrippina's. Can you persuade her to moderate her criticism of the Emperor?'

That criticism had indeed become sharp and open. At the suggestion of her mother-in-law Antonia, the widow of the Emperor's brother, Germanicus' sister Julia Livilla was married to Tiberius' son Drusus. Sejanus approved the match. He had cultivated the friendship of Julia Livilla and hoped that she would be able to ease the enmity which Drusus felt towards him, an enmity that was founded in jealousy, Drusus believing that Tiberius valued Sejanus beyond his merits.

The marriage, however, displeased Agrippina. She was not slow to tell anyone prepared to listen that it showed the Emperor's intention to set aside Augustus' will and name Drusus rather than Germanicus as his successor.

Sejanus laughed.

'I know you love her,' he said to me, 'but really she is

impossible. Do you know what I suggested to Tiberius? I said he might remind her that there are remote islands reserved for the female members of her family who step out of line. He wasn't amused.'

It was clear that Germanicus would not be permitted to return to the Rhine to pursue his dangerously independent policy in defiance of Tiberius. It was also clear, as Sejanus said, that he could not safely remain in Rome where he would be the focus for seditious elements whom Agrippina was all too willing to encourage. Now that I had, as it were, a foot in both camps, I could see the danger she represented, and yet could sympathise with her indignation. After all, like so many, I had felt Germanicus' charm.

At this point I should put on record my certainty that the suspicions of Germanicus' intentions which Tiberius, encouraged by Sejanus, entertained, were unfounded. Germanicus was indeed ambitious, but he sought glory, not power. I had several conversations with him in the weeks after his triumph, and never heard him speak disloyally of Tiberius, even though he was dismayed by the Emperor's unwillingness to allow him to return to the Rhine and pursue his plans for the conquest of Germany and the incorporation of the Germans within the Empire. But he was content to wait. He was after all the nominated heir, and Tiberius was already approaching old age. No doubt Agrippina was sincere in her suspicions. No doubt too she spoke freely of them to her husband. And no doubt he responded with a smile. But he didn't know what it was to feel resentment. He was the most open-hearted of men, and no one was ever less fitted to be a conspirator. I must make that clear.

The question of what was to be done with him solved itself. There was a small crisis in the east where the client-king of Cappadocia, Archelaus, had proved unsatisfactory. He was therefore arraigned before the Senate and it was resolved to incorporate his kingdom within the Empire so that it should come under direct rule from Rome. This task, responsible but not over-arduous, was entrusted to Germanicus. That made sense. No one could doubt his ability to reconcile the notables of Cappadocia to their altered status.

Then, before he departed on this mission, news came of a more serious crisis in Armenia. The king, Vonones, a good friend of Rome, was expelled by a faction that resented Roman influence and favoured an alliance with Parthia. Armenia is a sort of buffer-state between the two Empires of Rome and Parthia and therefore of great strategic importance. The revolution there could not be permitted to succeed.

Germanicus was therefore given new responsibilities. Tiberius requested the Senate to grant him *maius imperium* and supreme authority over all the eastern provinces of the Empire. The request to the Senate was of course a mere formality. The appointment testified, it seemed, to Tiberius' confidence in the ability and integrity of his heir apparent.

'Now,' said Sejanus, 'surely Agrippina will be quiet. If this doesn't convince her that the Emperor feels nothing but friendship for her husband, what will?'

The answer, alas, was nothing.

When I saw her, she asked me what I thought Tiberius meant by this appointment, and when I suggested that she should take it at face value, told me I was a sad innocent.

Tired of Rome, I sought and was granted a position on Germanicus' staff.

'Of course the Emperor approves your appointment,' Sejanus said. 'You can take it from me that he does. Why shouldn't he? You are loyal, aren't you?'

It was Tiberius' misfortune that he could trust only his dependents, his inferiors; therefore Sejanus and not Germanicus. This flaw was the product of his ingrained resentment; he had been used by Augustus, discarded by Augustus, recalled reluctantly by Augustus. Moreover, long years of subservience to the will of his formidable mother had soured him. He could not speak frankly with Germanicus. Indeed he could not speak frankly except to a few of his contemporaries, old drinking-companions. Or so it was said: that in his cups his tongue was loosened.

One of these companions was Gn Calpurnius Piso, a man of robust tastes, long experience in war, and with a judgement too often inflamed by wine. Piso felt for Tiberius, whose legate he had been in numerous campaigns, a dogged loyalty, tantamount to devotion. Now the Emperor appointed him Governor of Syria, and did so, it was believed, with the intention that he should exercise some restraint on Germanicus, should this prove necessary. He was afraid that in his zeal for glory Germanicus might embroil Rome in war with Parthia.

Did he, however, take into account the antipathy Piso felt for Germanicus? Did he even know of it? I cannot be certain, after so many years. Yet that antipathy was intense, so intense that it seems unlikely that Tiberius could have been wholly unaware of it.

Since I don't pretend to be able to read men's minds and interpret their feelings, I shall not myself offer an explanation for the hatred Piso felt. But I suppose that, among other things, he experienced the jealousy which men of grace and abundant charm provoke in those who lack such qualities and who are nevertheless conscious of their own merit and virtues. Moreover, since Piso was a habitual drunkard, and since it is well-known that addiction to wine may cause all resentments to fester, while distorting judgement, the appointment of Piso as a check on Germanicus was unwise.

Germanicus shone in the east. He won popularity wherever he went. Indeed, the Greeks and Asiatics, light-minded, mercurial, disposed to violent emotions, soon treated him as if he had been a divinity. His mission was successful. He restored order in Cappadocia, and installed a new king, favourable to Rome, in Armenia. Nor did he do anything to provoke war with Parthia. In short, he behaved in exemplary fashion.

Then he proceeded to Egypt. This was technically illegal. Egypt was an imperial fief, which no senator was allowed to enter without the Emperor's permission. Germanicus had not sought this. No doubt he thought it unnecessary in his case. Was he not after all Tiberius' designated heir? And in truth he only wished to visit the antiquities in which Egypt is so rich and which must attract any man of cultivated tastes. It may be that he exceeded his powers when, for instance, he relieved a famine there by ordering the release of stores from the imperial warehouses in Alexandria. But both the purpose and the result were admirable. Then again, it was perhaps tactless that he should issue an edict in which he deprecated the warmth of his reception by the people, for this served to draw attention to his unparalleled popularity. And Piso of course reported all that Germanicus did in letters to the Emperor, which put the worst construction on his acts.

Then Piso made a mistake. He countermanded an order Germanicus had given relating to the disposition of two legions. Since Germanicus was in possession of a superior *imperium*, Piso was both exceeding his rightful power and unquestionably guilty of insubordination. Germanicus accordingly ordered Piso to leave Syria. All this happened without the Emperor having been consulted.

Agrippina was delighted. She did not doubt that Piso had been sent to Syria by Tiberius in order to obstruct any measures that Germanicus took, and to do all in his power to render his mission a failure. She rarely mentioned Piso by name. She called him simply 'the Spy'.

'I am sure,' she said, 'that his reports to the Emperor are full of lies and slanders, and that the Old Goat licks his lips with relish as he reads them.'

For my part, I was not so certain. I considered that, with tact and good sense, the difficulties might have been resolved. But I had to admit I knew little of Piso's character. In any case my opinion was of no account. Piso, grumbling and furious, withdrew to the island of Cos.

And then Germanicus fell ill. I wasn't in Antioch at the time, having been sent on a diplomatic mission to the new King of Armenia, Zeno, the son of King Ptolemo of Pontus. This was agreeable. Zeno was a generous and gracious host, and I was able to ascertain that he was a true friend of Rome. But my absence means that what I report now is based on hearsay.

Germanicus was suffering from a form of fever, common, it is said, in Syria. This much is certain. He then seemed to recover, only to have a relapse. The most learned doctors were summoned and could not account for his condition. It is said that Germanicus himself suspected poison and accused Piso and his wife Plancina of being responsible. But it may have been Agrippina who was the first to speak of poison. She refused to believe that her beloved Germanicus was dying a natural death, and she ordered her slaves and freedmen to seek evidence of poison and/or magic practices. They examined the floor and walls of the chamber where Germanicus lay sweating and shivering alternately. They found human bones, signs of spells, curses and invocations. In particular it seems there were lead tablets inscribed with the name Germanicus, charred and blood-stained ashes, and other 'malignant objects effective to consign souls to the power of the tomb', as their report had it.

Germanicus, though very weak, then raised himself on his elbow and spoke, somewhat as follows:

'Even if I was dying a natural death, I could reproach the gods for parting me from my beloved wife, children, country and friends, and for denying me the glory to which I am entitled. But it is not the gods who are responsible for my condition, but rather these fiends in human form, Piso and Plancina. Tell my father by adoption, the Emperor, of my accusations. You will then have the chance to have my murderers hauled before the Senate and duly arraigned. I charge you with this duty. It is not for friends and loved ones to content themselves with mourning and walking in tears behind the funeral bier, but rather to carry out the dead man's will. Even strangers will mourn Germanicus. How much more therefore is it the duty of those who have loved me to avenge my death . . .'

At this point it is said his voice failed him and he fell back weeping. But Agrippina, though in tears herself, leaned over him and mopped his brow and dried his eyes, and kissed him, and besought him to rest. A shudder passed over his body, and he closed his eyes, and those watching feared that his spirit had fled. Yet in a little while, after Agrippina had touched his lips with wine, he spoke again, though more quietly, and with long pauses between the words:

'Show Rome my wife, the granddaughter of the divine Augustus. Display the weeping faces of our beloved children. Let the crowd share in their grief till it is roused in anger against my murderers. Any story of criminal instructions given to Piso will be hard to believe, harder still to prove; yet, once believed, once proven, impossible to forgive.'

And so he died.

It was, you may say, a remarkable speech for a man in the last extremities. Yet history relates other examples of deathbed eloquence. Certainly these were his last words, as subsequently related to me by Agrippina. She may have improved them, but at the time I did not question her sincerity.

At the time, yes . . . but now?

Agathon, who has read this, is puzzled and asks what it has to do with Caligula. I reply that it is impossible to understand the tragedy of Gaius Caligula if his biography is divorced from the story of his family.

VIII *

The story of Agrippina's return to Italy with the ashes of her dead husband is well-known, so well-known indeed that it has become embellished, and it's hard to say now what in the story is authentic and what is not. It is a story that is still recounted late at night, at dinner-parties when the slaves have been dismissed to their quarters, and also on long summer afternoons in country villas, to alleviate boredom with talk that is delicately spiced with scandal and subversion.

News of the beloved hero's death had of course long preceded the arrival of the widow at Brindisi. She had indeed delayed for some weeks, to allow public mourning to intensify; she knew, I suppose, how the expectation of her return would excite the People; and, like any deft storyteller, delayed in order to prolong the tension. Meanwhile in Syria, Piso, believing that Germanicus' death would give him the opportunity to resume his governorship, found he had miscalculated, and was at once arrested by order of Gnaeus Sentius Saturninus, whom Agrippina, with no authority other than that secured by her own will, had appointed commander of Germanicus' legions and governor of the province. So, even as Agrippina took ship for Brindisi, the wretched Piso was being dispatched to Rome, charged, for the time being only, with the sole crime of making war against Roman forces – as if that wasn't enough.

Tiberius sent two battalions of the Praetorian Guard to greet Agrippina and serve as her escort to Rome. With what some thought arrogance, others indifference, he placed Sejanus, whom all believed to have been Germanicus' enemy, in command. Agrippina herself regarded this appointment as an

41

insult. Throughout the journey to Rome she lost no opportunity to embarrass or humiliate him.

Before they departed from Brindisi, where she had been
received with rapture, while many tears were shed for
Germanicus, a curious incident occurred. A woman, by name
Martina, believed to be a dependant of Piso's wife Plancina,
had been arrested in Antioch, suspected of the murder. She
had a reputation as a notorious poisoner, or at least acquired
such a reputation after her arrest. She too was brought to
Brindisi, and lodged in a guard-room. The next day she was
found dead. There were no marks of violence, but traces of
poison were discovered in her hair. Some thought she had
committed suicide. Others were certain that she had been killed
so that she could not reveal the extent of the conspiracy which
had cost Germanicus his life. Years later Sejanus remarked to
me that Tiberius had sourly opined that she had been killed
precisely because 'the poor wretch had nothing to reveal'. I
have no view myself, being without evidence, though certainly
Tiberius' opinion was the best expressed.

Agrippina travelled slowly to Rome, her husband's ashes
displayed on a chest carried before her litter. She herself was
pale and there were dark circles under her eyes. These, like her
pallor, were doubtless renewed every morning. Her children
travelled with her, and looked sad, noble and composed. Years
later, young Nero winced as he recalled that journey.

'It was somehow shameful,' he said, 'though I didn't understand it as such then. But I did feel there was something false,
something exaggerated, playing to the passions of the mob. I
don't know how else to put it. And I was afraid . . .'

'Afraid?'

'Yes, I remember thinking how easily the mood of that
same mob might change. You told me once – and I've read
it since – that after Caesar's murder the crowd first applauded
Brutus and Cassius, and then after my great-grandfather Mark
Antony had addressed them, were eager to tear the self-styled

Liberators to pieces, though they had cheered them only minutes before. I didn't know that then, but the frenzy of the mob didn't please and excite me as it did my mother. On the contrary it frightened me.'

'Poor boy,' I said, 'poor dear boy . . .'

Poor boy indeed! He should really have been a girl and his sister Agrippina the boy. They resembled each other closely then, which was why I bedded both of them – I have ever found the androgynous irresistible. The younger Agrippina was – is? – an Amazon; Nero was scorned as effeminate and therefore cowardly. In truth he had a certain defiant courage, born of despair, I now think. Then his effeminate manner, his lavish use of scent and cosmetics, seemed to me the seductive play-acting of youth. Now I wonder if all this was not a species of protest against his overbearing and demanding mother, whom, I realise, he both feared and adored. She demanded more of him than he could give, and his affectations represented his way of denying her.

But I digress.

The triumphal funeral procession at last arrived in Rome. It seemed that the whole city had turned out to honour the dead hero, and demand that his murderers be punished. It was, as Nero was to say, frightening. No civilised man can be at ease before mass emotion. That day, I thought: 'Speak the word, and they will burn the Palatine.'

In the midst of the howling throng, young Gaius Caligula laughed and caught the flowers that the people threw on to the bier and into the carriage where Agrippina rode with her children.

Tiberius did not attend the funeral. Nor did the dowager-Empress Livia – she had always deplored displays of extravagant emotion. Nor, more significantly, did Antonia, mother of the (possibly) murdered Germanicus. But people said that Tiberius had prevented her.

Germanicus' ashes were laid in the mausoleum Augustus

had built for himself. Agrippina let it be known that Tiberius had been reluctant to consent to this. (Later I was assured that this was not so.) The crowd abandoned itself to an hysterical exhibition of grief. The Field of Mars was ablaze with torches. Later that night there was rioting in Trastevere, in the Suburra and in the Field of Mars itself. When dawn came, Rome looked like a city sacked by an invader.

Tiberius issued a stern reproof.

'Famous Romans,' he declared, 'have died before, but none has been so ardently mourned. I commend your devotion to the memory of Germanicus, my beloved son and nephew. But moderation should now be observed. After our first tears we should observe calm, as befits an imperial people. Remember with what restraint and dignity Augustus mourned his beloved grandsons and Julius Caesar his daughter. Remember how our ancestors endured the loss of armies, the death of generals and the destruction of great families, and did not give way to tears and lamentations such as are proper only for women. It is not for Romans to imitate hysterical and effeminate Orientals. Great men die: the Republic lives for ever. So I request all citizens to return to their ordinary occupations and, since the Megalesian Games are due to start, to their proper pleasures.'

The last reminder did the trick. The Games, and the opportunity to gamble which they offered, distracted the plebs, who in a few days seemed to have forgotten Germanicus, to Agrippina's surprise and disappointment.

Nevertheless there was still Piso's trial to come – and to look forward to. Tiberius, perhaps reluctantly, laid the case against his old friend before the Senate. He adopted a measured tone, which incurred the censure of all. Some thought his moderation amounted to an invitation to the Senate to acquit Piso. On the other hand, Piso's friends condemned the Emperor for having, as they thought, abandoned him. They put it about that when the time was ripe Piso would produce a document that would prove his innocence and implicate the Emperor at the same time. Feeling ran high. Piso, who had been kept under house arrest, found himself the object of threats and insults on his daily journey to the Senate. People cried out that he might escape the Senate, but not their vengeance. It was all very unseemly.

Whether such a document existed was never confirmed. Agrippina of course was certain that it had been destroyed by the Emperor's agents. It may well have been – if there ever was such a document. In any case it didn't matter. Piso escaped both justice and injustice. He fell on his sword, or cut his throat, I don't know which. Agrippina declared that this proved his guilt. I thought it evidence only of his despair. Tiberius then intervened to speak for the widow Plancina before the Senate.

So the murder of Germanicus was never avenged, if indeed he was murdered.

Of the months that followed I recall three conversations.

The first was with Sejanus. He called on me by night, with his face muffled that he might not be recognised in the streets. I thought the precaution ridiculous, especially when he told me it was for my protection, not his.

'The widow Agrippina trusts you, doesn't she? You loved Germanicus, didn't you?'

He threw himself on a couch. All his movements were rapid, decisive, and yet there was a curious languor to them also. Again, he made me think of a lion.

'It wouldn't do,' he said, 'if she learned that I was visiting you. She'd never trust you again.'

'Why should you care?' I said, and gave him wine.

'Why should I care?' He smiled. 'Like everybody,' he said, 'you're like everybody.'

'What do you mean? I should be offended.'

'What do I mean? Just this: you suppose, don't you, that

I'm as ambitious as I'm unscrupulous. Don't argue about the latter charge, I don't mind being thought unscrupulous. But ambitious? What should I be ambitious for? What could I be ambitious for that I haven't got – which is the Emperor's trust. That's enough for me. I'm his creature, you know. I would be nothing without him.'

'Just so,' I said, still wondering why he had come.

'I'm grateful,' he said. 'More than that. He's awkward, he's difficult, he's bad-tempered, he's suspicious as can be. See, I'm putting myself in your power when I speak like this.'

He held out his cup for more wine.

'Not bad,' he said. 'From your own estates? I thought so. Rome needs him, you know. Here in the city we can forget, if we ever realised, the extent of our Empire. You've travelled though, seen service on the frontiers, so you have some idea of what Empire entails. But do you know what it demands in application to business, in judgement, in good sense, if it is to remain at peace?'

'I've some idea,' I said.

'Good. Well, nobody excels Tiberius at the business of government, which is administration. He is rapid and certain in judgement. He is devoted to administration. He'll work at it half the night, you know. I've been told that he is even more capable than Augustus. He never goes wrong, except perhaps when it's a question of his own safety. But do you know the chief of his inheritances from Augustus? It's that the Roman peace will never be disturbed again by civil war. Do you see where I'm heading?'

I nodded, but kept silent.

'People call me a careerist, a low-born careerist. Let them talk as they please. My business is to see to the Emperor's security – and his peace of mind – so that he can devote himself to the work of government. I don't let anything get in the way of that. I don't intend to. I'm fond of him also in my way.'

'So?'

'So? This is good wine, almost as good as my own Falernian. Thanks. So . . . his security is threatened, his peace disturbed. I don't want to say anything against Germanicus, in any case he's no longer about to trouble us. He may have been the hero and the virtuous man you think he was. No point arguing. But his wife . . . a different matter . . .'

'What do you want of me?'

I was determined to make him reveal himself.

He smiled, a big cat's smile.

'Get that bitch off our backs,' he said. 'I don't care how. Throw a bucket of cold water over her if you like. Soft-talk her if you think that will serve. Or . . . or . . .'

'Or?'

'Just remind her,' he said again, 'that there are island prisons reserved for the female members of the imperial family who step out of line.'

My second interview was with Drusus. I have said nothing of him so far because till now I knew almost nothing of him. I mentioned only that he had suppressed the mutiny of the Pannonian legions, using very different methods from those employed by Germanicus. But because we had served on different fronts I had never till now spoken to the Emperor's son.

I was summoned to see him. I put it like that because it was framed as a command rather than an invitation. This displeased me. We might be living in an Empire; he might be the Emperor's son and, since Germanicus' death, his probable successor. Nevertheless I was of as good birth as he and, though his junior in years, to be considered his equal – in Republican terms. Augustus, as I knew well, had taken care to soften and disguise the realities of Empire by living simply, without pomp or ceremony, and maintaining the easy manners of Republican days. Above all things he detested servility; it embarrassed him. Tiberius likewise, to his credit, was angry if anyone addressed him as 'lord and master'; he regarded this as an insult. Drusus, it seemed to me from this summons, was of a different stamp. I prepared myself to be cold and reserved.

He had at that time a house on the Aventine, a cool villa set in a garden where fountains played under the ilex and pines. From its loggia you looked across the Circus Maximus to the imperial palaces on the Palatine. It interested me that Drusus had chosen to seclude himself here, at some distance from the bustle of the Forum and the daily scrutiny of other members of the imperial family and their slaves, freedmen, spies. His villa seemed like a country house within the city.

I was asked to identify myself by a guard, but was not searched. (Had that been demanded, I should have departed straightway, insulted. How innocent I still was in those days!) Then I was led through the corridors to a long room in the rear of the villa, that looked out over a second garden where painted doves flew among the trees and yellow roses clambered over a high wall.

Drusus lay on a couch. He was engaged in dictating. He waved a hand to me, as if negligently directing me to be seated, but did not interrupt his dictation. He was thickset as Tiberius, dark-haired, dark-eyed, ugly. His secretary was a youth – a Greek, I supposed, or perhaps an Asiatic – a pretty boy with loose lips and abundant curls; he wore a short gold-fringed tunic and his legs were long, soft, sand-coloured.

Drusus said, 'Write that up directly, and bring it back to be checked and signed. Now be off with you.'

The boy flashed him a smile. Drusus' eyes followed him out of the room.

Drusus said, 'My cousin Germanicus spoke well of you.'

I inclined my head, waited.

'My father also has a high opinion of your abilities.'

'I am honoured.'

'There wasn't much they agreed on. So this impresses me.

You're a soldier too, and I've no doubt you hope soon for a military command.'

'That would indeed be my wish.'

'And one that will be granted.'

He paused, took a straw from a jar that stood on a little table by the side of his couch, and chewed on it. There was silence but for the cooing of doves.

'I apologise for receiving you lying down. My back . . .' he said. 'Germanicus was not only my cousin but my brother-in-law. You know that, of course.'

Naturally I did. I had heard also rumours that Drusus and his wife Julia Livilla were at odds, though she had recently borne him twin sons (one of whom had died), and no one had dared question their paternity.

'As such,' he said, 'I bear a peculiar responsibility for Germanicus' children. You know them well of course. I should wish to know them better myself. But their mother makes that impossible. She guards them jealously, fears and resents, as it appears to me, any influence I might have over them. Of course she believes, doesn't she, that Germanicus was murdered, and even that this was done with the complicity of my father, if not by his direct command. What do you think of that?'

'I was not in Antioch when Germanicus died. I know nothing of the circumstances, except by report, which is all anyone who was not there knows. But to my mind it's absurd to suppose, even if he was indeed poisoned, that the Princeps had any hand in it. Absurd and worse, criminal. When people are consumed by grief, as Agrippina is, their judgement is faulty, they don't know what they are saying. I can't believe that she really supposes the Princeps to have been . . .'

'Quite so. It's the misfortune of our family that it is overstocked with impossible women. My grandmother the Empress, my stepmother Julia – though she had charm and I adored her for a time. The eldest boy Nero resembles her – in looks, I hope in nothing else. My own wife. Agrippina. All

49

impossible, all demanding, all irrational. What have we done to deserve them? I do not wish Agrippina to rear her boys to hate me, or my father; to believe we are their enemies. I wish them nothing but well. She trusts you? You are intimate with her?'

'Intimate?' I said, aware that I walked on dangerous ground that might at any moment give way beneath me. 'Not that. Yet I hope she trusts me.'

'Very well. That will do. I have a request to make, a request because it cannot be an order as I might give you an order were you my lieutenant in war: that you speak to Agrippina, seek to dispel these suspicions from her mind . . .'

The secretary returned, entering the room without knocking. I looked to Drusus to reprove him for this impertinence, but he only smiled.

'Lygdus, you've been quick, dear boy.' He addressed him in Greek.

'Not quick, master.' The boy's voice was high and fluting. I realised he was a eunuch. 'There's something here that puzzles me. Either I misunderstood your dictation, or you have made a mistake. Look here . . .'

Drusus studied the text. The boy stood by the couch, confident and relaxed, like one who knows that he is a favourite, to be granted liberties and forgiven what would be punished in another.

'Yes,' Drusus said, 'this doesn't make sense, it's not what I intended to say. Bright of you to spot it.'

He reverted to Latin and said to me, 'You will do that, won't you? As a kindness to me, and also as a public service.' He sighed. 'It's a lot to ask, I know that, and rather a bore for you. But important, don't you think?'

This time the smile, an unusually charming one that lit up his heavy and sombre features, was flashed in my direction.

'Lygdus,' he said, 'will you show the gentleman out, please, while I try to make sense of the nonsense I burdened you with. And when you return, give orders that we are not to be disturbed.'

As we were about to leave, he said, 'I've heard that the youngest boy, Gaius, is unbalanced. I hope that's not so. Is he?'

'Not to my mind,' I said. 'He's lively, high-spirited, but he has all his wits about him.'

'Not like his uncle, poor Claudius, then?'

'Not at all.'

'Good. One fool's enough in the family.'

At the door of the villa I gave the boy Lygdus gold.

'Are you Greek?' I said.

'No, sir, Syrian.'

'And you're fond of your master, I think?'

'He is very good to me.'

Unlike so many slaves, he looked me in the face as he replied, and didn't blush or seem embarrassed by what must have seemed to him a strange question – or rather, strange that such as I should have troubled myself to put such a question.

Agrippina had installed herself in a house in the Suburra, a popular quarter, one also where what is called vice flourished abundantly. She chose it of course to mark her difference from the imperial family, to hint that she could not trust her darling children to them, but relied rather on the love of the people to protect them. Some, the ancient dowager-Empress Livia chief among them, condemned this as hypocrisy. Agrippina had become for her an obsession. I know this because my mother and my aunts had to endure her railing, the venom she spat whenever she mentioned 'that woman', which she did all too frequently. I knew also that Livia had reproached Tiberius for his failure to intervene to defend Piso and Plancina against their accusers, all of whom, as she said, truthfully, were either inspired by Agrippina or acting directly on her behalf. My mother told me that Livia had complained of Tiberius' 'weakness', and compared her son unfavourably to her husband, 'always resolute and clear-sighted in a crisis'. 'Which is not,' my mother remarked, in a manner more caustic than was her wont, 'how she used to speak of Augustus when he was alive.' One had to remember of course that Agrippina herself was Augustus' granddaughter, and that Livia had always been jealous of Augustus' long-enduring fondness for his daughter Julia, who was the child of his earlier marriage to Scribonia – by all accounts yet another 'impossible woman'.

Agrippina's beauty had deserted her. It had been the product of happiness, which gave vivacity to her angular features. Now you saw that her nose was too long and too sharply pointed, and misery had caused the corners of her mouth to turn down.

She was not alone. To my irritation her companion was her brother-in-law Claudius.

(In the version of Gaius' biography which I shall eventually present to the younger Agrippina – if the gods will that I bring it to a satisfactory conclusion – I shall have to speak prudently, for Claudius, remarkably, is now our Emperor. How Germanicus would have laughed, how Tiberius would have curled his lip in scorn! And, of equal absurdity, she – that younger Agrippina with whom, under the rose, I knew so many passionate hours – is now his wife. To such degradation has ambition brought her! But now, in this secret version, I can say frankly what everyone said before that unimaginable hour arrived when he was named as Emperor, that Clau-Clau-Claudius, the stuttering, shambling, slobbering pedant, was as near to idiocy as it is possible to get while still being permitted to escape confinement. His own mother, that admirable lady Antonia, called him simply 'a monster', Livia detested him – he gave her 'the creeps' – and Augustus, usually indulgent to the young people in his family, simply asked whether this great-nephew might be mentally as well as physically deficient. As for Gaius' treatment of his uncle . . . well, more of that later.)

Now he greeted me with one of his ill-timed and ill-mannered jests. There are some stammerers who turn their affliction to good account, even using it in such a way that a quite ordinary remark may be given point and appear witty. Not so Claudius.

Fortunately Agrippina soon found his presence as irksome as I did myself, and dismissed him with the suggestion that his nephews and nieces might enjoy his company. So he left us alone, but not before covering his sister-in-law with slobbering kisses.

She said, 'I see he embarrasses you. He has that effect on many, poor Claudius. But my revered husband always troubled himself to treat his poor brother kindly, and it behoves me to do the same. Besides, the poor thing has a kind heart.'

'If you say so.'

'And kindness is something I have learned to value.'

What could I say to that?

'You have many loyal friends, myself among them. I owe so much to Germanicus, a debt far heavier than I can ever hope to repay. The least therefore I can offer you and your children is the promise that I am ever at your service.'

Was I sincere? I don't know. A man's life contains many hidden depths and large dark areas secret even from himself. Certainly, at that moment, I felt for Agrippina; she was magnificent in her obstinate solitude.

'They are all I have to live for,' she said. 'I shall never marry again. My own experience of a stepfather does not permit me to inflict such on my poor jewels . . .'

'And yet,' I said, 'your stepfather is now Emperor and the man on whom the welfare of your children, and the careers of your sons, must ultimately depend. That is why, conscious of what I owe Germanicus and mindful of the love I felt for him and feel for his memory, I now venture to suggest that it is rash on your part, however natural, to let your feelings about

Tiberius become general knowledge. It is not in the interest of your sons to treat him as your enemy.'

'I treat him,' she said, 'as I find him.'

I did not know how to continue. Her face was hard and cold as marble.

So I stayed silent. This is the fashion of our time when inertia is taken for wisdom; but in this instance I was playing no part. I was as baffled and, therefore, helpless as Germanicus himself had been when the mutinous legionaries received his impassioned speech, appealing that they return to their duties, as if he had never spoken.

Then she said, 'If it wasn't for the love that the common people bear to me and my jewels in memory of my dear husband, I should be tempted to give way to despair.'

This angered me.

I said, 'To trust in the constancy of the mob is folly. One day they cheer you, the next they call for your death. They are fickle and blow with the prevailing wind. They switch rapidly from misery to joy, and are unrestrained in either emotion.'

'Where did you learn such speeches?' she said. 'In books of rhetoric, I suppose. For my part I am schooled by experience, and I trust the innate virtue of the common people, even as I have learned the treachery of princes.'

'Germanicus himself was a prince, and a noble one,' I said. 'Listen, Agrippina, and as you listen do not forget that I speak as a friend and as one that loved Germanicus. By allowing the bitterness of your feeling towards the Emperor to become evident, you have placed yourself in a position of great danger. You have placed your beloved children in the same danger. Once, in the days of the Republic, there was free competition for office, and even for honour. Then opposed parties could vie with one another for the favour of the Assembly and in the Senate. Then it was possible to speak out against those whom you thought your enemies, and you might do so with impunity. But those days are past. The Republic is no more.

We live under monarchy, and monarchy does not permit open dissension. So, I tell you, the more loudly you express your suspicions of Tiberius, the more you parade your opposition to him, the greater the peril for you and your children. Have you forgotten how ruthlessly Augustus treated your mother Julia when her behaviour offended him? Have you forgotten how he consigned your brother Agrippa Postumus to an island prison? Have you forgotten your brother's unhappy fate? And do you, with your eyes open, invite such an ending for yourself and your sons? Consider, I beg of you, the reality of the world we are condemned to live in, and act according to its imperatives. I understand your anger. It is the anger brought on by great grief. But remember the wise words of Cicero: "time is the best medicine for anger."'

I was amazed by my eloquence, but Agrippina was not impressed. She looked on me as if she wished she was Medusa herself, and that her gaze could turn me to stone.

'You do not understand,' she said. 'You do not understand that defiance and the favour of the People are my only protection. Either that, or you have deserted me and mine, and attached yourself to those who conspired against my husband whom you pretend to revere.'

She got to her feet.

'I shall bid you good-day,' she said. 'You are no longer welcome in this house.'

IX

There is one other encounter I should record. Though I cannot date it precisely, it must have occurred some time in the two years after Germanicus' death. I know that because my mother served as the intermediary, and she herself died in 21.

The dowager-Empress Livia was, as I have said, an old friend of hers; more exactly perhaps her patroness. My mother had long been accustomed to attend her on public occasions. Livia had now ceased to appear in public. She let it be known that this was on account of her arthritis, but my mother thought she could really no longer put herself to the trouble. 'As for her arthritis,' she said, 'she has dosed herself for so long with her pet remedies that I shouldn't be surprised if in reality she is slowly poisoning herself.' Given that since her death, scandal has held her guilty of a number of other poisonings, I find this view of my mother's agreeably ironic.

But if she no longer appeared – deigned to appear? – in public, she had not abandoned her determination to know everything that was going on, and to influence the politics of the Empire which she interpreted, in feminine fashion, as the politics of her own family. I suppose that this was not, in the circumstances, unreasonable.

Be that as it may, I was summoned to attend on her, the summons being delivered, as I have intimated, indirectly, obliquely even, by way of my mother.

She had aged much since I last saw her, and was now a little old lady whose hair was thinning and who leaned heavily on a stick. Her right eye watered, but the left was still commanding, and her nose was now as curved as an eagle's beak.

'I'm told Agrippina has barred you from her house,' she said, abruptly, without preamble; and cackled. My mother had often remarked on her harsh discordant laugh, often provoked by the folly or misfortune of others. But I heard keen malevolence in that cackle.

'I'm too old,' she said, 'for palaver. I tire easily, so I keep conversations short. You've grown into a good-looking young man. Do your brains match your appearance?'

What could I reply to that? I suppose I blushed and bowed. She told me not to be a ninny.

Then she said, 'Do you know the one thing I have really learned in my long life? It's that most men are fools, and women too. However much they want something, they are impelled by some force to act against their own best interests. Agrippina was always a difficult girl. That she has turned against you is probably to your credit. What after all is in her interest? To engage the affection, trust and respect of my son the Princeps, in order to ensure the present well-being and future advancement of her children. So what does she do?'

She tapped her stick imperiously on the floor as if to command me to answer. But I remained silent.

'They're my great-grandchildren too,' she said, 'good children, if in need of discipline. She spoils them, doesn't she?'

My mother had stories of how Livia used to take a whip to Tiberius when he was a boy, and how, when the beating was done, there would be a passionate reconciliation. 'For years,' she would say, 'he believed himself to be her favourite, though the truth is that she loved Drusus in a different fashion, and he was jealous, even insanely, of Augustus.' That was the sort of gossip she liked to retail.

'So now,' Livia said, 'I hear that when she dined with my son, and he proffered her an apple, or it may have been a peach, which was natural because I have always insisted to him that eating fruit is good for the health, and he has never eaten enough, what does the silly girl do? She refuses it pointedly, and takes another from the bowl herself, and so makes it clear to all the company that she supposes my son may be trying to poison her. Can you imagine anything more stupid, anything that runs more certainly counter to her own interest?'

She tapped, three times, with her stick, and a maid brought her a cup of wine.

'It's for my health,' she said. 'These days talking makes my throat dry. I won't offer you any because a young man like you shouldn't drink wine before the sun goes down. I'm in bed by then, now, at my age. But I recommend this wine. It's Pucinum, from the gulf of Trieste where the grapes are exposed to a sea breeze.'

She sighed, sipped her wine, and for a moment closed her eyes.

'I sent her medicine,' she said, 'a remedy the Princeps used to find good. It relieves the nerves and is good for tension. Oregano, rosemary, fenugreek, wine, oil. She sent it back with a message saying her nerves were in good order, there was nothing wrong with them. Such a lie, so silly, and not a word of thanks. She'll be saying now I intended to poison her myself. At my age! Ridiculous! You're wondering why I sent for you?'

I waited. We were in the garden room of her villa, Primaporta, near Veii, just beyond the eighth milestone on the Via Flaminia. There was a wall painting behind her which gave the illusion of a pavilion set in a luxuriant garden, with abundant flowers, laurels and fruit-trees amongst which birds flew freely, all but one nightingale housed in a cage.

She said, 'Drusus will make a good Princeps, better than Tiberius, if he lives. But so many die . . .'

For a moment, so distant all at once did her voice sound, as if it was coming from far in the past, I could not be certain whether she was speaking of her own son Drusus, himself in fact long dead, or Tiberius' son, her grandson.

'You know my dear husband's boast? That he found Rome

of brick and left it of marble. How do you destroy marble? Are you an engineer? Can you answer me that?'

'Sculptors chip it,' I said, 'and make something new and beautiful of it.'

'And many botch fine pieces in the making,' she said, quick as a dog's snap. 'What's made can be unmade, what's done can be undone,' she said, now speaking low, muttering, as if to herself, my presence for the moment forgotten.

Then she said, 'I'm too old to be discreet. People think I dominated the Princeps, and it's true he often took my advice, so that it was said he did what I told him to do. But it wasn't like that. It was a partnership, certainly, but one in which I always had to think before I spoke. Do you understand what I'm saying, young man?'

I said I did, though that wasn't true, merely polite. To tell the truth, as far as I remember it, I was bored. She was rambling.

'Now I don't care,' she said. 'I say what I think. I'm too old to be afraid of the future. That makes me bold.'

(For my part, I don't find that fear of the future diminishes; indeed, because I no longer trust it, and know that the god Fortune has deserted me, it stretches out a waste land, chilly, dark, empty of reward, glory, even respect.)

'You can't speak to Agrippina,' she said, 'but someone must look out for her poor children and see that she doesn't ruin them.'

'Drusus,' I said, meaning the Emperor's son, 'is doing that. He has already proposed taking, I'm told, the two elder boys, Nero and his namesake Drusus, into his household. But you must know that, my lady.'

She turned away.

'Drusus,' she said, 'looks strong, but is weak. He is a good boy, but . . . I'm sleepy. Go away.'

X

A strange, inconclusive conversation, and I couldn't understand why she had sent for me. Later, when I learned how Tiberius sought to exclude her from all public business, and to shun her company, so that she could find no occasion to bring troublesome matters or complaints to his attention, except in letters which I daresay he never read, I thought that perhaps I was only one of a number of young men whom she summoned, as if seeking to convince herself that she was still at the centre of affairs; and that it had been her intention to question me exactly, but that, weary, her mind failing as senility took hold, she could not keep to her purpose, but instead spoke, almost at random, indiscreetly, irritably, at the last pathetically. I have more sympathy with her now that I find myself in the same condition, though yet far short of old age.

I never spoke to her again. A few months later I was assigned, at my own request made to Drusus, to the army in north Africa. Drusus was pleased to agree to send me there because the commander in the war against the Numidian rebel Tacfarinas was Quintus Junius Blaesus, who was Sejanus' uncle. It suited Drusus to have someone willing, as he put it, 'to play for my side'.

It is not to my present purpose to give an account of that scrambling and irregular war. Enough to say that I acquitted myself in a manner worthy of my ancestors, that Blaesus won victories which nevertheless achieved nothing, though they secured for him the title of *imperator*; and that, after his recall to Rome, his successor P Cornelius Dolabella, a scion like myself of the old nobility, and a friend of Drusus, efficiently ended the rebellion when, following my advice, he lured Tacfarinas into a trap and killed him.

I remained in north Africa for another two years, engaged in projects of reconstruction, the success of which may now be measured by the province's great prosperity and its value to Rome as one of the chief granaries of the Empire.

In that time I did not return to the city for more than a few weeks every year. I was therefore distant from the events which led to what appeared the unstoppable rise of Sejanus. Nevertheless I have taken great care to discover exactly what was happening in Rome then, and the account which follows is authentic.

The most important event was the death of Drusus in 23. At the time there was no reason to think it other than natural. He had complained for some months of fatigue. His limbs felt heavy and he could work for only short stretches of time. The Emperor sent for physicians from Alexandria and Athens, to consult with those from his own household. It may be that there were too many opinions for any course of remedial action to be effectively pursued. I do not know. In any case I have no confidence in any doctor. In certain moods it seems to me that it is the gods' will whether we live or die, and that all attempts to deny this are mere frivolity.

It was known of course, in circles close to the court, that Drusus and his wife Julia Livilla were on bad terms. There had never been much affection between them, though twin children, a boy Tiberius Gemellus and a girl Julia Livia, had been born to them in 19, and no one had questioned Drusus' paternity. But Julia Livilla was a difficult woman, given to resentment. She was the younger sister of Agrippina, and neither beautiful, being stout and heavy-featured, nor intelligent. She had come to despise her husband because he accepted the superiority of Germanicus, and she was intensely jealous of Agrippina. She was given to tantrums, which bored Drusus. It was commonly said that they never slept together after the birth of the twins, and that Drusus took the Syrian boy or eunuch, Lygdus, to his bed. Certainly he did not scruple, as I have related, to display affection for him. It is natural for a woman to come to despise a husband who prefers boys, and there was talk of others besides the Syrian. She had all the more cause for resentment because, like her mother Julia, she was highly-sexed. The story went that, when it was proposed she should have a guard of her own, Cornelius Dolabella said, 'Well, one every now and then.'

But, in truth, it was the Prefect of the Praetorians, Sejanus himself, who became her lover, though he was still married to his wife, whose names escapes me. (I could set Agathon to look it up, but the matter is unimportant.) If it had been anyone else I daresay Drusus would have been happy enough. He had a robust contempt for the idea of honour, in the context of marriage anyway, and he might have thought that his wife would be easier to live with, if there was someone ready to satisfy her lust, and capable – no easy matter – of doing so. But he was jealous of Sejanus, whose influence over his father he both resented and thought dangerous. Once, in a quarrel over some quite trivial question, he lost his temper with Sejanus and struck him on the mouth, causing it to bleed. Sejanus took the blow without making a fuss or offering to return it, remarking afterwards only, 'What a pity that the Emperor's son and heir has such bad manners and is no more capable than a child of governing his temper.' But I've no doubt he was wounded in his pride, which was very great, and he must have taken an even greater delight in cuckolding Drusus.

Tiberius did not weep when Drusus died, though he sat by the bedside throughout his son's last hours. But he moved from the chamber like a man who has aged twenty years, and it was after this that he took to calling Sejanus 'the partner of my labours' and to treating him as a substitute son.

This seemed to me understandable. I had, as I have already

remarked, a considerable respect for Sejanus' ability and I believed him to be truly devoted to the Emperor.

It wasn't till a couple of years after Drusus' death that I was given cause to think differently.

I was in Corinth, a city notorious for immorality. I should say that, on my return from north Africa, I had found myself denied immediate employment. Perhaps I had done too well there. It is dangerous to excel in times of tyranny, such as Rome was now entered upon. So I went travelling, and resolved to see the famous cities of Greece and Asia of which I had previously only read or heard tell.

In Corinth then, one night, I visited a brothel, as is customary there, for it is well-known that the stews of Corinth offer rare and superior pleasures to the connoisseur. I had indeed delighted myself with a tawny Armenian girl so cunning in the art of love that I was all but deceived by the passion she feigned. Afterwards I rested in the chamber set apart for that purpose, and amused myself by observing the other clients. One, whom I recognised as a senator, the grandfather of a friend of mine, was so exhausted by his exercise that his chest heaved, the sweat streamed from his brow, and he slobbered at the mouth. Yet the expression on his face was beatific, and I was certain that in his mind he was preparing himself for another onslaught. Every now and then he murmured, only to himself, 'Oh the choice limbs, oh the dear little pudenda . . .'

I called for wine. The boy poured it for me with his face averted. His hand shook. He spilled some. His short tunic rose up as he dabbed at the little pool. His legs were soft, dusky. He was scented, yet smelled of fear. I took his arm between my thumb and forefinger, just above the elbow, and pressed hard till he yelped.

'Look at me,' I said.

Reluctantly he submitted. His lips quivered.

'What are you doing here?' I said, still pressing on his soft brown arm.

Then I got to my feet and, not releasing him, gave money to the woman who kept the house, and commanded a room. I set the boy on the bed and stood back.

'You recognise me,' I said. 'Why did you think you could hide here?'

He shook his head and began to cry.

At last, 'It's my aunt's house,' he mumbled. 'I didn't know where I could go.'

'What are you afraid of?' I said.

It had irritated me that, though I recognised him as Drusus' boy, I had for the moment forgotten his name. Now, as I stood over him and saw, with a stab of pleasure, fear make him ugly, it came back to me.

'Lygdus,' I said, 'there are things I want to know.'

Perhaps it was his name, or my altered tone, I don't know, but he collected himself and in a little began to talk. Yes, of course, he was afraid. He had been his master's favourite and his Ganymede, and now his master, whom he had loved, truly loved, was dead, and . . .

'He was poisoned,' he said. 'He was poisoned. I know that. He knew it himself. And so I was afraid. I was the one who fetched him what he asked for, and gave him the watered wine he drank, and he was poisoned, and so . . .'

'But nobody thinks he was poisoned,' I said.

'But he was. She hated him and she killed him.'

'She?'

'Yes, of course, but I knew if there was any suspicion, I would be the one accused. They would say I had been bribed . . .'

'By whom?'

'I don't know and it doesn't matter. That's what they would say, and how could I prove myself innocent? They would have me . . . so I ran away.'

'Yes,' I said. 'I see it now. It's the way things are. Stop crying. Weeping is for women. Men must remember . . .'

'Men,' he said, looking up, and his lips attempting a smile. 'Men, indeed, but such as I ... I can't forget, but may I not weep?'

I gave him money, told him he was not safe there, that I had come upon him, and recognised him; therefore so might others, worse disposed.

He did not thank me. It was good Fortune had given him the gold, ill Fortune that made the gift possible.

'I loved my master,' he said again, meaninglessly.

Then, his long eyelashes wet with tears, he summoned up the coquetry that was, I suppose, natural to him, and looked an invitation.

'You should leave Corinth,' I said. 'Bury yourself somewhere more remote.'

All the things that happen to one in life are like the leaves on a tree in summer. What we hold in our memory is no more than the last few leaves that cling to the branches when the winter winds have blown. If I still see his tear-stained face, if the fear that set those soft legs quivering is still alive in my memory, it is because that brief encounter, that staccato conversation with a frightened boy, tore from me whatever illusions I retained.

It had not been hard to set aside the rumour that Germanicus had been murdered, not hard to judge that Agrippina's certainty was rooted in misery, resentment, hatred. But I did not doubt for a moment that the eunuch Lygdus spoke the truth, and this showed me what Rome had become, what we had, from generation to generation, made of Rome; and from that night on, I knew myself to be a cynic, without illusions; and Rome to be a killing-field. Remember this, I tell myself, when you come to write about poor Gaius. Yes, poor Gaius.

XI

Yes, poor Gaius. It's absurd that, now, I should feel pity for him. Nevertheless . . .

I saw him soon after my return to Rome, spring 26. (I must have Agathon check the dates before I write the other version for Agrippina. It seems to me that I'm in danger of telling my story, rather than Gaius'. But one can write only what one knows.)

He was staying with his father's mother, Antonia. The daughter of Mark Antony and Augustus' sister Octavia, she was respected by all, a strong-minded and virtuous woman. If anyone could have been a good influence on the boy Gaius, it was she.

It was my habit to visit her soon after any return to Rome; she had been a lifelong friend of my mother and my aunts. She had adored Germanicus, and liked to talk of him with one who had served under him. At the same time she had no patience with her daughter-in-law's conspiracy theories. She thought Agrippina supremely tiresome, and would not even concede that she was a good mother.

On the contrary. 'I grant you she's a devoted one,' she said, 'but a good mother would not try to rear her children to be instruments of revenge. Fortunately Nero is too sweet-natured to have any such thought. As for Drusus I can't be certain. He believes his mother does not love him as she loves his elder brother – who by the by is scared stiff of her – and so he is desperate to win her love and will do anything to secure it.'

'And Gaius?' I said.

'Gaius? You know perhaps that he is living with me now? He

was too much for his mother, who lacks patience, as you will remember. And Gaius needs careful handling, that certainly.'

'I recall him as a spirited small boy, who could be enchanting.'

'The small boy is still there. He emerges from time to time. But Gaius is moody, fitful, suffers from night terrors, alternates between periods of wild energy and extreme lassitude. I love him dearly, but I don't, I confess, know what to make of him.'

She paused, sighed: 'And though he's strong-willed, he is also too easily influenced and spends his time with the sons of eastern kings who are, to speak frankly, not what I would wish.'

Then she sent for him.

He entered awkwardly, as one who expects reproach or rejection: a lanky youth with straw-coloured hair, a big mouth and long lower jaw, and eyes of a blue like the Sicilian sky at noon. I suppose he was then fifteen. It was hard to believe I had carried him about that Rhineland camp on my shoulders while he hurled commands at the adoring legionaries. Antonia reminded him who I was. He affected to be delighted. Perhaps it was not affectation, but his talk soon became wild, wandering, inconsequential. Yet in it all there were streaks of intelligence. He threw his arms and legs about as if they were under imperfect control. Even when he sat on a stool by his grandmother, and allowed her to stroke his hair, his legs twitched. He talked of the Games, for which he had an inordinate enthusiasm; of the lions – 'Do you think man is a beast of prey himself?' he asked; and without waiting for a reply said, 'For my part I've no doubt. The philosophers who pretend otherwise, and prate of virtue, are cowards who have had their teeth drawn. That's what I think, and when I say that man is a beast of prey, I'm not insulting him. For there's nothing finer or nobler to my mind, and the beasts of prey are far more admirable creatures than the bald-headed sophists and pedants who preach a morality that is merely an excuse for their own weakness. You're a soldier, you must agree.'

And he gave me a sudden and charming smile in which, for the time it might take a sparrow to fly from one branch to another, I saw the small boy who had thumped his wooden sword on the table and proclaimed himself commander of the legions.

Of course I also thought he was speaking wildly, showing off, and was not sincere. It's the habit of adolescent boys to try out extravagant opinions.

It wasn't Antonia who told me that young Nero was becoming an embarrassment to the imperial family. She was too proud to make such an admission. But I hadn't been long back in Rome before I learned that it was common knowledge that his effeminacy aroused the derision of at least that part of the mob which retained the vigour of Republican days, and which did not share the general feeling of loyalty to the family of Germanicus. So when he appeared in the imperial box at the Games, which was but rarely since they were not to his taste, 'offending his refinement', as someone remarked, there would be cries of 'fairy prince', 'pansy', 'girly-boy', and such like insults.

'He's so heavily rouged,' my informant said, 'that you can't tell whether he blushes or not to hear such catcalls, such expressions of contempt. It's shocking, really. His father, the blessed Germanicus, would have been overcome with shame.'

'And the Emperor?' I said, keeping to myself my thoughts about Germanicus, now less favourable than they had formerly been. 'The Emperor, what's his reaction, seeing as how, with his son dead, he has named Nero as his heir? Or so I have been told.'

'Not exactly his heir, though it's true that he took Nero and his brother Drusus by hand, and commended them to the

Senate. How does he react, you ask? What would you expect? He despises the mob. So he curls his lips and hoods his eyes, and nobody knows what he is thinking. But I did one day see him lean over and press hard on young Nero's shoulder as if offering support. On the other hand, since, as you must know, Agrippina loses no opportunity to spread scurrilous rumours about Tiberius and to show how thoroughly she loathes and distrusts him, I can't suppose he is altogether dismayed to find one of her brood so despised. Of course there are others who say that he and Nero . . . But you know what a sink of iniquity Rome is when it comes to gossip and scurrility. For my part I don't believe these stories. Pansy boys were never Tiberius' type. He prefers something altogether more masculine, preferably German . . .'

And he told me of how one day Tiberius had incurred the fury of the mob by refusing to consent to the death of a blond young gladiator, 'who,' he added, 'he then took into his household where he acts as the Emperor's Ganymede. Charming times we live in, I must say. When I think of how my revered ancestor Marcus Porcius Cato denounced the immorality of his generation, which was nothing compared to that of today, well, words fail me.'

But they didn't. He went on in this vein for at least the next half-hour.

'This,' I thought, 'is real decadence: to pose as a moralist in order to have the pleasure of expatiating on all that is deemed vicious.'

'Mind you,' the descendant of the virtuous Cato said at last, 'the stories about young Nero may be exaggerated to discredit him and the family of Germanicus. I shouldn't be at all surprised to discover that they all originate from the circle around Sejanus, even from the man himself. You do know by the way, don't you, that he's the lover of Drusus' widow, Julia Livilla – and held that post even while her husband was alive. But then Drusus preferred a beastly little Syrian eunuch, can you imagine? That said, not all the gossip about Nero is false. I myself know a senator – no names, no pack-drill – to whom he wrote asking for an assignation and offering himself. Fact: he showed me the letter. I've never read anything more disgusting. And to think the boy is the great-grandson of the Divine Augustus!'

'Indeed, yes,' I said.

'Not that that signifies, of course. We all know the road Augustus followed to get the Divine Julius to name him his heir. He certainly warmed Caesar's bed for him. There's no doubt about that, though it's not safe to say such things. One has to guard one's tongue everywhere nowadays. Still, it may not be treasonable to recall that my grandfather once told me that as a young man, long before he became Augustus, when he was not even Caesar but was known as Gaius Octavius Thurinus, grandson of a moneylender as you will recall, he used to shave his legs with red-hot walnut-shells, to make himself more attractive.'

Young Nero's legs were also smooth, but it may be by nature rather than art. He had been a pretty child. He was now a pretty youth with dark wavy hair, a soft skin, charming profile and lips that trembled too readily when he was distressed. That was frequently: he was an unhappy young man. Certainly he was far from being the debauched creature scandal would have him be. He was shy, graceful, timid and, as I soon discovered, still affectionate. He had a taste for poetry, delighting especially in Anacreon, Callimachus, Meleager and Theocritus among the Greeks, Propertius among the moderns, and he wrote pretty verses himself, in both languages. I found him to be intelligent, far more so than his glorious father. Being so, he understood the precariousness of his position.

'The Emperor has been kind to me,' he said. 'And why not? He is my great-uncle after all. And I respect him. I'm sorry for him too, even though he's not what you might call sympathetic. He's a lonely old man, often wretched. That's my opinion anyway. It's not a position I would care for, and yet . . . It frightens me, the prospect. But I know he can't look at me without remembering that the people and even the legions preferred my father to him, and without thinking of my mother, whom he regards as his bitter enemy. And I'm sure Sejanus encourages his suspicions. Again, it frightens me. But what can I do?'

I have condensed many conversations, chance remarks, into a single speech, for convenience. He often spoke in this way, during that summer when we saw much of each other. If he seized the moment and made love with an ardour and a vigour that surprised me, it was, I now think, because he so feared the future. He often wept afterwards, not for shame.

'If only,' he said, 'I could live in Greece as a private citizen, and write poetry and drink wine by the sea . . .'

Poor Nero. I should have taken him to the east with me. But of course that was impossible. It would have been seen as a step to conspiracy.

XII

I spent three years in the east, strengthening the frontier, glad to be out of Rome. I pause on that last phrase. There was a time when it could not have been written by a man of my birth. That was in the era of politics, when free men competed against each other for office and responsibility. Then Rome grew rich, the bounds of Empire were extended, and the practice of politics was corrupted by money. Greed flourished. Violence prevailed. Order was broken, honour first despised, then forgotten by all but a few.

One of these was the Emperor himself. Many thought him a hypocrite because he sighed for the Republic. Doubtless historians, certain of their own virtue, will depict him as such. They will sneer as they set his professions of regret for the lost Republic against the monstrous treason trials that proliferated and disgraced the last years of his life, the last years of that reign which in his heart he despised. But they will be blind, even wilfully, to the cruel necessity to which he was subject.

The family of Germanicus was destroyed, all but utterly, while I commanded the legions in Asia. Once in the years of my sojourn there I sailed across the Euxine to Colchis, the land where Jason planted the dragons' teeth that sprang up as armed men eager to destroy him. On the return voyage, I thought of how Medea, infatuated with the Greek adventurer, slew her young brother Absyrtus and scattered fragments of his flesh on the waters to delay her avenging father. Rome was no less savage.

Sejanus, fearing Agrippina whom he knew to be his enemy, fearing the consequences for himself should Tiberius, already almost seventy, die, caused spies to be inserted into her household, so that they might find or devise evidence of seditious intent to be laid against her. The reports he forwarded to Tiberius were compelling. Years later when, as Emperor himself, Gaius Caligula had me examine them, and then, having had my summary, read some of these documents himself, he wiped a napkin over his sweating brow and said, 'It's impossible that the old man should not have believed this evidence. It stinks of treason.'

Some of that evidence was supplied by the middle brother, Drusus. Sejanus had suborned him, with the promise that he would persuade Tiberius to name him as his successor. This was enough. Ambition and the lust for power destroyed whatever natural affection the young man might have had. He had long been jealous of Nero; now he even allowed himself the liberty of retailing, even with embellishments, his mother's bitter and ill-judged criticisms of Tiberius.

Then in an attempt to provoke the foolish woman into still more rash behaviour, Sejanus had his agents advise her that it was the Emperor's intention to have her exiled and young Nero put to death. Only one course of action was open to her, they said, only one hope of safety: she must flee Rome with Nero and seek the protection of the legions stationed on the Rhine. There, she was reminded, the glorious memory of Germanicus was still held dear. There she would find support. Showing unaccustomed caution, she declined the bait. But the discussions within her household that preceded her decision were reported to Tiberius in a manner which led him to believe that this treasonable plot had initially won her favour, and been rejected only as too dangerous.

The Emperor had himself by now abandoned Rome and retired to Capri, the better, gossip said, to indulge his vices. (This was nonsense, but more of that later.) He did not return to the city even for his mother's funeral, only sent a eulogy to be read on his behalf by one of that year's consuls. Being removed from the city, he was, as I have come to realise, at the mercy of whatever reports Sejanus chose to make. He was enveloped in a web of lies and deceit.

Even so, his response to the stories about Agrippina and Nero disappointed Sejanus. Instead of having them arrested and charged with treason, he contented himself with sending a letter to the Senate – this being by now perforce his only method of communicating with that august assembly, in which previously he had been accustomed to speak in debate as if an ordinary member. In this letter he complained of the hostility Agrippina showed him, and spoke also, sorrowfully, of the 'flagrant indecency' of Nero's conduct. Given the rumours already circulating concerning his own way of life on Capri, that must have had some senators sniggering – behind a hand raised to conceal their lips – and others sweating lest their own lusts and misdemeanours be exposed.

Word of this letter enraged a portion of the mob – or so it seemed. While the senators hesitated, not knowing what Tiberius wished them to do, and not daring to guess at what this might be, a crowd outside the senate-house demonstrated in support of Agrippina and 'the blessed family of the glorious Germanicus'. It appeared spontaneous and has been received as evidence of the enduring popularity of the dead hero. But I have no doubt it was organised by Sejanus to alarm the Emperor.

What did Tiberius mean by that first letter, so vaguely couched? Later he told me that he hoped it would persuade Agrippina to desist from agitation and Nero, whom (to the boy's horror and dismay) he had married to his own grand-daughter, little Livia Julia, to lead a more virtuous life, or at least seem to do so. I find this hard to credit, an excuse formulated in retrospect. My own opinion is that his mind was in certain areas already confused, and that, in any case given by nature to vacillation, he wrote that letter without clear intention. It was an expression of his general discontent.

Be that as it may, Sejanus did not desist. He crossed over to Capri to tell Tiberius that he was in great danger. Conspiracies surrounded him. His own household was not to be trusted. And he told him of how one of Agrippina's freedmen had lately left her house disguised as a dealer in precious stones. He had first given Sejanus' agents the slip, and was not apprehended till he reached Lyon. A letter was found on his person. It bore no direction, but the wretch had been questioned and, under torture, had revealed the name of the intended recipient.

Then he showed Tiberius the letter. One sheet read as follows:

> As for the old man himself, it will be time enough to determine what is to be done with him when we are in control of the State. I know you have feelings of residual loyalty, and these shall be respected. Therefore you yourself may conclude in consultation with my son who, being tender-hearted, to some extent shares your sentiments, whether he be imprisoned on some island, less salubrious than that where he now lurks, or whether he shall be more conclusively disposed of. I am bound to say that, for our greater security, I favour the latter course, for who knows how many adherents he may still have, or whether his continued existence might become a focus for disaffected generals.

Was this letter genuine? It may have been, for Agrippina was as rash as she was bitter. (Even if it was, I can't believe that young Nero knew of it, or the conspiracy it was evidence of.) It wasn't, as Tiberius himself remarked, in her hand, but that meant nothing. Nor was it in cipher – surely an elementary precaution in the supposed circumstances.

For my part, I'm inclined, while conceding that nothing would have pleased Agrippina more than Tiberius' death, to think that it was concocted by Sejanus. What is certain is that Sejanus used it to fan fears which already gripped the old Emperor. Moreover he appealed to his generosity too, by telling him that his own utter loyalty meant that he himself was the first target of the conspirators.

'Whenever anyone approaches me with a plea or a petition,' he said, 'I wonder if he is the murderer they have dispatched. I try to reassure myself. "He's been searched by my guards," I say; "he can't possibly have a weapon concealed." And then I wonder if my own guards may have been suborned. It is to such imaginings, unworthy of a man, that my devotion to your person and your interests has condemned me.'

This was what convinced Tiberius: that Sejanus should confess himself afraid. It also excited him, just as he had been excited by the quivering legs of that German boy lying on the sand awaiting the death from which the Emperor reprieved him. So he consented to the arrest of Agrippina and Nero. He wrote again to the Senate, more explicitly. A vote of thanks for his deliverance from 'vile conspiracy' was passed with no dissenters. Some sycophants called for the death penalty. But Tiberius, to Sejanus' disgust, could not bring himself to consent to that. Agrippina was sent to the island of Pandateria where her mother Julia had previously been imprisoned, poor Nero to the island of Pontia, where some of Julia's lovers had been held and died.

I knew nothing of this for weeks. When I heard of it my first thought, I confess with shame, was for my own safety. Had I not myself been one of Nero's lovers? Now, a second cause for shame presents itself to me: Sejanus did not think me of sufficient importance to have me removed from my command. Instead, he wrote to me in terms apparently friendly, yet with an undercurrent of menace. I was to know that he trusted me, because I knew he could destroy me. And so I did nothing, said nothing, thought much, fearfully. I dreaded that Nero would find the means to communicate with me. Now I reproach myself for that fear and torture my sleepless nights with the certainty that, had he done so, I would for my own security have betrayed him to Sejanus and Tiberius.

XIII

Gaius meanwhile continued to live with his grandmother Antonia. He still associated with the scions of eastern royal families – the Thracian princes Polemo, Rhoemetalces and Cotys – young men brought to be educated in Rome and kept there as security for the good behaviour of their fathers, client-kings of the all-powerful Empire. They were loose-living young men, given to deep drinking and fornication, proud of their birth, resentful of the impotence to which their once free and independent kingdoms had been reduced. I never knew them well, but I cannot think their influence on Gaius was anything but harmful. That certainly was Antonia's opinion. She would have had her grandson abjure their company, but it is difficult for an old woman to bridle a mettlesome colt. In the end she always yielded to Gaius' sulking or cajolery. She loved him well, but not wisely, and assured herself that he displayed but the natural wildness of youth.

'After all,' she would say, 'my own father Mark Antony was what they call a roaring boy, forever in scrapes as a young man. I rather fancy that my dear Gaius takes after him. He certainly has a good deal of his charm. And whatever my father was as a boy and a youth, nobody can deny that he became a great general and a formidable and serious politician.'

There was, however, one thing to recommend these eastern princes: they took not the slightest interest in Roman politics. Gaius showed himself absolutely indifferent to the arrest of his mother and brother. Quite simply, he never spoke of it, or indeed of them. I have it from his sister, the younger Agrippina (for whom, I have to remind myself, the revised version of this

79

memoir is being written – though, to tell the truth, I have to my surprise become so engrossed in this exercise of memory that I pursue it for its own, and my, sake; which makes it all the more certain that whatever I eventually offer her will bear little resemblance to what I write now, for myself).

Where was I? Yes, I have it from her that for some years he never spoke of his mother, or of Nero, even to his sisters, to whom nevertheless he was devoted. Indeed when the younger Agrippina once tried to raise the matter with him, he looked at her – so she told me – 'as coldly as if he had been the Mouth of Truth cut into the rock of the Capitol' and said, 'We have nothing to do with all that. It's quite simply something that belongs to another life. For your own sake you must believe that.'

When, the following year, Sejanus turned against his other brother Drusus, who had, as I have written, played an important part in the destruction of Nero and Agrippina, and persuaded Tiberius that Drusus too was plotting against him, Gaius merely muttered, 'He always was a mad fool.' Drusus was arrested, and confined in a dungeon under the palace on the Palatine Hill where he fell into madness and died raving, having eaten his bedding. Gaius made no comment, but he must have realised that this death brought him closer to danger – or the throne.

Agrippina responded to the news of Drusus' arrest by refusing to eat. The prison governor, alarmed by the possibility that she might starve herself to death, and that he would be blamed, ordered that she should be fed by force. She resisted and, struggling with the guards, received a blow which cost her the sight of her left eye. She wrote angry and indignant letters denouncing her guards, the governor, Tiberius, the world. The governor had them intercepted. Supposing that the day would come when he might make use of them, he hid them in a secret place. Later he presented them to Gaius, who read them dry-eyed and gave the former governor gold.

'Why not?' he said. 'I despised him.'

Nero died, or was murdered. I have never known which. This was Sejanus' version, given in a letter to Tiberius and kept by him in a casket opened after his death:

> The miserable prince seduced one of his guards, a Calabrian of low intelligence, and persuaded him to abet his escape from Pontia. The other guards who suspected the liaison reported it to the governor, who informed me in my turn. I commanded that a close watch be kept, and the pair were apprehended as they tried to embark in a boat. A struggle ensued in which both were killed. I regret to have to inform you that Nero displayed shocking cowardice in his last moments and died pleading for his life like a woman.

I have never forgiven Sejanus for the cruelty and contempt of that last sentence. Nobody knows just how the young man died or what truth there is in this account. I suspect very little. Sejanus, now married to Drusus' widow, Julia Livilla, was drunk with power. His character, formerly admirable, had been corrupted. It is my opinion that he ordered that Nero be put to death, and concocted this story. Alternatively, he may well have had a guard ordered to seduce, or allow himself to be seduced by, Nero, in order to provoke the attempt to escape which he describes.

Frankly it no longer matters.

But what does? Agrippina – the younger, that is – is now married to the ridiculous Claudius, her uncle and Gaius's, that shambling oddity, drunkard, glutton and buffoon. And he is Emperor – the man whom Tiberius refused to allow to address the Senate, for fear that they would laugh; a man whose previous wives have cuckolded him almost under his nose. Agrippina's predecessor, Messalina, only fifteen when Claudius married her, was more promiscuous than any Egyptian dancing-girl, and for years the Emperor, master of the world, did not notice. Gaius used to say that no woman was by nature chaste; his successor might have picked that wife to prove this true.

But I digress. Why not? Though I am not yet old and still bear a resemblance to the young man I was, in body and face if not in mind, I find on the second bottle – and I'm now on the third – an inability to concentrate, to keep my mind fixed on the work in hand. Instead the line of past loves and murdered friends disturbs my vision. The gods long since abandoned Rome. We pay them mouth-honour only. I have reached a point at which I no longer believe even in omens, which nevertheless I search out, though indifferent to the future. It's commonly believed that Gaius became mad. I am not so sure. The horrid possibility presents itself: that he displayed his sanity by taking Rome as the hell it is. 'Remember,' he once told Antonia, 'I can treat anyone exactly as I please.' He spoke truth there. Was that mad?

It was undoubtedly Antonia who saved his life. When Drusus was arrested and Agrippina was still in prison and young Nero dead, she took Gaius and brought him to Capri to the Emperor. She arrived the day after he celebrated the marriage of his German boy, Sigismond, to a Greek girl called Euphrosyne. Years later she recounted their conversation to me. I now reconstruct it as best I can.

'It's strange,' she said, 'how we have remained friends.'

I picture them, two old people, the bent and twisted Tiberius, with the corners of his mouth dragged down, and the white-haired, rather plump Antonia, whose face retained an expression of serenity despite all the suffering she had endured, and I see them sitting on a terrace under a pergola of roses in flower and gazing out over the sea, which was Tiberius' last delight.

'And yet,' she continued, 'everyone tells me that you are the enemy of my family, sworn to destroy them.'

Tiberius would have looked away, unwilling to meet her candid gaze, and have muttered his reply.

'We could never be enemies. I remember gratefully how you refused to credit the vile rumours that held me responsible for Germanicus' death.'

She brushed that aside.

'I knew they were lies,' she said. 'I knew you could never harm your dear brother's son. But now two of his grandsons have been condemned by your command.'

He did not reply, she told me. He looked away and his hand trembled. He gulped wine, and shuddered. Then at last he mumbled something about the evidence being incontrovertible.

She told him she had arrived a day earlier than intended because she no longer cared to advertise her movements precisely. And she had brought young Gaius Caligula with her because – and she paused long enough to compel him to look at her – 'Because,' she said, 'I am afraid of what may happen to him if he is not with you . . .'

He did not answer.

She said, 'I am afraid to anger you.'

He shook his head.

She said, 'I am suspicious of some of his new friends. They talk wildly. They encourage my boy to drink heavily, and I fear the talk is then seditious. They feed him with stories to your discredit and invite him to speak rashly and stupidly. He is not stupid. Indeed in his way he is extremely intelligent, far more intelligent, I have to say, than Germanicus was, or than either of his brothers; but perhaps precisely because his intelligence is both acute and wayward, he does often speak foolishness. And I have discovered that at least two of his new friends are false friends, who have associated themselves with my boy, in order to provoke him to indiscretion.'

Here, she told me, she paused, hoping that Tiberius would speak. But the Emperor remained silent and would not meet her eyes. He looked out over the sea which was as empty as it was beautiful.

'I realised then,' she said to me, 'how utterly lonely he was, how isolated, how wretched, weighed down by the burden of Empire which he now found intolerable. But I had come for a purpose, and I would not let it go.'

'I don't know how to say this,' she said. 'I fear that, however I put it, I shall anger you.'

He made a vague gesture, as if to placate her or dismiss such fears. She took hold of his hand, and even in the sun of a summer afternoon, it was cold.

'Someone told me,' she said, 'that these new friends, these false friends, had been intimates of Sejanus. They were described to me as his protégés, his creatures. So I had them watched. One of them on several occasions went straight to Sejanus' house from the supper-parties he had attended with my boy, straight to his house on the Esquiline, and remained there a long time, as if making a report. Tiberius, my boy is wild and uncontrolled in his language. But it is only talk. He is easily led, because he has no confidence in himself, and so it would not be hard to lure him into saying stupid things, even to talk treason. So I am afraid for him, horribly afraid; I believe that one day, perhaps very soon, Sejanus will come to you and say that he has evidence that my boy has engaged in sedition, and witnesses to prove it. That's why I beg you now to take him into your own household. For his security.'

Tiberius gave no sign that he had heard her. But she knew him, and therefore knew that he was turning over what she had said in his slow, deliberate fashion. So she continued.

'Did all the evidence against my boy's brothers come to you by way of Sejanus?'

'I have never,' she said to me, 'been so nervous as while I waited for an answer to that question.'

'I trust Sejanus,' he said at last, and it seemed to her that the words were drawn unwillingly from him.

'Where there is trust,' she said, 'there is opportunity for treachery. Brutus could not have killed Caesar if Caesar had not reposed an infinite trust in him.'

Again he made that vague sweeping gesture with his hand, and now it seemed to her that it was a feeble attempt to push reality away.

She plucked up still greater courage. 'I was braver than I knew I could be,' she said to me, remembering, and flushing to remember.

'Nobody else will dare to say to you what I am now going to say. In giving your entire confidence to that man, you have isolated yourself. He has made of you a thing of mystery in Rome, and mysteries are always feared. You made him what he is, but can you be certain that he has not escaped your control? He tells you, I am sure, that he never acts but in your interest. But are you certain that he is not preferring his own? Agrippina has been your enemy, I do not deny that. She is a foolish woman, foolish, bitter, and unbridled in her speech. But are you certain that her sons, still little more than boys, were not made to appear your enemies by the contrivance of that man, Sejanus? It is not difficult in Rome today to procure evidence, or what seems to be evidence, of criminal thought.'

'Sejanus has never told me a lie,' the Emperor said.

'I felt desperate then,' Antonia told me, 'so desperate that I risked everything. "My dear Tiberius," I said, "you mean only this: that he has never told you a lie which you have detected." And then,' she continued, smiling at me now, 'I thought of Julia and of how Tiberius had trusted her and been deceived, and I said, "My dear, this is not the first time you have been betrayed by affection, and been deceived because you thought others must be as honourable as you are yourself. Listen, my dear," I said, "if what I say now echoes, as I believe it must, suspicions which you have had and yet denied, then you must know that you are as much the victim of this man, Sejanus, as were Nero and Drusus, or as I fear my poor chick, Gaius Caligula, may be. I suggest that you ask Sejanus to let you have a report on my boy, and I wager that he will come to you, his eyes brimming with tears, to present you with evidence that is calculated to destroy him. Has it not occurred to you that the chief, indeed the only beneficiary of my grandsons' pretended plots, has been that man Lucius Aelius Sejanus, whom I dare to call your evil genius."'

'And that was where you left him?' I asked. 'To revolve these matters in his mind?'

'No,' she said, and blushed again. 'I was still more daring. I told him of how in Rome now he was spoken of as a monster who had abandoned himself to the most shameful vice. I even dared to relay a story I had heard, of how, while sacrificing one day, he had taken a fancy to the acolyte, the young boy who carried the casket with the incense, and how he had rushed through the ceremony in order to hustle the lad out of the temple and assault him.'

'And?' I said.

'And there were tears in his eyes and he muttered of how the Roman people were ever scurrilous and loved nothing better than to exchange scandal, how like tales had been told of Augustus and Julius . . . But I persisted. I told him I had tracked that story to its source, which was none other than Quintus Junius Blaesus, who was, as you know, the uncle of Sejanus. He protested, feebly, that he could not believe it was in Sejanus' interest that men should despise him or view him with horror. I said it is in his interest that you should be thought unstable, cruel, capricious, near to madness. Then people will hold to Sejanus as the only man capable of restraining your savagery. It is because I know you are not that monster that I have dared to speak as I have done. If you were such a man I should not see the morrow. He looked at me as one who has abandoned himself to despair. "If what you say is true," he said, "I would wish that I might die tonight." And so I left him, weeping, and myself near tears also.'

XIV

So Antonia saved her boy's life. I've no doubt of that. Without her intervention Sejanus would have conjured his destruction as he had that of his brothers. And yet Sejanus was not by nature either cruel or malevolent. As I have written, I found him intelligent, dutiful, even sympathetic. If you had told the young Sejanus what he would do, what crimes he would commit, then I believe he would have looked on you with horror, and fled to some wild place to escape that future. Yet, slowly, insensibly, that future crept up on him, and the lust for power came to dominate his mind and take utter possession of his being. There is no other explanation. If I was a poet, I might make a tragedy of his life.

It is not to my purpose to recount his fall. The story is too well known. Suffice to say that Tiberius prepared the destruction of his favourite in anxiety and fear, for he was now persuaded that Sejanus aimed at the supreme power, incited to that goal by Julia Livilla, and that his own life, or at least his liberty, was threatened. Moreover, aware of his own unpopularity, from which at other moments he derived a bitter satisfaction, he could not be certain that the orders he gave for Sejanus' arrest would be obeyed. He had to rely on the second-in-command of the Praetorians, a fellow by name of Macro, a lewd intemperate man who had been first advanced by Sejanus and had recently been excluded from his confidence. Tiberius cannot have been certain that Macro would obey him; and feared that instead he might break his confidence and betray his intentions to Sejanus.

On the island the old man must have sweated. He had a

boat waiting for him at the landing-stage, in case the news was bad. But where could he have gone? To which legions? And why should he still care to escape death, at his age?

Gaius said, years later, 'It frightened me to see him so afraid. I knew then what I would rather not know, not remember. Of course I had been told about it before, had read of how Julius himself was cut down in the theatre of Pompey, and how my great-grandfather, Mark Antony, chose death before dishonour, falling on his sword. Truly, there is no guard against the malignance of Fortune and the gods.'

He liked, sometimes, to speak like that. Like an actor. Often indeed in hexameters. You couldn't be sure whether he was truly pompous or engaged in self-mockery. Even after his illness he was capable of that.

I anticipate.

Tiberius won, came through. The Senate, hearing his letter read, turned on Sejanus. Macro had already bribed the Praetorians who, with only two exceptions, deserted their Prefect of seventeen years. Scum, I thought when I heard that, even while being grateful that they did. How old was I before I discovered that you can despise and approve actions simultaneously?

Sejanus was strangled in the Mamertine. His children were put to death. So were scores of those thought to support him, or who had for one reason or another offended the mob. A disgusting episode, but necessary.

Afterwards Gaius and Macro formed an alliance, in bed and out of it, men said. Others preferred to believe that Macro prostituted his own wife to the young prince.

Tiberius did not neglect his education. He saw to it that Gaius learned to speak Greek correctly and with a good (Athenian) accent. He had him study philosophy and history, and master rhetoric. One of his teachers, a Greek from Antioch named Demetrios, told me that he had rarely known a pupil more adept at making extempore speeches. It is of course easy for princes to win praise. Nevertheless I am inclined to believe this Demetrios, for I have heard Gaius speak well in the Senate, in the Popular Assembly, and to a legion that was disgruntled and in which discontent simmered. On each occasion he won over his audience, and did so in a style suited to them. For instance, his address to the legions was full of humour, well-laced with jokes, some of them filthy, unbelievably filthy. 'And,' said a centurion, veteran of thirty years service, 'at least half of them were new to me.'

Gaius was very certain of his own taste, which admittedly was that of a callow youth. He had no time for either Homer or Virgil. He said once that the only good thing about Plato was his decision to ban the reading or recitation of Homer in his Republic. He dismissed Livy as a pompous bore. But he greatly admired Sallust and relished his sardonic humour. One might argue with his judgements, but at least they were his own.

Mostly his own anyway. He fell under the influence of the Jewish prince Herod Agrippa, who was his senior by some twenty years. A dissolute fellow, he had come to Capri to escape his creditors and to try to ingratiate himself with Tiberius, in the hope that would make him a king like his grandfather, Herod miscalled the Great. Or if not a king, then a tetrarch. He soon realised that his hope was vain; Tiberius despised him. As a Jew he was accustomed to being despised, so cultivated the young prince who would, after all, be Emperor himself before long. Then he remembered that Livia, the Emperor's mother, had lived to be ninety, or something like that, and sighed. Still, he had a fund of stories that amused Gaius.

'I'm not a whole Jew,' he would say, 'only a half-Jew. The religious Jews detest me, which is why, when you wear the purple' – he loved that sort of ridiculous phrase – 'you should set me to govern them.'

'Is it true,' Gaius asked, 'that the Jews believe there is only one god?'

'That's what their god told them,' Herod said. 'Thou shalt have no other gods but me.'

'But that doesn't mean that other gods don't exist, merely that they are forbidden to worship them.'

'That indeed is how it was in the beginning, when Moses led our people out of bondage in Egypt, but now things have moved on, and the most religious of my compatriots – and, I hope, future subjects – assert that the Jewish god, who must never be named, is the one true divinity.'

Gaius picked his nose.

'That's absurd,' he said, 'either there are lots of gods, or none. They worship Tiberius in Asia, I'm told. He says it's ridiculous. I don't agree, though of course I never argue the point with him.'

XV

I returned from the east. The Emperor summoned me to report. Tiberius no longer came to Rome. He had set off two or three times for the city since Sejanus' death. Each time he had turned back, overcome, it was said, by nausea. On one occasion he found that his pet snake, which he had adopted because snakes inspire revulsion in most men and women, was being eaten by ants. His soothsayer told him it was a warning that he should beware of the mob. He replied that he needed no such warning. All his life he had despised the easily roused fury of the people. The reception of Agrippina bearing the ashes of Germanicus had served only to intensify his contempt. Now, men said, he was afraid. I couldn't believe this. I was certain that he longed for death. Why then should he fear it, no matter how it arrived?

Yet, I was searched as I stepped on to the landing-stage, and searched again at the gate of his villa. His German boy, no longer a pretty youth, but a sturdy fellow whose yellow hair was now thin and whose face was burned the colour of brick by the sun, received me as if he had been a senior officer of the Republic. He saw my surprise, but did not acknowledge it. He was perhaps the only man Tiberius now trusted, if, that is, he was still capable of trusting anyone.

I found the Emperor at work, poring over accounts which the Treasury had sent him. His desk was piled with documents awaiting his attention. He fished among them for the last report I had sent from my province. He discussed it for some time, rationally and in detail.

'In the end,' he said, 'all that is left is duty.'

He called for wine, which the German fetched.

'I had a great respect for your father,' he said, as he had every time I had been summoned to his presence in the twenty years since our first meeting. 'He served with me in Illyricum, a good soldier and an honourable man, a true Republican. And I have found you worthy of him. That is why I was never disturbed by your friendship with that hellcat Agrippina, though much information was laid against you.'

He drank wine, throwing it to the back of his throat as legionaries drink the rot-gut served in the taverns of frontier towns. It was thin, sour, greenish stuff, the wine of the island. There wasn't a tax-gatherer in the Empire who didn't serve better wine. He looked out over the shimmering olive trees to the blue intensity of the sea.

'Duty,' he murmured, 'and to what end? They will howl with delight when they learn of my death, and Gaius . . . My father Augustus – my stepfather Augustus – spent years brooding over the succession. He rejected me twice, rejected me till there was no alternative. And now there is no alternative to Gaius. If I was ten years younger, then perhaps my own grandson Tiberius Gemellus, but he is only fourteen. A good boy, a handsome boy, why should I think of burdening him with Empire? So it is Gaius. Rome deserves him and he deserves Rome. A sink of iniquity where every day someone sends to me denouncing this man or that man, women too, for treason. Augustus declared he had restored the Republic . . . a lie. He was always a liar, my revered and now divine stepfather. If we had really restored the Republic, what then? You've served on the frontier . . .'

'We should have lost the Empire,' I said.

'And so?' he said.

'It is a law of nature. All things must grow or decline. We could no more have refused Empire than we could fly.'

'Alexander,' he said, 'wept because there were no more

worlds to conquer. I have wept because we have conquered so many.'

I never saw him again. That's my last memory, and his head seemed to have been carved from the cliff that rose behind him. It was grey in the evening shadow.

He was soon dead. There are different stories told. Some say he died naturally, which was not surprising, given his age. Others suggested that he was murdered by his German servant, who disappeared with his wife before Tiberius' funeral obsequies were celebrated. (But why he should have done so, I cannot imagine.) More recently, the word is that Gaius himself was responsible, for it has been hinted that Tiberius intended to change his will and nominate his own grandson Tiberius Gemellus as his successor. But there is no evidence of this, and my own last conversation with the Emperor contradicts it.

News of the death was greeted with general rejoicing. He had never been popular in Rome. Now the cry was 'To the Tiber with Tiberius'. It would not have surprised him; he was a flinty aristocrat whose contempt for the people was absolute. But he was also, I believe, the most wretched of men.

Part II

I

'It's the morning of the world,' I heard a butcher cry.

'The Golden Age returned,' another sweaty fellow with a red bandana tied round his forehead shrieked; and, as if to prove it, began to dance a jig.

When word came that the young Emperor was approaching the city, the mob surged to greet him. Nothing, I swear, had been seen like this in Rome since Agrippina brought the ashes of the hero Germanicus from Brindisi. Only this time, instead of wails and lamentation, there sounded paeans of joy. Gaius appeared, and was greeted with cries of 'star', 'chicken', 'baby', 'pet'. A veteran, who swore he was one of those who had carried the Emperor as a boy on his shoulders round the camp, and given him his nickname of Caligula, was so swamped by offers to stand him a jug of wine that I am ready to believe he could have drunk himself to death before the sun went down.

And it must be said Gaius himself looked splendid. He still had a good head of yellow hair, or at least his barber had set it to make it seem as if he did; and he stood upright and unarmed in his carriage, and extended his arms as if he wished to embrace the whole city. And perhaps he did.

I made my way to the Senate. When Augustus died, there had been a debate, as you remember, before the supreme *imperium* was granted to Tiberius. Indeed he himself had protested that the burden was too heavy for one man to bear, which some thought hypocrisy, and I now believe to have been honesty, Tiberius' first and most sincere attempt to salvage something from the wreck of the Republic, and persuade the Senate to resume its former share in the government of the Empire. But he was refused. 'O generation fit for slavery,' he would often mutter as the years passed.

But now we had no debate. Tiberius had been a general of renown, an experienced administrator, a great servant of Empire, when the Conscript Fathers had deliberated on the succession to Augustus. Gaius was a boy in his twenties. He had never served in the army. He had held no official post. He had had responsibility for nothing. For four years now he had been kept on Capri away from public life and the public eye. Yet no questions were asked, no arguments raised. With one accord, we consented to deliver to him the supreme *imperium*. Not a voice dissented when he was granted powers which, when Julius took them for himself, had provoked his murder.

And I confess that I too remained silent. Silent and ashamed.

I returned to the house I had inherited from my mother on the Aventine, through a city drunk with wine and joy. I had married again that summer. My wife Caesonia was the widow of a fellow-senator. She had been married to him when she was seventeen and he seventy, his fifth or sixth wife. That marriage gave her status. Her own birth was insignificant. My mother would not have approved the match, but Caesonia had been my mistress, intermittently, for years. I wanted a son. She was free. We married.

This is not my story, but Gaius'. Yet of course Caesonia was to be part of his life too, poor woman. So it is relevant to say here that, though she failed to give me the son I sought, she brought to my bed an intensity I had never previously experienced, and a variety I had scarcely imagined. I did not choose to ask her where or from whom she had learned such tricks and devices of love-making as even the most expensive courtesan of Corinth cannot to my knowledge match. Perhaps they were natural to her, but I think not. They spoke even then of schooling in the most extreme depravity and obscure and compelling delights. Besides which, I have to say, even a whiff of her body and its musky odour excited my manhood. Never have I felt more alive than in the year and a half of that marriage. It may even be that the spell she cast over me accounted for the complacency with which I watched Gaius' first essays in the exercise of supreme power. Nothing that happened in the Empire mattered one half as much as the pleasures to which Caesonia introduced me in our marriage bed.

She herself took a lively interest in Gaius from the first. There was nothing unusual about that. All the ladies and young women and girls were on edge, seeking to attract the young Emperor's attention. It didn't matter whether they were married or not. Our ancestors may have set a high value on the married state and talked even about the sanctity of wedlock (see the elder Cato, passim). Then, in later generations, husbands discovered how easy, and often delightful, it was to shake their wife loose and find another. Before long the ladies themselves learned the lesson so that now, in our days which poets rightly style degenerate – a state of affairs which nevertheless most of the poets I have known find perfectly agreeable – divorces are initiated by wives as often as by husbands, and no self-respecting married woman is without a lover. So it is not surprising that the question of who should be the first to lure the Emperor into marriage was, as Caesonia said, 'the only topic when we meet together'. I should say that most of my wife's lady-friends were younger than she, and I doubt if any thought Caesonia with her thick thighs and rather stout figure a candidate for the imperial bed.

In any case for some months they were all to be disappointed. Gaius showed no interest in any of them. His affections were divided between his sister Drusilla and the actor Mnester, for whom he developed a passion the moment he cast eyes on him, which was indeed in the first week after he arrived in Rome. Mnester, a man of my age, was himself a notorious pederast; it must have come as a surprise to him to be the pursued rather than the pursuer. He was prudent enough to let himself be caught, though his taste was said to run to slim ephebes and lithe young acrobats rather than to lanky, bony young men with bad breath. All the same I could never be sure that the Emperor's passion for the actor was not in large part simulated. He liked to shock the respectable, and the sight of the Emperor hanging on the neck of a middle-aged actor going bald at the temples, and slobbering kisses over him, certainly did that. When Antonia, who alone dared to speak frankly to Gaius, warned him that such behaviour would cause him to be regarded with contempt and that while Emperors could endure hatred, they could not survive contempt, he laughed and said, 'Please remember, Grandma, that I can do anything I choose.'

It amused him to demand the utmost respect for his lover's performances in the theatre, which by the way were excessively mannered and decidedly old-fashioned. On one occasion Gaius was irritated to find a certain equestrian chattering throughout. So he had him arrested, and then sent him as the bearer of a sealed message to King Ptolemy of Mauretania. Just to make sure he delivered it, the wretched man travelled with an escort of six soldiers from the Praetorians, who were instructed to see that he handed the letter, seal unbroken, to the king himself. Which done, with the miserable creature trembling in terror, the message was: 'Do nothing, either good or bad, to the bearer of this letter.' Nobody can say that Gaius lacked a sense of humour. But I anticipate and run ahead of my narrative.

If his passion for Mnester was itself a piece of play-acting, that for his sister Drusilla was very different. She was the sister closest to him in age, only a year separating them. As children they had played together, apart from their brothers and sisters, and conversed in a secret language of their own. I can't remember how it was formed, except that they had their own peculiar names for things and also reversed words so that case or tense endings preceded the stem; for example, the singular of the noun *annus* would decline: *usann, eann, umann, iann, oann, oann.* It used to infuriate Agrippina when they spoke it in her presence, because she couldn't bear not to know what her children were saying and doing. She suspected them of being disrespectful, which I suppose they often were. Not even Agrippina got everything wrong.

I dwell here on his love for Drusilla – a love which was undoubtedly consummated – because it holds at least one of the keys to his peculiar character. There are of course some who, now that he is safely dead, dismiss Gaius simply as a madman, therefore of no interest. This is not so; if it were, I should not be troubling myself to write this memoir. Certainly he often behaved madly. There were many who thought that the gods had cursed him and deprived him of his wits. But he was more interesting than that.

Drusilla . . . he felt safe with her, as with no one else except perhaps his grandmother Antonia. She represented for him, more completely than any other being could, the childhood idyll from which he had been snatched by circumstance or fate. Think of it: he was an adored small boy, the darling of the legions. His father was a favourite of the gods, especially of Apollo, for his smile was like the rays of the summer sun. (Poets used that line often, too often; nevertheless it was the impression Germanicus made.) They had a mother who loved them passionately, but whom the children nevertheless feared. Consequently all six of the children grew up to be liars; poor Nero, the one I knew best, lied as easily as birds sing, while being nevertheless kind, gentle, sympathetic, lovable. But they all told lies. (I can't send this stuff to my Agrippina; it will have to be utterly recast. She tells lies herself as naturally as she breathes.)

Then their father died. Their mother told them, time and again, that he had been poisoned by order of his wicked uncle, the Emperor, who feared him and hated him because he was so popular with the army and the People. She told them this with such emphasis and conviction that they could not but believe it, as indeed she believed it herself. They found that they had inherited his popularity; so they grew up knowing themselves to be the darlings of the crowd. But Agrippina also instilled in them the knowledge that they were surrounded by enemies, bent on their destruction, and these, she said, were controlled by Tiberius. She taught them to think of the old man as a master-spider weaving webs to entrap them. So they grew up also in fear; in fear and resentment, for their mother insisted that they had been cheated of what was rightfully theirs.

Sejanus then sought to lure Agrippina and her sons into treasonable activity. When she was arrested, this proved to her younger children that everything she had said was true. There was indeed a conspiracy, aimed at their family. Nero was held prisoner, and either murdered or, conveniently, 'killed while trying to escape'. Drusus was arrested, and either murdered or starved to death, his wits having fled. Their mother was attacked by a guard and lost an eye. Then she too died, mysteriously.

Is it to be wondered at that young Gaius and Drusilla should hold each other close, should confide only in each other, should trust none but each other? There were no other arms in which either could find security. If, as is said, Antonia found them entwined in the same bed, both exhausted and both weeping, who that has any understanding of fear and loneliness can pretend to surprise?

The law prohibits incest, and in Republican Rome it was viewed with peculiar horror as something corrupting and offensive to the gods (some of whom nevertheless indulge in the practice). The vice seemed all the more repulsive because it was known to be the custom in some royal houses of the east for brothers to be married to sisters; the Ptolemies of Egypt are one example. So the liaison between Gaius and Drusilla was dangerous.

Fear of the law and, even more, fear that their infatuation with each other might be discovered by Sejanus' agents was another unspoken reason for the urgency of Antonia's visit to Capri when she persuaded Tiberius to take the boy into his household. She hoped that their incestuous love was a phase of their disturbed adolescence, to be killed by separation, and then forgotten.

Gaius, who learned on Capri to assume the mask of a consummate hypocrite, gave her reason to suppose her hope well-founded. If he occasionally corresponded with his sister, he did so in the most ordinary and casual manner, his letters being brief, dull, factual and devoid of any terms of endearment. Drusilla had the self-control to reply in like vein.

But as soon as he was free of Tiberius and invested with the purple, he cast aside the restraint he had imposed on himself. Indeed I have been told that the very first night he took up residence in the imperial palace, he summoned his sister to his bed. Drusilla responded at once. She had never loved anyone but Gaius; poor girl, she never would. He on the other hand was notoriously promiscuous. Even on Capri he couldn't entirely subdue his appetites. Some say that he raped the wife of Tiberius' German favourite (and former catamite), and that the old Emperor had summoned him to answer this accusation when, fortunately for Gaius, he was taken ill and died. Nevertheless, at this stage of his life, if he loved anyone truly, it was Drusilla.

II

Within only a few weeks of his accession he resolved to embark on an act of piety. He would sail for Pandeteria and the Pontian islands to retrieve the ashes of his mother Agrippina and his brother Nero that they might be reverently placed in the family tomb. Being well aware, as Tiberius had never been, of the value of influencing the opinion of the people, he ensured that this intention was well publicised. In passing, I may observe that he had given thought to what I might call public relations. He remarked to me that Augustus had been a master of that art.

'Look at his *Res Gestae*,' he said, referring to the record of his reign which Augustus issued. 'I've studied it carefully, and there are no lies in it at all, and yet there is scarce a sentence which expresses the absolute truth. But everybody now accepts it as utterly authentic history. Magnificent . . .'

So he had established a committee to study the best way of presenting imperial policy and his own acts to the public. He gave it one of his favourite freedman, a very intelligent Greek from Tarsus called Narcissus as its secretary, and invited me to be its chairman. Perhaps I should say now that from the moment he became Emperor he showered favours on me, and made it clear that he reposed complete trust in me, because, as he said, 'My hero-father had a high opinion of you, and besides you carried me on your shoulders when I was a little boy. Even my mother used to say what a fine bold part you played in quelling that famous mutiny on the Rhine.'

So I was close to him, and for this reason you may accept everything I relate as authentic.

He also invited me to accompany him on his quest for the family ashes. I say 'invite' because it was indeed couched as an invitation, though there was naturally no question of refusing.

'It's right that you should be with me,' he said, 'after all, you were one of my brother Nero's lovers,' and he cackled and dug me in the ribs with his elbow.

'Poor Nero,' I said. 'I accept of course but I must tell you that when you have held a live body in your arms, there's little satisfaction to be expected from gazing on the ashes it's been reduced to.'

He thought that an excellent joke, then, as so often, broke off abruptly, in mid-laugh.

'Poor Nero certainly, but we must look on the bright side. If he hadn't been one of that man's victims and was still alive, I shouldn't be Emperor. That's not a thought that pleases me. So it was perhaps all for the best.'

He was in high spirits on the voyage. Even the wretched galley-slaves responded to his cheerfulness and sang their work-songs less mournfully than usual. Admittedly he told them that he would be seriously annoyed if he found any of them looking gloomy. That was a joke to him too.

We reached Nero's island first, a sad barren place, sharp rocks baking under a merciless sun. At Gaius' insistence the governor paraded the convicts in his charge, and then showed us where Nero had been confined.

'I'm afraid my predecessor had orders to treat him harshly and deny any request he might make,' he said

'It's fortunate for you, my good man,' Gaius gave the governor a wicked smile, 'that you are not your predecessor. If you were, do you know what I would do? No? Guess? . . . All right then, I would have handed you over to two of the most villainous-looking rogues in your charge, and told them they were free to do whatever they chose to you.'

Even though he had been assured that Gaius was speaking

of how he would have treated his predecessor, the governor trembled. It was clear that he was thinking how easily the Emperor might decide to amuse himself by presenting him to the villains as a surrogate. I imagine he was a very happy man when Gaius transferred his brother's remains to the splendidly engraved urn we had brought.

Even then, Gaius had a last joke for him.

'In honour of my visit,' he said, 'I desire that you give all the convicts a holiday from their labours. But if any escapes, you shall take his place.'

Then he selected a peculiarly evil-looking brute, a red-haired Gaul with a squint in his eye, and amnestied him.

'I need a new guard for the imperial closet,' he said. 'Poor brute, looking like that, how could he fail to turn criminal?'

At night, as we sat at our wine on the ship's deck under a summer moon, Gaius said, 'I do intend to be a good Emperor, you know.'

'I don't doubt it,' I replied.

'But what makes an Emperor good?'

'Well,' I said, 'that's not so easy. We've had only two. Three, I suppose, if you include Julius.'

'Four, counting my great-grandfather Mark Antony.'

'Most people don't think of him as an Emperor,' I said, 'but I suppose you're right, and he really was one. The lesson he teaches is clear enough: don't fall in love with the Queen of Egypt.'

'There's no Queen of Egypt. Even I know that,' he said. 'If there was . . .' and he giggled, 'then I can't swear as I shouldn't, not if she was like what Cleopatra was, by all reports. But I'm serious. What makes an Emperor good?'

What did I answer? What could I have answered? Poor boy, he really was serious and he really did want to know. I suppose I talked about the necessity to respect the Senate but at the same time to control it, to keep the confidence and trust of the legions and see that they were paid on time, and that their term of duty was not extended arbitrarily, to ensure that taxes were collected and justice done . . . I don't know. What I do remember is that he listened carefully, brow (as they say) furrowed, that every now and then he interrupted to say something like, 'Yes, that's good' or 'I'll remember that,' or 'I hadn't thought of it that way'; and sometimes he just nodded. I talked for a long time, going well beyond the range of answers to the question he had posed, so that I ended by giving him what amounted to an outline course in Roman constitutional history, theory and practice. I had never known him quiet for so long, except for an evening spent in Tiberius' company on Capri, when the young prince never spoke except in monosyllables, and then only when asked a direct question.

When at length I finished or broke off, fearing I had bored him, he thanked me profusely and said, 'I'm going to keep you by me to keep me doing my duty the right way. For the first time you've made me understand why the Old Man always spoke of the Empire as his "burden". I thought it was just his usual sour grumble, but now I see what he meant. It's a great responsibility, isn't it? I must be worthy of it. When we get to Pandeteria, I'll swear an oath to that effect, and make a sacrifice. To which god, do you think?'

'Jupiter,' I said, 'it must be Jupiter, but in my opinion the sacrifice should be made at Rome.'

'I see that. But there will be no harm swearing the oath twice and making two sacrifices. Surely that will please him?'

He gulped down his cup of wine which he hadn't touched since I started talking, and poured himself another. Then he leaned forward with a broad happy smile.

'Tell me,' he said, 'just exactly what did you and my brother Nero do together?'

I obeyed. What else could I do?

'Not my taste,' he said, 'but then unlike Nero – he was really a girl, wasn't he – I've never fancied mature men.'

My face must have betrayed scepticism because he crowed with laughter.

'I see you're thinking of Mnester,' he said. 'But that's a joke. I mean, Mnester's my private joke. Of course I adore him but it's the parade of adoring that amuses me. Anyway he may be thirty-five but you couldn't call him mature, not if you'd heard him giggle in bed. But really he's a joke and I expect I'll soon be tired of it. Generally though, if I can't have a woman, I prefer a boy, though not a girly-boy like Nero but a tough muscular fellow, an athlete or a street-boy. You can pick up some really juicy pieces in the taverns of the Suburra, stinking of the stable some of them. I discovered that when I was quite young and used to slip secretly out of my grandmother's house. Of course I won't have to do that now when I can have anyone I choose fetched for me. But it would still be fun to do it the old way, in disguise perhaps. What do you think? You know, I get a terrible headache if I can't have sex every day.'

So, in moonlight, with a gentle breeze blowing from Africa, we sailed, talking of sex, for the island that had been his mother's prison.

He was cheerful in the morning, and evidently had no headache. Then, as the island came in sight, he said, 'Poor Mother, she consumed her life in hatred. We all disappointed her because we couldn't hate as much as she did. Drusus perhaps, but not the rest of us. I'm grateful to my grandmother, for this as for so much else. She taught me that hatred is a waste of time and energy. She used to say, "You try to direct it outwards, but the result is always the same. The more fiercely you hate, the more fiercely you burn up, till there's nothing left of you." I don't think I'm capable of hate.'

III

Gaius was determined to rule well.

'The people love me,' he said. 'I must be worthy of their love.'

It was early morning, before a meeting of the council he had convened to advise him. He looked out over the city and the swelling murmur of voices – hucksters crying their wares amid the cries of coachmen, draymen, touts for schools of drama, dancing and rhetoric – may have sounded like love in his ears. I don't know. I record, from memory, his pronouncements, and I don't know which were sincere, which spontaneous, which calculated. But then I believed him because I wanted to.

I had respected Tiberius, even admired him, while certainly, as I have written, pitying him also. But Rome and the Empire now required an Emperor who was eager, energetic, ardent to lead as well as to serve. When Gaius bestowed on me, or the company, that frank boyish smile, which spoke of his delight in the opportunity offered him, it was possible to believe he would indeed be that leader. Though in appearance gawky, and in movement awkward and ungraceful, he had nevertheless inherited Germanicus' charm, as Nero had, though in a different, more vigorous and masculine form than that poor boy.

Now he outlined to me the programme for government he would put before the council. Since so many now speak of him as acting only on caprice – so malicious have been the judgements delivered since his death – I repeat it here, that future generations may judge how well-considered, liberal and sensible it was, how virtuous were his intentions.

First, he announced that he would hold special games in honour and memory of his mother. By doing so he would please the people and discharge a filial obligation.

Then his grandmother was to be invested with all the honours granted to Livia. She would be Antonia Augusta.

'I wish the people to understand that I do not reign alone, but am supported by the whole imperial family, and the elevation of Antonia, to whom I owe so much, signifies this. Besides, if such as we do not honour familial bonds, how can we expect that the poor should do so? Augustus understood that the foundation of a strong Republic is the solidarity of family structures. That's right, isn't it, Lucius?'

'So I understand,' I replied.

'My family was destroyed, or torn apart by malice. But the destruction was made possible by our legal system which encourages men to denounce others for crimes and inform against them, and be rewarded for their testimony. I intend to put a stop to that. There will be no more trials for treason unless I myself and a committee I shall appoint to advise me have considered the evidence, questioned the informers, and tested the case privately. And anyone whom I discover to be acting from malice and bearing false witness will be punished, in whatever way is appropriate to his rank. I want this determination of mine to be published.'

He made that promise good, getting three senior senators with much experience of pleading in the courts to draw up a document which he himself first scrutinised carefully.

At the same time he declared that there should be no 'retrospective justice'. So he abjured the opportunity to take revenge on those who had been responsible for the conviction of his mother and brothers. He ordered potentially incriminating documents stored in the Bureau of State Security to be burned.

No one could fail to be moved by the magnanimity this displayed.

Next he revoked all sentences of exile, and allowed those condemned by them to return to Rome.

'A new reign,' he said, 'should offer a new life to those who have erred and suffered for their mistakes.'

Likewise he ordered that books banned by the previous regime might be published.

'An Emperor should not fear criticism,' he said.

'Tiberius disdained it,' said the aged Senator M Cocceius Nerva, an intimate of the late Emperor, who had been one of the few regularly summoned to Capri. 'He disdained it, nevertheless found it expedient, even necessary, to follow the example of Augustus and impose a censorship. He used to say that what did not trouble him in his private capacity might nonetheless endanger the Republic.' He looked at Gaius and saw him frown. 'Naturally,' he continued, 'I do not make this point in opposition to your generous intention, rather and merely as something you might consider.'

Nerva coughed, delicately, into his sleeve, as if to deprecate his own words, while nevertheless holding to his opinion. Though his family was undistinguished, provincial parvenus from Narnia in fact, his father and uncle had been partisans of Mark Antony, remaining loyal to him, for which reason Gaius held this present representative of the family in respect. Yet after Actium and the destruction of the Antonian faction, they had served Augustus with equal loyalty, and one, but I forget which, had been made Proconsul of Asia. Modest, deferential, yet never yielding his own judgement to whatever was the consensus of the day, this Cocceius Nerva had been one of the few whose advice was sought, and sometimes followed, by Tiberius. Once, when I asked him to account for the manner in which his family had ridden the stormy seas of two lifetimes, he smiled and said, 'We kept our heads down and rarely raised our voices.'

Now the frown left Gaius' face and he grinned:

'We shall bear what you say in mind, and not forget you

if your warning is proved wise. But at any rate, for the time being, this Emperor does not fear criticism . . .'

He broke off and for a moment seemed distracted.

'I'm told I'm already a god in some parts of Asia,' he said. 'Can a god be damaged by criticism from mere mortals?'

This was not a question which any of us hastened to answer. Had I done so, I might have remarked that once in Galatia I saw villagers hurl the image of their local god into a refuse pit because he had failed to satisfy some demand they had made.

'I had thought of giving an order that, in honour of my accession, all debts should be cancelled.'

'That would certainly be popular,' Quintus Lollius, not only a sycophant, but a nobleman himself burdened with debt, responded.

'Not with the bankers or the tax-collectors, who have already compounded for this year's taxes,' Cocceius Nerva said.

The Emperor smiled.

'You are right as ever, Nerva. That's what they told me at the Treasury. So I've abandoned the plan. Pity, really. It would have amused me to see the bankers' indignation. Now I come to the last item on today's agenda: the question of the consulship. It's proper that this being the first year of my reign I should hold one consulship myself. But who should be my colleague? Who is worthy?'

Nobody replied. The consulship has of course long been an honorific post. It belongs to that part of the constitution which may be styled decorative. Not since Republican times has the consul been expected to act as head of state or to command an army. Indeed, even in the last years of the Republic, military commands were usually held by proconsuls, since it was expedient that they should last more than the single year of a consul's office. Now the consul has few duties, except to lead (if he chooses) the Senate, and conduct sacrifices and suchlike routine and purely formal business. But in those years when an Emperor chooses to hold one of the consulships himself, the choice of his colleague becomes important, because it signifies where favour rests, and therefore even the direction that state policy may take.

Nobody, as I say, replied. Nobody was willing to suggest a name, lest it be thought that he was proposing someone who might appear, if only temporarily, the Emperor's equal. Almost everyone around the table would have been delighted if the Emperor chose him as his colleague, but no one dared to propose himself. I remembered how Tiberius had lamented the passing of Republican days when men competed openly against each other for office; and now we waited, like servants, to hear the name that the Emperor might pronounce.

Do I include myself in this collection of cowards? No, for Gaius had already revealed his intention to me, during our voyage back from Pandeteria. He thought it a splendid joke, and I chose not to argue with him.

Now he got up and strolled round the table. Nobody turned to look at him. All kept their gaze lowered. Every now and then he would stop and tweak the lobe of a councillor's ear, and say, 'Have you really no suggestion to make?'

At last he tired of this teasing and resumed his seat. Speaking in the most formal and dignified manner that he could muster, he said: 'Since none of you chooses to advise me despite my invitation, I must make the decision myself.' His eyes sparkled. 'There is one member of my family who has never held an official position in the State. It is time that was rectified.'

At this point he was interrupted by Lollius, who guessed where the Emperor was heading, and thought to gain merit by anticipating his announcement.

'Indeed yes,' he said, 'though your cousin, the late Emperor's grandson, Tiberius Gemellus, would normally be thought too young to receive such an august honour, yet in the first year of what will, I trust, be your glorious reign, and considering the paucity of other candidates, even, alas, in the imperial family, I can think of no one more appropriate, no choice that would be more popular, or contribute more to your own reputation.'

Gaius heard him out, and when he had finished, grinned broadly.

'An interesting suggestion. Little Tiberius Gemellus . . . do you know, I hadn't thought of him, had quite forgotten him, but no, I think not, he is still too young, still a schoolboy in fact. It would look absurd, and the Emperor must never seem absurd. No, I was referring to my beloved father's brother, the distinguished historian Claudius, grandson of Mark Antony . . .'

'Claudius – Clau-Clau-Claudius,' exclaimed Marcus Aemilius Lepidus, laughing with the freedom he felt permitted to him as the Emperor's brother-in-law. (For he was married to Drusilla and had borne being cuckolded by Gaius with a truly aristocratic equanimity, all the easier to assume because his own taste ran to boys and he had, he once admitted to me, more than once slept with Gaius himself.) 'My dear Gaius, you can't be serious. This is one of your jokes, and a very good one, if I may say so. But I know Claudius well, and can speak freely since he is not only my uncle by marriage but also a cousin of my mother. Why, you might as well make your horse a consul as Claudius. It would be no more ridiculous.'

'My horse? Incitatus? That's another interesting suggestion and one that I'll bear in mind for the future. Incitatus would certainly make a very handsome consul and a digni-fied one too. And he's certainly more intelligent and much more beautiful than many who have been consuls, including, if I may say so, Marcus, your own great-grandfather, the Triumvir, whom my great-grandfather Antony described as an adequate message-boy. No, it's going to be Claudius. He has his disabilities, I grant you, and both Augustus and Tiberius were prejudiced against him on that account, but he is the brother of my late hero-father, and in granting him the consulship which he has long desired, I shall honour my father's memory and so please the people. Besides, like I said, he's a distinguished historian. His history of the Etruscans runs to I don't know how many volumes, and has been highly praised even if nobody has read it.'

IV

Was Gaius playing a game, enjoying a private joke? It was hard to tell. Even then he would fly from one extreme to another, baffling those he spoke to and those who observed him. This decision to grant Claudius a consulship infuriated Marcus Aemilius Lepidus. He could hardly contain himself till the meeting was over. Then, as we left, he took me by the sleeve and led me to a quiet corner in the palace gardens.

'You must stop it,' he said. 'If anyone has influence over the Emperor, it is you. And yet you sat there silent. If he persists with his intention, and makes Claudius consul, he will make a laughing-stock of us all. And from my study of history and knowledge of men, a regime may survive being hated, but not ridiculed.'

'But Gaius is popular,' I said, 'he is popular as neither Augustus nor Tiberius ever was.'

'With the mob, with the stinking mob, I grant you. But we all know how fickle the people are. They will applaud an actor or a gladiator one day, and howl him down and throw dung at him the next. But with the people who matter – the Senate, the provincial governors and the generals – his popularity is by no means assured. He's at best on probation. They all think of him as a mere boy and they're watching him carefully. We Romans demand one thing of our leaders, and that is dignity.'

'Competence also, I should have thought.'

'A reputation for competence has to be earned, but dignity is something that is displayed. Both Augustus and Tiberius had dignity, and both also showed themselves supremely competent. That is why their supremacy was tolerated, why their authority was accepted. Tiberius wasn't loved, not even liked, but he was respected and feared. As for Augustus, I'm too young of course to have my own memories of his reign, but I've heard my father and uncles speak of him. When he presented himself as the benign "father of his country", that was a pose, a pretence. The mob may have acknowledged him as that, but people like us – I mean, our fathers, people of some standing in the Republic – knew the claim was fraudulent. Yet they kept quiet because they saw that it lent him dignity and reinforced his authority, and that made for stability in the Republic. Gaius isn't in that position, and if he is allowed to make a drunken clown like Claudius consul, nobody who matters is going to take him seriously. And you know, as I do, that if the head of state isn't taken seriously by people who matter, he won't be head of state for long. There: I've spoken my mind.'

'Indeed,' I said, 'and you needn't fear that I will report your words. But in turn I must say this. It's a mistake to think of Gaius as a lightweight. I have found more strength of will, and perhaps also of character, in him than I had expected. As for Claudius, well, it may be that the best thing is to treat his elevation as natural and proper, and to regard it, as the Emperor himself said, as an act which honours the memory of Germanicus, and indeed Antonia his mother, the new Augusta.'

'She can't stand him. You know that. She can't bear to be in his company.'

'It's not so much that he embarrasses her. He bores her. He embarrassed Livia, that's true, and Augustus, who had a horror of dwarfs and any sort of physical disability. But, you know, though he is odd and, as you say, often drunk, he's not entirely negligible. Unlike the Emperor, I have actually read some of the histories he has written. They don't sparkle, they don't amuse, as for example Livy's do, but they are solid, respectable pieces of work. I admit I was surprised to discover that. It made me wonder if we haven't underrated him.'

No doubt now that Claudius is our Emperor, this conversation seems ill-judged. It would certainly be rash to reproduce it in the version of Gaius' biography I shall send to Agrippina. Even though I acted as his defender, it's clear that I felt in a position to patronise him and couldn't take him altogether seriously. But then nobody did. He was the fool of the family. That was generally agreed. Nothing indeed reveals more surely the contempt with which he was regarded than the fact that Sejanus had never troubled himself with him, never sought to implicate him in any of the largely imaginary plots against Tiberius by means of which he destroyed Nero and Drusus. He simply didn't think for a moment that Claudius could be any danger to him, any hindrance to the achievement of his ambitions.

Even now, separating the man from his office, it's difficult to find anything to respect, let alone admire. Though I spoke in defence of his historical writings, I knew that they were plaguey dull, the work of a pedant. Gaius' sisters all used to tease him, calling him 'poor old nuncle' and Agrippina herself used to imitate his stammer and his ridiculously old-fashioned style of speaking. She told me once that when she was quite a young girl, he had made advances towards her, fumbling her breasts, pawing her thighs and trying to thrust his hand between her legs.

'Horrid old pervert,' she said. 'Now of course that I'm grown up, I can laugh at him. But even when I was a small girl I hated it when he kissed me, which he thought his right as my uncle, all wet and slobbery, ugh.'.

And now she is his wife. I suppose being on the receiving end of his wet kisses is a small price to pay for being Empress.

Lepidus was unconvinced by the defence I offered.

'It's a mistake,' he said again. 'It invites ridicule. Tiberius, you remember, even refused a request from the Senate that

Claudius be permitted to address them. I daresay he knew that Claudius himself had put some senator up to propose this, in exchange for remitting a gaming debt, I've been told. But it shows what Tiberius thought of him.'

'Look,' I said, 'if you're so concerned, why don't you ask your wife to speak to her brother about it. I'm sure she has far more influence over him than I have.'

'Drusilla?' he said. 'No, I couldn't do that. It's not for women to meddle in public affairs.'

He looked very young and handsome as he said that, flushing because of course he knew that I knew that he knew how things stood between his wife and his brother-in-law.

'How old-fashioned you are, my dear,' I said. 'I admire you for it, of course. The old ways were better than ours are today.'

V

That autumn Gaius fell ill. For some days he complained of being overheated. He suffered blinding headaches that incapacitated him for hours, compelling him to lie in a darkened room. His physicians were at a loss. Then they advised him to leave the city, escape its bad air. He must go either to the mountains or the sea. Drusilla therefore arranged that he be carried to his villa at Aricia, in the hills overlooking the sacred lake of Nemi. The journey weakened him. He developed stomach pains and vomited anything he ate or drank. He was bled, copiously, but grew only more feeble. He lay sweating on his bed and when he fell into a feverish sleep, woke screaming and in terror on account of his dreams. His tongue swelled and turned black, his eyes and skin were yellow. There was talk of witchcraft, also of poison. Now he shivered when he did not sweat. He cried out that demons were pricking him with sharp knives. In rare conscious moments he wept and howled curses.

Word spread that he was on the point of death. Some recalled how his father Germanicus had died. Others hastened to pay court to his cousin, young Tiberius Gemellus, who was assumed to be his heir. One of the first to do so was Macro, the Prefect of the Praetorians, in terror because so many suspected him of having murdered the young man's grandfather Tiberius. He brought with him his wife, into whose bed he had introduced the Emperor. The loyalty he owed Gaius was forgotten in his eagerness to ingratiate himself with his successor.

Then it was reported that Gaius had recovered. Men fled

from Tiberius Gemellus; his antechamber was empty as the desert of Arabia. This was premature. The next day Gaius rose from his bed, took a few uncertain steps, and collapsed. For two nights and a day he lay in a coma. Once again crowds flocked round the young prince. Riots broke out in the city, with much burning and looting. Macro hesitated, then declined to order the Praetorians to suppress them. There was no Emperor, he said, to command him to kill fellow-citizens, and he would not take that responsibility on himself. The consuls – two mediocre senators, for Gaius and Claudius had not yet assumed office – urged him to do so. But he dared not. All was confusion. The rioters proclaimed their loyalty to Gaius. They cried out that their beloved Emperor, the child of their hero Germanicus, had been poisoned – just like his father. They swarmed round the house where Tiberius Gemellus was now in effect their prisoner, with no respectable person brave enough to approach him. I am told he conducted himself well, as befitted his birth. But his house was stormed and set alight; he had to escape by a sewer. He fled to Nemi, accompanied only by a few slaves. It was his intention to display his loyalty to Gaius. But everyone knew how many had flocked to the young prince at the first word of Gaius' illness. That was enough. Drusilla, saying there was revolution in the air, ordered the young man to be arrested. He was then hit on the head and his throat cut.

This inexcusable murder nevertheless found apologists. They said she was disturbed, overcome by grief and fear, therefore not to be held responsible. Her husband Lepidus was appalled. From that day he never permitted himself to be alone with his wife.

He came to me in tears.

'What has become of us?' he asked, time and again. 'Have we descended to the level of wild beasts? Are we so degenerate?'

What could I say? There was no reply, safe, prudent or

comforting. I clasped him to me, and saw to it that he had wine enough to drink himself to oblivion.

Strangely, from the moment of that murder, Gaius began to recover. He stopped sweating and shivering. His eyes lost their frantic look. Drusilla told everyone that the poison was being expelled from his body. Some said that the killing of the young prince had broken the spell which necromancers in his employ had laid on the Emperor. This absurd theory was widely believed. In Rome the riots subsided, but only because the mob was sated, and had gathered more loot from the houses and palaces they had ransacked and burned than they could have hoped for.

Drusilla, now in full charge, had Macro and his wife arrested. He was hurried to a cellar and put to death, without trial. As for his wife, she disappeared. Certainly she was never seen again. No doubt she too was murdered. Drusilla let it be known that the prefect's treason was manifest, therefore no trial was necessary. When, subsequently, a senator nerved himself to protest, it was stated that Macro had been killed resisting arrest. It was intimated to the senator that, for his health's sake, he should absent himself from the city, and indeed from Italy. There was no need to repeat this message.

Gaius rose from his bed and gave thanks to the gods for his deliverance. He ordered that a medal be struck in commemoration. He talked of granting his sister the title of Augusta and, when he was well enough to address the Senate, demanded that she be officially thanked for having saved the Republic. This demand was not resisted.

Before his illness he had talked often, warmly to me, of his intention to make the Senate once again an equal partner in government. There was no more of such talk. Instead he ordered a list to be made of all those who had hurried to ingratiate themselves with Tiberius Gemellus and show that they were ready to hail him as Emperor. The length of the list dismayed and frightened him. It was never published, though this had been his original intention. But from now on he never felt secure. The terrors that caused him to shriek out in his illness still disturbed his mind. He slept little, and then fearfully. Three hours a night was the most he managed, and that with the aid of wine. Then he would wake from his painful dreams, his body twitching and his mind racing. He would stalk the corridors of the palace and, in an attempt to divert his mind, would ponder ambitious plans: throwing a bridge over the Forum to join the Palatine to the Capitol, cutting a canal through the isthmus of Corinth, constructing new harbours for the corn-fleet in the Straits of Messina, building new aqueducts, conquering the remote fog-shrouded island of Britain. Nothing was beyond him, except sleep. Once, in the darkest hours, his nightmare so filled him with terror that he choked the boy he had taken to his bed to death. Fortunately the youth was of no significance, a common prostitute or rent-boy.

He still had good days, when he was cheerful, even genial, energetic, and in such moods he could be captivating. His humour was perhaps even more wayward than formerly, and it was still less easy to be certain what he meant seriously and what as a jest. How to take for instance that dinner-party at which after a long silence while he crumbled bread and drank three or four cups of wine, he broke into a cackle of laughter and, when one of his guests asked whether they might share the joke, said, 'It just occurred to me that I have only to nod my head once, and your throats will be cut straightaway'?

It was that remark which caused a wit to say, 'Caligula is in jugular vein tonight' – and then look horrified by his temerity.

Even Drusilla was worried, made anxious by his unpredict-ability, and turned to me for advice, or perhaps comfort.

'You're the oldest friend we have,' she said, laying her hand on my sleeve and purring like a cat, 'the only person who's been a friend of all the family. I know how fond of you poor

Nero was, for instance. He once said to me that if I was in trouble, I should go to you.'

'Poor Nero indeed. I could do nothing for him.'

'You made him happy for a little, and not many managed that. In any case you've been a friend ever since you came to us as my father's young legate in Germany. He loved you too. I've seen letters he wrote to our grandmother in which he spoke so warmly of you.'

'That was too generous,' I said, 'but your mother found me a disappointment and in time came to dislike me, I think.'

'Oh, Mother,' she said, and smiled, for a moment looking just like Nero as I remembered him waking beside me. 'Everyone disappointed Mother. I certainly did. She expected so much, made such high demands. So she came to dislike most people. Poor dear Gaius was terrified of her, you know. But that's beside the point. Which is, of course, that he positively doted on you when he was a small boy and you used to carry him about the camp on your shoulders. You remember that, don't you?'

'Yes, I remember that. When he was in high spirits he was an enchanting small boy. The soldiers adored him, but I don't need to tell you that.'

'They did . . . all the same . . .' She hesitated; she had such a light way of speaking, like a sparrow or canary hopping from twig to twig. 'You remember the mutiny?'

'I couldn't forget it.'

'We were terrified. I think even Father was terrified, though he didn't show it. But you were so calm.'

'Not how I felt.'

'Well, that's how you seemed. It's how we perceived you. And it . . . it helped us to try to appear calm ourselves. You saved us. That's what we all believed, all us children, I mean. So none of us – I really mean none of us, not a single one – could ever wish you harm. You do believe that, don't you?'

What could I say?

I said, simply, 'Drusilla,' as gently as I could.

'Do you think me attractive?'

'What man wouldn't?'

'And yet you've never . . .'

'Never?'

'Made love to me, tried to seduce me, get me into your bed, as you got poor Nero.'

We were at Nemi again, looking over the lake and the grove sacred to Diana the huntress. It was a pale-golden afternoon in late October, and the water of the lake was dark and still as silence. I wanted to stretch out my hand and trace the line of her lips with my finger.

I said, 'Poor Nero fell into my bed, really.'

'Yes,' she said, 'and I won't. Of course.'

I nearly said, 'You're a married woman, and Lepidus is a friend. I don't seduce the wives of my friends.'

But that would have been as untrue, in every way, as it was pompous. I had seduced several wives of friends, and in any case Lepidus was hardly that, though I admired and respected him. Nor did I speak what was in my mind: you sleep with your brother the Emperor, it would be as much as my life is worth to . . . Instead, I said, 'This isn't what you want to talk about.'

'No,' she said, 'it isn't.' And I flattered myself I caught a note of regret in her voice.

'It's Gaius. He's not well, he's not fully recovered, I don't know what he is going to do or say next. It's never been like this before. I love him, you know . . .'

She blushed and lowered her eyes. The long lashes lay on cheeks that were dewy with starting tears.

'No, not that way, though we do that, and I consent because it's how he needs me, or needs me most immediately or most urgently. So I'm not ashamed, though the world – and my grandmother – would think I should be. But he's disturbed, in his mind or spirit or whatever you choose to call it. Disturbed and frightened. He doesn't know what he wants or what to do. So he goes to extremes, drinks himself out of his mind, night after night, and sends one of his guards down to the Suburra to bring him a woman or a boy. Always of the lowest sort. I've seen some of them and they disgust me.'

You're jealous, I thought; now I believe I was mistaken. It wasn't jealousy that had brought her to speak in this unguarded manner to me. It was fear and concern and love.

I said, 'He's young and a bit wild, but there's nothing so unusual in such behaviour. I could supply you with the names of a score of young nobles who carry on in much the same way.'

'I've no doubt you could.' And for the first time there was a note of amusement in her voice, making it lovely. Then it fled. 'But it's not the same thing, not at all. It's not as if he gets pleasure from it. He's unhappy, so unhappy. He's the Emperor of the world and he's unhappy.'

'There's no law says an Emperor should be happy. Tiberius was miserable.'

'But he had reason to be. Everybody hated him, nobody loved him, not even that German catamite he is said to have doted on. I'm told he robbed him and fled even as the old brute lay dying. Do you think Tiberius corrupted my brother?'

'No,' I said. 'I don't believe Tiberius corrupted anybody.'

'Marcus thinks he did.'

'Marcus?'

'My husband, have you forgotten?'

'He knows nothing about it.'

'Anyway, that doesn't matter, one way or another. But Gaius, he's so unhappy and afraid. You know he takes the omens several times every day, and they're always bad. They frighten him. Yesterday, he said to me, "It's only a matter of time before somebody sticks a knife into my neck." What do you think we can do?'

It was worse than I had thought. She looked at me with pleading in her eyes.

At last I said, 'We must get him out of Rome. To the armies. He's a child of the camp, remember.'

VI

There were several reasons why I made Drusilla that suggestion. Had she sought them I would have restricted my reply to those which pertained to the arena of public affairs. They were genuine enough.

There is a truth which we must not speak and which Augustus contrived to conceal. It is this: the power and authority of the Emperor rest on the legions. He called himself Princeps, first citizen, rather than Imperator – emperor-commander – and pretended that he had restored the Republic. But Republican institutions were now a facade, hiding the secret of Empire. No troops, except the Praetorians, were stationed in Italy; the armies were deployed along the frontiers. But Augustus kept for himself the governorship of all but one province in which there was a military establishment. Those which remained the responsibility of the Senate were bereft of troops. The Princeps made all military appointments without reference to the Senate. It follows therefore that to be successful, indeed secure, an Emperor must win the loyalty of the legions and their commanders, and retain their confidence. If this is ever denied him, then the secret will be disclosed, and an Emperor will be made far away from Rome, in Germany, or Spain or Asia or on the Danube.

As the victor in the Civil Wars, Augustus, though himself but an indifferent general, secured for himself that loyalty and confidence. Though after Actium he rarely took the field himself, and indeed scarcely left Italy in the last thirty years of his reign, his control of the armies was never threatened. He relied first on his old lieutenants, chief among them

Marcus Vipsanius Agrippa (himself the grandfather of our new Emperor, Gaius), and then on younger members of the imperial family, Tiberius and Drusus, and Germanicus; and was fortunate to find them competent.

Tiberius was in his mid-fifties when he became Emperor, and his own military career was over. But it had been distinguished, he was Rome's greatest living general; and after the mutinies which followed Augustus' death, and which I have described, his authority was never questioned by the army.

Gaius, however, had become Emperor without any military experience. Tiberius had preferred to keep him under his eye on Capri, and had not trusted him with a command. He was young and untested and, though he had certain advantages, being the son of the hero Germanicus and having himself been when a small boy the 'darling of the camp', as I had said to Drusilla, that was twenty years ago, the centurions who had known and adored him had mostly retired, many of the private soldiers too.

So it was desirable that he should put himself at the head of his legions, make himself known to them, earn their regard. And I had no doubt this could be done, provided he took with him a reliable and experienced second-in-command, for which position, I confess, I could think of no one better qualified than myself.

But there were two other reasons why I thought it desirable to get Gaius out of Rome.

Drusilla's account of his nervous and disordered condition did not surprise me. It chimed with my own observation, even if it went further. She had given what she thought to be the causes. I did not dispute them. She knew her brother, and I accepted what she said about the damaging consequences of his upbringing. Indeed I would have gone further: his overbearing manner and erratic behaviour, his wild speech and the fear that oppressed him, all betrayed a lack of self-confidence, which could be eradicated only by achievement; this itself was a good reason for advising that he should put himself at the head of the army, that unrivalled school of character.

It was clear to me however that everything that was disturbing in his behaviour was aggravated by his addiction to wine. Since he had recovered from his illness, he started drinking soon after he rose. Indeed many mornings he was in so nervous a condition, hands shaking, body sweating, suffering from nausea, that he was incapable of conversation, let alone attention to business, till he had downed two or three cups of sweet wine. Then he drank promiscuously throughout the day, erring, as one of his physicians put it to me, 'as to quality, quantity, frequency, time and order'. There was probably not an hour between rising and retiring that he did not drink, usually wine, sometimes strong beer. If he was rarely thoroughly intoxicated – at least till late at night – he was never truly sober. His addiction to liquor provoked his lustfulness, so that night after night, as Drusilla had said, he had his guards or slaves fetch him bedmates of the lowest and most despicable sort, male or female being indifferent to him. Sometimes too he himself sallied forth from the palace, disguised as a common bravo, in search of adventure or seeking release from his inner wretchedness in mean taverns, brothels, even the gutter. Drink also distorted his memory, or obliterated it, so that many mornings he had no awareness of what he had done, where he had been or with whom the night before.

Many drink heavily without destroying their ability to work and engage with others as reasonable beings. Tiberius indeed was one such. He would often go drunk to bed, but he would rise in the morning sober, and ready to spend hours at his desk occupied with the administration of the Empire. His drinking may have contributed to his melancholy, moroseness, misanthropy; but it did not unfit him for business, as Gaius' addiction to liquor seemed to be doing.

Finally, I thought it good to get him away from Drusilla

– a reason which evidently I could not offer her. I doubt if Gaius himself was perturbed by this incestuous relationship. The people, if they had learned of it, would have been equally unconcerned. It is after all common among the poorer plebeians for girls to surrender their virginity to their fathers or, failing that, uncles or brothers. But the Senate, however debased, still counted for something; and respectable people will not trust an Emperor who flouts the law and disdains religious prohibitions. And, though the Empire is founded on power, iron force, it functions most smoothly when there is trust between the different organs of the State. Gaius' reputation could not survive the full exposure of his incestuous affair. It was bad enough that he had been known, at dinner-parties, to command a senator's wife to leave the room with him, for a purpose none could fail to guess.

He responded with the naive enthusiasm that was one of the most attractive features of his character to the suggestion that the time was ripe for the legions on the frontier to have the pleasure of making the acquaintance of their Emperor, and even come under his command.

'You are right,' he said. 'I am a soldier's son. I belong in the camp, away from this city which stifles me.'

Before we set out for Germany, he was engaged in a project which has aroused much derision and has led many to question his sanity. Naturally no one openly spoke like that then. But very often what is said subsequently is thought previously.

On what appeared to the world to be a whim, pure folly, he ordered his engineers to construct a bridge of boats across the Bay of Baiae, a distance of three miles. This was a considerable undertaking, as you may imagine. Merchant ships were requisitioned, to the irritation of their owners and captains, also of merchants whose trade was interrupted, so that some fell into bankruptcy. They were anchored, and chained together. Then boards were laid across them, as it were a floor, and earth was piled on the planks and beaten smooth by gangs of slaves.

'What is he doing?' men said.

'Making an Appian Way across the waves,' was one reply.

When the work was done Gaius rode across, dressed as Alexander, and whooping with joy. His favourite horse Incitatus arched his neck and pranced boldly, as if expressing his pride in carrying so great a hero.

Some cheered, others shook their heads, most looked on in mute wonder.

Gaius himself was happy as the small boy I remembered in camp.

'It holds,' he said, 'we'll test it more throughly tomorrow.'

So the next day he emerged from his villa dressed as a charioteer, and commanded me to join him in the waiting car. Then, behind two mettlesome horses, we careered across the waters, followed by a division of the Praetorians, some in chariots, some on horseback, some on foot. When we reached Baiae, having set off from Puteoli, he supervised the disembarkation, as I may call it, carefully, and took particular note of how smoothly the troops were deployed. Then he inspected them, praised their discipline, and gave orders for the return journey.

Like so much that Gaius did, this exercise has been subjected to mockery and harsh criticism. One absurd suggestion was that Gaius was seeking to emulate the Persian king Xerxes who, in his Greek war, also constructed a bridge of boats across a bay. The only basis for this calumny was that one evening at dinner, when the talk turned to military matters, Gaius had been heard to express interest in, appreciation of, this engineering feat.

A still more ridiculous notion has been floated by one scribbler who styles himself a historian. He says that Gaius was attempting to disprove a prophecy which the astrologer Thrasyllus had made to Tiberius, to the effect that Gaius had no more chance of becoming Emperor than of riding a horse dryshod across the Bay of Baiae. Now I admit that Gaius took note of everything astrologers said, so that some believed he was entirely guided by the most recent prediction offered him, even if it contradicted that on which he was already acting. This is true, though in other moods his attitude was more robust. Once for instance, when an astrologer told him that the sun would be so hot at noon the next day that it would kill anyone who ventured to remain in it, Gaius had the man tied to a chair and set out in the courtyard that he might test for himself the value of his prediction. The man survived, which amused the Emperor who said, 'Since you haven't died, I should by rights have you put to death for making a false prediction.' This thought so amused him that he did nothing about it. Nevertheless there are many who believe that he did have the astrologer killed – even though the man continued to practise his art very publicly for many years.

One should never underestimate the credulity of the public – or the credulity of intellectuals. I sometimes think they will believe anything. How else to explain the eagerness with which so many repeated – and, for all I know, still repeat – that story about the prophecy Thrasyllus made to Tiberius? I'm not denying that he may indeed have spoken thus. But that anyone should not have seen that Gaius had no need to ride his horse across the bay to disprove the prediction, since he was already Emperor and its hollowness had been exposed, is frankly extraordinary. Or would be if men were not such fools.

In fact Gaius had a good reason for this exercise. It wasn't a caper. It was an experiment. And it had a purpose, or rather a double purpose. It was first a training exercise for the corps of military engineers which Tiberius had created but which had been seldom employed. It was a demanding exercise to test their ability; and they passed the test to the Emperor's great satisfaction.

Second, Gaius, from the day he first realised that he would be Emperor if he trod carefully and survived Tiberius, had one ambition: he would pursue his father's work, achieve the triumph which the caution of Tiberius had denied Germanicus, complete the conquest of Germany, and extend the bounds of Empire by surpassing Julius Caesar and successfully invading Britain. He had, if fitfully, studied the writings of military thinkers and strategists and had concluded that engineers were of the utmost importance. The more skilful they were, the more audacious a commander could be. He liked to quote some authority – but I forget which – who wrote that 'supply and engineering are the sinews of war'.

I mention this, in itself no great matter, because so many have portrayed Gaius as not only wild and even crazy, but stupid. This last he certainly wasn't. At some point in his lonely and frightened youth, he had read deeply, for many hours at a stretch, and, once grown, remembered much of what he had read. He could quote whole paragraphs of Sallust, for example, especially relishing the history of the war against Jugurtha. He thought his style superior to Cicero's, which he condemned as 'florid, self-admiring, tiresome even in his private correspondence'. But then he couldn't be expected to find much to admire in that lawyer-politician, who had moreover slandered Mark Antony, of all his ancestors the one whom Gaius most revered. Indeed I believe that privately he thought of himself as Antony reborn, though he had none of the beauty for which Antony was famed. That said, he certainly didn't lack the charm to which all who knew, or have written of Antony, have borne witness.

The prospect of leading the army into Germany did much to restore the Emperor's health and calm his mind. He even drank less, and so slept better, though never alone – he had a horror of waking without a bed-companion.

Nevertheless there were difficulties. The generosity or extravagance he had displayed in the early months of the reign had been costly. One can win popularity by remitting taxes, but government and war both require money. Moreover, though the bridging of the bay had been, in Gaius' opinion, completely successful, it had one unfortunate consequence: many of the ships he had commandeered had belonged to the grain-fleet, required to bring corn from Egypt. Its schedule had been disturbed. There was a danger of bread shortages, of all things the most threatening to civil order. Not even releasing stores from the reserves could satisfy demand. There were riots, if only small and sporadic ones. Gaius sought to shift the responsibility by accusing merchants of hoarding grain in order to raise the price. Some were arrested and their goods confiscated. But it was several weeks before supplies returned to normal, and in this unsettled time Gaius could not leave the city. So the German campaign had to be postponed.

He had remitted many taxes, and abolished some. Now he had to impose new ones, and those which would bring in money immediately. One ingenious device, the brainchild of the freedman Narcissus, was to levy a 5 per cent tax on the cost of civil trials and all legal fees. There was something to be said for this. Since the rich go to law more readily, more frequently, and certainly more expensively, than the poor, it hit those best able to pay. On the other hand, it hit them at a time when they were already incurring high expenses, since going to law is never cheap; it was therefore bitterly resented. In time too it had an unlooked-for side-effect: fewer people brought civil actions since they had become more costly. The returns therefore diminished.

Other taxes were less justifiable. One on the daily earnings of porters and prostitutes was particularly absurd; either it was impossible to compute their earnings, or, if this was done, they merely raised their fees. Of course Gaius never himself paid for the whores and rent-boys he had brought to his bed; it should, he said, be sufficient reward for them to have served the Emperor. Like many who spend lavishly, he was mean in small things.

Financial straits are corrupting. Gaius had, as I have written, brought the treason-trials that had disgraced Tiberius' reign to an end. The professional informers were discouraged; some were exiled, a few imprisoned on charges of false witness. It seemed that the crime of *Maiestas* might happily become rare in our lawcourts. But, alas, *Maiestas* was a useful crime; it gave such opportunities for the confiscation of property. So treason-trials were resumed.

Gaius made a joke of it: 'I always wondered why Tiberius was so ready to believe people were compassing his death. Now I know. It was simply because he was such a close-fisted old miser. But I need the money to extend the bounds of Empire. And how else am I to get it?'

There were other ways. The friends of his youth, the Thracian princes, Ptolemo, Rhoemetalces, and Cotys, were restored to their hereditary kingdoms, which Tiberius had made imperial provinces. Each however had to pay a substantial sum for the privilege. Gaius boasted that the money they paid was more than the provinces had paid in taxes over ten years; 'and,' he said, 'because I know my friends well, they remain firm allies of the Republic. So I lose nothing and gain much.'

In Africa, in Mauretania, however, his policy was different. There he deposed the king, Ptolemios, declaring that he was an enemy of the Republic and plotting rebellion. There may have been some truth in this; the king's family had shown their resentment of our suzerainty. But Gaius had a more urgent motive. Ptolemios had a well-stocked Treasury which was immediately confiscated. Mauretania, a rich country, was made an imperial province, and its taxes doubled.

So, one way and another, Gaius accumulated the money he needed to prosecute war.

Let me at this point interject a personal note. I myself have been reproached for having failed to dissuade him from the course on which he had embarked. My critics have observed that I had previously approved Tiberius' decision to fix the bounds of Empire where Augustus had left them, and had expressed my approval in numerous Senate speeches. Therefore, they say, I was negligent of my duty, and indeed betrayed myself and my own integrity, when now I made no effort to restrain the Emperor. But Gaius was a mettlesome colt who would not be bridled, and the most I could hope to do was to exercise a moderating influence on him during the subsequent campaign. The truth is, that if an Emperor is determined to have a war, there is nothing you can do to prevent him.

Besides, the idea of war was popular. Men were bored with the long peace. Young men sought glory, the People looked forward to a succession of victories, all those who remembered how the hero Germanicus had been thwarted by the timidity of Tiberius rejoiced. There was expectation of booty, much talk of the riches of Britain, famous for its pearl-fisheries, and of slave-markets thronged with handsome and muscular young Germans. In short the prospect of the imperial war cheered everyone up. Half a dozen poets set to work composing epics in its praise, before the Emperor had even departed from Rome.

VII

Then that departure was further delayed. Drusilla fell ill. For some months she had been troubled by a persistent cough. She was pale and easily tired. She lost weight, though she had always been slim. She had no appetite. She began to cough blood. She developed a fever and took to her bed.

Gaius was distraught. He commanded his physicians to heal her. When they failed, he threw them into prison and summoned others. He consulted the omens several times a day. The wisest soothsayers predicted her recovery, and then all but the most foolhardy found urgent reasons to leave Rome. Some of the new physicians advised sea air. Drusilla, now very weak and barely conscious, was transported in a litter carried by relays of slaves to a villa on the Bay of Naples. There she died. The Emperor hurled himself on her body as if he could prevent the soul from slipping away. 'Am I not a god?' he howled in his grief, tore his clothes and scratched his face till the blood ran. For three days he lay, weeping, by his dead sister and only true love. Then he had the physicians who had advised the move strangled because they had, he said, 'deceived him and cheated his beloved sister'.

I feared for his sanity.

His uncle Claudius arrived to express his condolences. Gaius would not see him. He cried out, 'That such a creature as Claudius should live and Drusilla die.'

I advised Claudius to return to Rome if he valued his life. He stammered indignantly, reminding me that he was the head of the family and declaring that his place was by his nephew's side. I said that I couldn't guarantee that the head of the family would keep his own head on his shoulders if he didn't immediately obey the Emperor's command and depart. I don't think he has ever forgiven me this blunt speech, though it may have saved his life.

Gaius at last emerged from the death-chamber, white as the snow on the mountains, and staggering, half-drunk. He said, 'How terrible to feel her body so wasted, so lifeless.' Rumour fastened and fed on these words. It was whispered that he had had intercourse with her after her death; in later years I have heard senators swear that semen had been found even on her grave-clothes, and that her husband, Lepidus, had remarked, 'I have catholic tastes myself, but I draw the line well short of necrophilia.' That story too was widely believed, though absurd. It was not in his style. For all his weaknesses he was an honourable man. Besides, he had no sense of humour and was incapable of wit.

Gaius, overcome by grief, now declared that Drusilla had become a goddess and was to be worshipped as such. One senator, Livius Geminius, obsequiously swore that he had indeed seen the Emperor's late sister ascending to the heavens; his reward was rich – one million sesterces. From this day, whenever Gaius had to take an important oath, even at a public assembly or an army parade, he swore by Drusilla's divinity. 'There is no other way,' he said to me, 'that I can better demonstrate my sincerity.' In his misery, he resented his other sisters, Agrippina and Julia Livilla, simply because they were alive and his beloved Drusilla dead.

Agrippina said, 'For the first time in my life I am afraid of my little brother.'

Her fear softened her harsh features. Her upper lip trembled as her brother Nero's used to do. Her eyes filled with tears. She seemed for a moment Nero reborn. Was that why I now took her in my arms and kissed her, to calm her fears, as I had been used to calm his? I would like to think so now – now that I dislike her, find the thought of making love to her repugnant. But it was different then, if I am to be honest, at least with myself. She responded eagerly, thrust her tongue into my mouth. That was how our first affair began. It was then a matter of only a few nights. That did not distress me. Though I found her desirable and her resemblance to her brother Nero added piquancy and also tenderness to our love-making, she could neither excite me nor satisfy me as Caesonia did. Had circumstances been different I have no doubt she would have been determined to continue our affair. She detested her husband, with reason, for Gnaeus Domitius Ahenobarbus was notorious for his arrogance and cruelty. Indeed he was an entirely despicable character who had once killed one of his freedmen for refusing to drink as much as he was told to, and on another occasion when driving through a village on the Appian Way had quite deliberately run down a small boy and killed him. He was also dishonest in financial affairs and a compulsive liar. So it is not surprising that Agrippina should have fallen into my arms and taken me to her bed. But she broke off our affair because she was afraid that Gaius would be angry if he learned of it. Or so she said. She may have been speaking the truth. She sometimes does; even today, I'm told.

Soon she had other reasons to fear her brother. The first was, on the surface, trivial. Gaius had always resented or, rather, been ashamed of his descent from his grandfather Marcus Vipsanius Agrippa. It mattered not at all that Agrippa had been a great soldier, the man who won the victories that were credited to Augustus, and a great servant of the Republic, responsible too for many fine buildings in the city and for the restoration of more than a score of temples. His birth, however, was humble; that was enough, too much, for Gaius. We had already learned to avoid mentioning him; one of the Emperor's first acts had been to cancel the annual commemorations of Agrippa's victories at Actium – admittedly that was gained at the expense of his other grandfather Antony – and in Sicily, where he had defeated Gnaeus Pompeius.

But now he found that whenever anyone mentioned his sister's name, which had also of course been his mother's, he was reminded of this low connection, and therefore it was forbidden to mention it in his presence. Instead he nursed a fantasy, which he may really have come to believe, that his mother had been born of an incestuous union between Augustus and his daughter Julia, the wife successively of his great-uncle Marcellus, who died young, Agrippa, and Tiberius. Perhaps he thought this possible because of Julia's notorious promiscuity, and it may have amused him to believe that Augustus, who passed so many laws against immorality and who exiled Julia on account of her scandalous behaviour, should have practised incest – just as he did himself. 'Who else should gods lie with?' he once asked me, adding, 'but you realise, my friend, that anything and everything is permitted to me.'

I pitied him now. There's no question but that he was utterly wretched. However perverted his love for Drusilla, it was the very fibre of his being. Nothing and nobody could console him. He ran away. With only a small escort of guards he galloped through Campania, careered down the coast of Calabria, crossed over to Sicily, pronounced the place 'loathsome', and went back to Rome, all this in fewer than ten days. Apart from the guards, his only companion was the young Parthian prince, Darius, who had been sent to Rome as a hostage and whom Gaius had taken a fancy to on his arrival at court. He had made him a household pet and the boy had ridden with us in his chariot when he cantered across the bridge of boats at Baiae. It was easy to understand why he favoured him; with his long black hair curling in ringlets, dark lustrous eyes, heavenly legs and smooth tawny skin, soft – one guessed – as rose-petals, he was certainly adorable. But fourteen, his probable age, is too young to be sodomised and I can't believe the youth enjoyed the Emperor's attentions, which nevertheless he had to endure. Whether he in any way served to distract Gaius from his grief is to be doubted. In any case Gaius soon tired of him, as one does of passive beauty. I have often wondered what became of him.

When Gaius returned from Sicily, he immediately ordered a period of public mourning for his sister. The conditions he imposed were rather severe. It was to be a capital offence to laugh, bathe, or dine with one's parents, wives or children while the period of deep mourning lasted. Fortunately, as my wife Caesonia remarked, these prohibitions were so strict that nobody could be expected to observe them.

The boy Darius proving insufficient consolation, Gaius now decided to get married. He had already disposed of his first wife, Livia Orestilla, divorcing her after only a few days of marriage because, he said, she had once corrected his pronunciation of a Greek word. Now he summoned Lollia Paulina, wife of the proconsul Gaius Memmius. He had never seen her but somebody had told him that her grandmother had been a famous beauty. 'So was mine,' he said, referring, I suppose, to Julia rather than Antonia, the latter being more admired for her character than her looks. (This was surprising actually since she was the daughter of Mark Antony, the most beautiful man of his generation, and Augustus' sister Octavia, said by everybody to have been far more beautiful, if less seductive, than the Egyptian queen, Cleopatra.)

No matter. 'So was mine,' said the Emperor, and announced that the children of his marriage to Lollia Paulina would there-fore be as beautiful as Venus or Apollo. Unfortunately, what-ever the grandmother had been, the granddaughter proved a disappointment; she was pretty enough, but dull, placid and rather fat. He called her 'the honey-coloured cow' and discarded her almost at once, forbidding her ever to sleep with another man. 'No one,' he said, 'should have the Emperor's leavings.' This was absurd, given his propensity for whores and rent-boys.

All this was a distraction from the business of preparing for the campaign. On the other hand there was something to be said for having the Emperor distracted. The work went on faster. Arrangements were no longer disturbed, or reversed, a few hours after they had been agreed and put in train. That said, when people declare that Gaius was nothing but a liability, I have to differ, speaking from more experience. Some of his suggestions were actually rather intelligent, even helpful. I wish I could call examples to mind.

One day, soon after his return to Rome from Nemi where he had been brooding, as he said, on the malignancy of fate, he summoned me. I was surprised to find him genial.

He said, 'Did you know about the priest of Diana at Nemi?'

'Something, my lord,' I said. Unlike Tiberius he was pleased to be addressed in this way, though, on account of my position and long friendship with the family, I did so only when I was more than usually uncertain of his mood or of the direction he wished a conversation to take.

'I didn't,' he said. 'Sometimes I think nobody tells me anything. What do you know of him?'

'Only generalities, my lord. Only generalities: that he's a runaway slave who wins the priesthood by slaying the incumbent, but how frequently this happens, or whether there is a set date for him to do so, or anything of that sort – of all that I'm ignorant.'

'There's no set date,' he said, chewing his nails. 'No set date, and for a long time no challengers. Outrageous, don't you think. Disrespectful to the goddess. I discovered last week that the priest had held the position for twenty years, and do you know how often he had been challenged? Twice. I put that right. I ordered one of the estate slaves, a slimy fellow from the Tatar mountains, to escape and bring a challenge. Which, I'm delighted to say, was successful. Diana will be pleased. Now it remains only to devise a means of making the challenges regular. And well-advertised. It's good sport.

You should have seen the old priest's face when he stepped out of the grove and found a challenger waiting . . . Hilarious, that's what it was. I was absolutely convulsed.'

'Are you sure, my lord, that the goddess approves arranged challenges?'

'I've no doubt at all. Remember, I know her mind. She comes to my bed at the time of the full moon.'

There wasn't much to say in reply.

He smiled, his happy urchin's smile.

'Come,' he said, 'let's have a treat. Let's go see Incitatus in his stable.'

I have heard stories that the stable of this favourite horse was lined with gold. This is not true. It was marble, and his stall or box was ivory. He had a team of slaves to tend him, and when he was led out, wore a collar studded with emeralds, this jewel having been chosen because Gaius thought it set off his silky dark bay coat to perfection. Which indeed it did; in certain respects the Emperor's taste was impeccable.

He whinnied when he recognised the Emperor's voice.

'It's a special call he keeps for me,' Gaius said, and gave him an apple, which a slave brought on a silver salver.

Gaius then put his arms round the horse's neck and cooed gently to him, muttering endearments in what I took to be a private language that only horse and Emperor understood. He covered his neck with kisses, and Incitatus responded by taking the Emperor's ear very gently between his lips and nuzzling it. In a little while Gaius drew back and kissed the horse on its lips in turn. For a little longer they petted each other, and everything was, as the saying goes, merry as a marriage bell.

'I adore that horse,' Gaius said. 'He's far more intelligent and loyal than any of my subjects.'

'He's certainly very beautiful.'

'So why am I still discontented?'

He stuck out his lower lip and kicked the turf.

'I'm going to marry again. An Emperor must have a consort. Otherwise he'll get crabbit, like old Tiberius. So I want a new wife. I think I'll take yours.'

VIII

I had looked for tears and protests from Caesonia. She had often told me that I was not only her husband, but her one true love; and, though, on account of her earlier promiscuity, I could not absolutely believe this, nevertheless I did not doubt that she loved me. All my life I have been too trusting.

She saw the dismay on my face.

'What did you expect?' she said.

'At least a semblance of sorrow, a display of some sort . . .'

'My dear husband,' she said, 'for so I suppose I may still address you, if for the last time, we both know how things stand. Therefore it would be foolish to pretend they are not as they are. Whatever our personal feelings we must submit to the Emperor's will. There's no more to be said.'

She smiled with, I thought, a certain complacency. It occurred to me that perhaps the idea of being the Augusta appealed to her.

'But can you live with Gaius?' I said.

'I shan't know till I've tried. But – and this may surprise you – I don't see why I shouldn't. I heard one of your aunts once call me an old whore. It may be that an old whore is just what the Emperor needs. And, do you know? – he brings out the motherly instinct in me too.'

'We could have had children of our own to satisfy that,' I said.

'Indeed we could have, and I daresay I would have liked that. There's nobody, my dear, whose children I would rather have had than yours. But there it is, and it's no use crying over spilled wine, as my grandmother used to say. You can't think it sensible that I should refuse the Emperor. Where would you be if I did? So we must make the best of it. In any case, it's a different sort of maternal feeling I have for him. There are times when he seems to me like a little boy lost, and that's appealing to an old whore like me. I don't know if you can understand that, but there it is. I know what he needs, you see.'

'And what's that?'

'To lay his head on my lap and weep, so that he can give way to the tenderness that is locked up in him, and of which he is all too probably ashamed.'

'And you don't care that he has insulted me by telling me so casually that he will have my wife?'

'As he might take this house or your estates, you mean?'

'More than that,' I said.

'So a wife is a more valuable possession than estates?'

'You're laughing at me.'

'This is foolishness,' she said, and took my hand and made me sit by her. Then she kissed me and stroked my cheek. 'Foolishness,' she said again. 'Did you protest when he said that? No, you didn't. Did you think I would decline this gracious offer? Of course not. Or did you just hope that I would weep and sob and give way to hysterics? That would be stupid. As I have said, things are as they are. We don't live in the days of the Republic when women were expected to be virtuous, and the marriage bond was respected. You yourself have been to bed with Agrippina though you have always protested your love for me. So there it is. I shall be the Emperor's woman and you still his loyal and obedient servant.'

'You speak as if you despise me,' I said. 'Or do you merely extend your famous pity to me also?'

'All women pity the men they lie with. How could it be otherwise?'

When I asked her if she despised me, I looked for her

assurance that she did. I despised myself for my acquiescence. But what else could I have done, short of inviting death? Curiously I did not hate Gaius, scarcely even resented his theft of Caesonia. Was this because I had accepted him as he was, and the Empire as it is, or because I was contemptible, resolved to survive, no matter what? And is such a resolution contemptible? I do not think so. Once of course our Roman sense of virtue, of what becomes a man, would have compelled me either to avenge the insult or to fall on my sword. But virtue belonged to the time when we were free men. No one can afford to be virtuous now in this generation of slaves.

I argued this question once with Seneca, more than once indeed, but it is one particular conversation that I recall.

He had withdrawn from Rome, to a villa in the region of Sulmona, which he had inherited from the father of his first wife. Sulmona was the home town of the immoral poet Ovid, and Seneca prides himself on his stern morality. The conjunction amused me. I have always enjoyed Seneca's company – at least he has a mind – while finding the tragic dramas on which his fame rests ridiculous, arid, derivative, and bearing very little relation to reality. Gaius incidentally was of this opinion too, and thought nothing of them or indeed of his philosophic and moral essays. He condemned them, and also Seneca's speeches, as 'sand without lime'. So Seneca was wise to absent himself from the city in Gaius' time. But the conversation I recall took place some years later.

Seneca is a couple of years younger than I am; yet, probably because he never enjoyed youth, has long seemed older. His manner is grave, even pompous; there is no lightness in him. Curiously, though he was brought to Rome when still only a child, he has never lost the harsh accent of his native Spain. Perhaps this is because he has never really listened to other people, or moved happily in good society. His knowledge of the world is theoretical, as was that of his father, an old bore who spent his latter years writing about imaginary civil and criminal cases, and drawing moral lessons from them. I don't think my Seneca ever visited a brothel in his life, unlike his younger brother, M Annaeus, who was rarely out of them, preferring those where there was a selection of German boys, though finding time to father a charming son, young Lucan, who, unlike the other members of this scribbling family, shows real poetic talent. But I digress.

Though I speak now somewhat contemptuously of Seneca, I admit that I enjoyed arguing philosophy with him, he belonging to the school of the Stoics, and I myself favouring, by reason of my experience, that of Epicurus. But what brought on this conversation in Sulmona I can't now recall.

I spoke of the humiliation I had endured at Gaius' hands, and of the pain I had felt when deprived of Caesonia.

'Should I have acted?' I said. 'But how, and indeed why, since there was nothing efficacious I could have done? So I followed the prescript of the master, Diogenes of Oenoanda, who taught that there was nothing to fear from the gods, nothing to feel in death, and that evil times can be endured, this in a world where virtue as our fathers conceived it is now extinct.'

'My poor friend,' Seneca said – it was his habit to express the sense of his own superiority by this patronising mode of address – 'my poor friend, virtue can never be extinct, for, if it were, you could not conceive of it. Your response to evil is submission; mine is detachment and the contemplation of higher things. You judge that virtue is extinct, because this acquits you of responsibility for what you do, and allows you to wallow in sensuality, which, I may add, is a perversion of the philosophy you pretend to be guided by. I, on the other hand, trust in the attainability of virtue, even in evil times.'

'Your argument is as fallacious as it is impertinent,' I said. 'I recognise virtue. But I early concluded that I could not afford it. If I had followed the path of virtue, I should be dead. I turned away from it, and still enjoy life. I should not have survived

Tiberius, let alone Caligula. As it is, I am here with you on this terrace, gazing out over a delectable view, and eating these first figs of the season – which are delicious by the way – with a fine pecorino cheese and this admirable wine you have provided. Which is better? To be a handful of grey ashes, or sitting here in the sun and discoursing of philosophy?'

'It is better to follow virtue so that your soul may be in harmony with the divine.'

'But if Gaius had commanded me to cut my throat, or sent his guardsmen to do it for me, where would my soul have been then, even granting for the purposes of argument that such a thing as the soul exists? Which however I doubt, for while I have seen bodies and have delighted in the pleasures of the flesh, I have no acquaintance with what you call soul, and therefore take leave to doubt its existence.'

'But that is impossible,' he said, 'for if it were not, then life would be meaningless.'

'As it may be.'

'The world is ordered and therefore has meaning. What is the true end of man but an active life in harmony with nature, that is to say, a life of virtue, for that is the law of the universe and the divine will. Only right conduct produces happiness. Have you been happy, my friend?'

'Happy? There have been moments. Even this is one when I look from your terrace down on the pale road winding through the olive groves and feel the soft sun of evening on my cheek.'

'Happiness requires purity of heart.'

'Really? Do you know that someone once suggested that to Caligula. I think it was Caesonia, poor woman. And do you know what he replied? That every man acquires it in his own way, and that he himself found it in the company of the dead, especially those whom he had himself condemned to death. What do you make of that?'

'It's of no interest. The Emperor Gaius was mad.'

'Do you think so?' I said. 'I have moments, in the black of night, when it seems to me that he was sane, horribly sane; that he had seen the void and accepted it, knew human life for what it is, or may be: a vast emptiness. He once said, when I was bold enough to speak of Drusilla whom he had truly loved, that it didn't matter, her death didn't matter, it signified nothing. His grief hadn't lasted because that was impossible. Grief, he said, is vanity. We indulge in it to persuade ourselves that we are not what we are.'

'What he was, you mean. My poor friend, Caligula was a murdering lunatic. We are well rid of him.'

The shadows had now crossed the pale road through the olive trees and obscured it. From the town below came the sound of singing, a girl's voice, pure and melancholy as she sang a song of love betrayed, or something of the sort.

'I don't dispute that,' I said. 'We are indeed well rid of Gaius. He was too much for us. He saw things too clearly. Perhaps that was indeed lunacy: to realise and accept that nothing lasts. Since nothing endures, he said to me once – we were standing at night, a colder night than this, on the bank of a northern river, and the vast blackness of Germany stretched into the invisible beyond – since nothing lasts, he said, the only reality is sensation, the sensation of a moment and, for me, that sensation is most vividly expressed in a moment of killing when I am completely free, free from all memories, all illusions. And to think, he added, with that laugh of his – you remember that schoolboy's cackle – that old Tiberius was afraid of this freedom, did not dare to grasp it, as I have.'

'My poor friend, you are obsessed with that lunatic.'

There at last he spoke truth, recognising my obsession. But was Gaius Caligula a lunatic? I have never been sure.

IX

At last, after so many delays, so much uncertainty, such procrastination, Gaius made ready for his German expedition. By this time many had come to the conclusion that he would never set out for it. 'He talks a better war than he will ever fight,' one elderly senator said to me, before quickly retracting his words or trying to pass them off as a joke, lest I should repeat them. I could not blame him for being unwilling to trust my discretion. In a despotism no man will speak his mind without immediately regretting his rashness. As it happened, I was to be trusted, but he was scarcely culpable in his fear.

Gaius insisted I should accompany him as his senior legate, indeed as his second-in-command.

'I remember how you saved us in Germany when I was a child,' he said yet again. 'You are my talisman. Besides, I sometimes think that you are the only man in Rome who understands the world as I do myself, and who has no more illusions than I have.'

'If you say so, Caesar,' I replied.

In truth, I would have avoided this dangerous post of honour, had that been feasible. But of course it wasn't. To disobey the Emperor, or devise some excuse that would make it impossible to do as he bid, would have been sheer folly, and, though I have in my time been accused of much, and even of many crimes, no one has ever called me a fool. Besides, I still believed, in my self-conceit, that I might be able to exercise a moderating influence on Gaius. He was not to my mind beyond redemption.

There was an unfortunate incident before our departure. In

accordance with tradition, and the requirements of religion, Gaius prepared to sacrifice an ox to Mars to ensure a successful campaign. He looked impressive as he approached the altar, suitably robed in priestly garments, and wearing an air of solemn dignity such as he could assume when he chose. It was indeed his ability to play the part required of him in suitable fashion which persuaded me that in spite of his vagaries and his erratic behaviour, something might yet be made of him. Yet, on this occasion, he was unable to sustain the role. Dressed as the *popa,* whose duty it was to knock the victim out, he swung his mallet three or four times around his head while uttering the appropriate prayer, but then, instead of bringing it down on the sacrificial victim, he felled the assistant priest who was waiting to cut the ox's throat. Few thought this an accident, even fewer when the Emperor burst into peals of laughter. All thought it an evil omen.

Gaius himself was in no way concerned, and this was odd because he was in so many respects morbidly supersitious. I have known him for instance abandon a day's hunting simply because he had seen a black cat, a creature that invariably caused him to break out in a cold sweat, and for which he felt a peculiar horror. But now he merely remarked: 'It is clear that the god favours me and would have me strike down my enemies in like manner. My expedition is therefore well begun.'

So we set off the next day at top speed. Indeed Gaius set such a pace that the accompanying cohorts of the Praetorians, being out of condition on account of soft living in the city – and many with hangovers after the night's carousing with the prostitutes they were leaving behind – could scarcely keep up. Gaius thought this a great joke, but yielded to my plea that he should make the following days' marches shorter.

'You must cosset and pamper the Praetorians,' I said. 'They are the pillars on which your power rests.'

'Must?' he said, frowning. '"Must" is a word that does not please me.'

'Nevertheless . . .' I said, and left it at that. But he took my advice, though the day would come when he forgot it. I mention this here to silence those critics who assert that I had no influence over Gaius, and that I owed my survival merely to my sycophancy. The truth is that, at this stage, Gaius was not yet deaf to good counsel and, for the reasons I have already given, retained confidence in my judgement and even, I believe, affection for me.

Caesonia later told me that he had grumbled about me that evening, before saying, 'That word "nevertheless" which he uses to deter me from my chosen course would offend me in any other mouth.'

The cheers that greeted his announcement that the next day's march would be shorter convinced him both of my wisdom and of his own popularity. This was still real. Men remembered that he was the son of the hero Germanicus, and there were still some centurions left who had served under him as raw recruits and had adored him. Besides, for all the centurions, Gaius still, in his enthusiasm for martial glory, offered a sharp and welcome contrast to Tiberius, whom they despised for his miserliness and whose betrayal, as they saw it, of their popular commander Sejanus, they had so bitterly resented. Therefore the Praetorians approved Gaius and hoped for much from him.

Throughout the march north Gaius was in high spirits. Even his jokes and jests were kindly. He was happy to be with the army. He was looking forward to the war, and looking forward too to testing himself, and proving himself a worthy son of his father. He impressed the soldiers by his energy and his powers of endurance. There were several days when he abandoned his horse and marched at the head of the column. As a child he had learned many of the legionaries' favourite marching songs, and now he gave the lead to the singing.

Sometimes too he had Caesonia descend from her litter, and march at his side, dressed as a legionary herself. When, one day, she remained in the litter, only showing her face through its curtains, he roared out that if anyone wondered why his wife wasn't by his side and keeping in step, it was because 'the poor bitch has blisters', and all those within hearing joined in his laughter and cheered loudly, calling out to Caesonia that they had all been there before her. Further north, when she kept to the litter for several days, he did not hesitate to assure the men that she was suffering from woman's troubles, which, he added, 'we're all lucky enough to be free from.'

'Stuff and nonsense, Caesar,' came a voice from the rear of the column, 'we all know that it's because you've been rogering her so hard that the poor cow can't walk. Don't think we didn't hear you at it last night.'

Instead of being angered by this insolence, which, in Tiberius' time, would have earned the man a good scourging, Gaius glowed with pleasure, and insisted on the man being brought before him, rewarding him first with two gold pieces and then with a kiss on either cheek.

On the march Gaius indulged in none of the eccentricities of dress that he was accustomed to, eccentricities which had already aroused the anger and contempt of senators and other conservatively-minded men and women in Rome. Certainly these were in marked constrast to the decorum and decency that had characterised both Augustus and Tiberius. There were no appearances in silk tunics or women's dresses (this in honour of his bed-mate the Moon goddess). Instead he wore the uniform of an ordinary soldier, except that, when the weather was fine, he put on the breastplate of Alexander the Great, which at his command had been brought from the great king's tomb in Alexandria. In short, he did nothing to offend the soldiers. Even the discipline he imposed was fair as well as firm, and there were no executions.

Moreover he conducted himself suitably, and with a grace

that his figure did not promise, at each of the cities and towns
we passed through. He listened carefully to the addresses
which the municipal dignitaries favoured him with, only rarely
yawning and always hearing them to the end without inter-
ruption. He refrained from making jokes about the uncouth
dress of those Gallic chiefs who had not yet learned Roman
manners, and did not mock their often clumsy attempts at
speaking Latin. He listened patiently to the grievances of the
provincials and, when it was possible, gave instructions that
they be redressed. He paid due honour to local deities, and
in Lyon sat on the judges' bench and dispensed justice in
exemplary fashion. At dinner-parties given by the notables
of the municipalities, he conducted himself so graciously that
reports of his behaviour sent to Rome were not believed; and
he made no attempt to seduce the wives, daughters or sons of
his hosts or the other provincials. The truth is, he was happy
and at ease, for the first time since the early weeks of his reign.
Caesonia told me that he was even sleeping at night – 'Five or
even six hours unbroken, and with no nightmares, no evil or
disturbing dreams. Not once since we left Rome has he woken
up screaming or bathed in sweat. I would say he was a new
man, if I wasn't certain that what we are seeing is the real
one. He recognises the change himself. Just yesterday he said,
"I don't know what's happened to me, but I am comfortable
in my skin." If you want my opinion . . .' She paused.

'Caesonia,' I said, 'when haven't I? You know that I've
always valued it. I still do, even when you have been taken
from me.'

'There's nothing to be said about that.'

'Of course there isn't. Which is why I have never till this
moment referred to it. But don't think I don't miss you.
However . . . what was it you were going to say?'

'You won't repeat it though, will you?'

'Promise.' A promise that I have kept to this day, and only
now, when nothing matters any more, and nothing can matter

to my poor Caesonia, or to Gaius himself, do I feel released from it.

'You know what his upbringing was,' she said, 'how he was trained in hypocrisy, thanks to that old monster on Capri, how his life was in danger if he spoke rashly. You know all that. But he survived and when he became Emperor felt his power as an intoxication. Yet all the time he was still only a frightened boy, and one who didn't really believe he was capable of anything. So he tried to impress and dominate the world, simply to calm his fears and his sense of his own insufficiency. He felt inferior to the senators and to all those who had experience of command. You must remember he had never been allowed to occupy any official post, had never served in the army or governed a province. So it's not surprising that he behaved as he did. He's not proud of it, you know. Indeed – and this is something else you must never repeat – he knows he has made many mistakes, even committed crimes, as well as offending so many. "Do you know," he said to me just the other day, "since I became Emperor, the only place where I have felt comfortable and been at ease has been watching the Games in the arena and hearing the crowd cheer me." Then he added, and this should make your ears tingle, "If I hadn't had your ex-husband to rely on and to advise me, I should have run away and hidden myself in a remote cavern, and shunned human society." But now, in the army, he feels at home. It's that simple.'

I wish it had been. If Gaius could have continued in the course he set himself these few weeks, he would still be alive and be regarded as a good and much-loved Emperor.

But, alas, he was soon to be diverted from it.

X

I had been too long from the armies. That was what I thought these first days on the Rhine. There was exhilaration in the sounds of the camp, in the sight of soldiers going about their duties, in the smell of the horse-lines, in seeing the gates closed as the long northern twilight faded, and the bugles commanded the changing of the guard.

The Emperor experienced the same surge of pleasure. Several times he remarked, 'This is my natural habitat,' or 'This is where I was raised,' or even 'I feel as if I have come home.' He was encouraged too by the rapturous reception the legionaries gave him, and delighted in having the veterans crowd round him, with their memories of his father, and their wounds to prove the length and hardship of their service.

But it was not long before our mood changed. I say 'our', for Gaius and I, at this time, were of one mind. Once the first exhilaration of being with the legions began to fade, it was evident that all was not well. There was no snap to the drill. The men paraded with dull and even dirty weapons. Not only had there been no punitive expeditions across the Rhine and into Germany to maintain peace, impress the tribes, collect tribute and take hostages, for two years now, there had also, I discovered, been no training exercises either. In short the troops went through the motions of performing their duty, but only that, and did so in a lackadaisical, slovenly manner. Drunkenness was rife, and a number of the centurions had installed their Gallic or German whores even in their military quarters. As for the men it was soon clear that they spent more time in the tavern and the brothel than in the field. Too many were fat, and others short of breath, red-nosed, bleary-eyed, and incapable of concentration. They mingled too freely with the local population, which was not surprising since so many had had children by local women, and, as always happens when discipline has been relaxed and men can spend time lounging about in villages or the disreputable quarters of towns, corruption was common, and an inventory of stores would have found evidence of pilfering and of state property being sold for private benefit. To be blunt, wherever one looked, one saw things to disgust and dismay; to anger also anyone such as myself who was accustomed to the long-established high standards, rigorous discipline, efficiency and smartness of the army.

It was of course the fault of the commander. Gnaeus Lentulus Gaeticulus was a man, unquestionably, of good family, and his career had been not undistinguished. He was a contemporary of mine, and in my youth I knew him well. Indeed soon after the mutiny of 14, Germanicus had appointed him one of his junior lieutenants. He had an easy manner and a pleasing appearance: middle-sized, light-limbed, with a soft, rather girlish face, surmounted by abundant curls. At first the men were inclined to mock him, even to hold him in contempt; I believe that some of the recruits used to imitate his rather mincing walk. But he soon showed himself brave and capable of surprising endurance on campaign. Moreover, perhaps because he wished to give the lie to the innuendos that his somewhat effeminate appearance provoked, he won himself a reputation as a great womaniser, something that always pleases the legionaries. Actually of course our soldiers are wonderfully tolerant with regard to sexual morality. One of our fellow-legates, Marcus Labienus, a grandson of Julius Caesar's general, lean, silent, grim and unprepossessing in appearance, always chose one of the prettiest recruits to be his body-servant – and nobody thought it stopped at that –

but was nevertheless adored by the troops on account of his matchless courage and devoted care for their well-being.

Gaeticulus was a favourite of Tiberius, who employed him to spy on Germanicus and report on his state of mind and ambitions – a task, you will remember, for which both Tiberius himself and Sejanus had tried to recruit me. He therefore basked in the sun throughout the old Emperor's reign, was never suspected of disloyalty and given a succession of important and rewarding jobs. His elevation was not entirely undeserved. He was intelligent and had great charm, remaining good-looking even after he lost the sight of an eye in the Mauretanian war. I always enjoyed his company, except when he gave free rein to his salacious humour; his mind was utterly filthy and he had a stock of grotesque and repulsive stories. That was another reason why the troops loved him.

So now, to discover how my old friend was neglecting his duty, had let things slide, was painful, as painful indeed as to find that the soft girlish face was now fat and double-chinned, the once abundant curls had given place to baldness, and the somewhat slanted and always flirtatious brown eyes – I say flirtatious since he could never resist trying to exercise his charm – were now dull and without expression.

It was painful too that he had not, even at the moment of our arrival, evinced any pleasure in seeing me again. Indeed, to judge from his manner, we might never have known each other in our salad days, never talked the night away, never exchanged the most intimate of confidences. It didn't occur to me then to ascribe his coldness and indifference to finding me so evidently the Emperor's chosen lieutenant and most trusted adviser. It wasn't till later that I knew the depth of his detestation of Gaius. I hadn't then understood how completely he had abandoned the party that remained devoted to the memory of Germanicus, itself, however, explicable by the fact that the elder Agrippina was one of the few he had never succeeded in charming. Indeed, even in those distant days of our youth, she distrusted him and would speak of him coldly, even with contempt. Nor did I realise that, astonishing as it may seem, he had not only admired Tiberius, but in his own manner adored him. Strange that I have had to live so long to begin to understand the complexities of the heart, its utter and irrational waywardness.

It now strikes me as probable that the deterioration of his character, which was so exactly reflected in the demoralised state of his command, was the consequence of the death of the old Emperor and his replacement by Gaius. It was as if Tiberius had been the anchor that held him to duty, and that, now the anchor was raised, he was drifting hopelessly towards his shipwreck. I do not think this too fanciful an explanation.

Gaius for his part reciprocated Gaeticulus' dislike and contempt. Within a few days of our arrival he was referring to him as 'the old woman'. He took pleasure in humiliating him, upbraiding or contradicting him even before the troops, and in watching the general having to swallow the reproofs and insults.

There was a young man on Gaeticulus' staff whom the Emperor took peculiar pleasure in baiting. He was called Valerius Catullus, a connection of the dissolute, but talented, poet of the late Republic. This Catullus had no such gifts. He was a tall, loose-limbed youth, with long legs, narrow hips, and soft arms. His face, rather silly when animated, had in repose a deep sensual sadness. It was clear that Gaeticulus found pleasure in his company; so Gaius responded by humiliating him too. That wasn't the only reason. Empty-minded and vain as Catullus seemed to be, he nevertheless possessed an ease of manner, a natural buoyancy, that served to reproach the Emperor's awkwardness. Moreover Catullus appeared impervious to the insults and gibes that Gaius directed at him, and this infuriated him. If we had been in Rome, Gaius would have had him put to death. But here it was different; he wasn't the same man given to cruel impulses that he was unable to resist. He had a serious interest: restoring the army to a pitch of efficiency that would make his conquest of Germany possible. Catullus was a mere irritation, no more annoying really than a fly buzzing round your head while you are trying to work.

Catullus survived Gaius, if only just. Years later, quite recently in fact, he said to me, 'Well, I've you to thank in the first place, and Caesonia in the second. She liked and protected me.' (I felt jealousy like a dagger in the ribs, at these words.) 'But then I knew Gaius for what he was. That was what he couldn't forgive me for. We were schoolfellows and then, when we were fourteen, briefly lovers. It's been put about, I know, that I used to boast I had sodomised him to the point of exhaustion. I suppose I may have said that in my cups. But really, it wasn't like that. I had a certain tenderness for him, don't you know? He was so awkward and shy and unhappy. I could never believe he was absolutely a monster, on account of those hours we spent together when we were young. And I think, beneath everything, he retained something of a feeling for me. I know I was later condemned to death, but I heard that Caesonia had said that in his heart he was happy that I had managed to give him the slip.'

How calmly he said that! How extraordinary that he should be capable of such calmness. How much he has forgotten! Or, perhaps, what a liar he is and, like the most accomplished liars, capable of believing his own lies, these imagined or revised stories.

But I digress again, or at least anticipate.

Marcus Aemilius Lepidus came north, ostensibly as an emissary from the Senate. He was accompanied by Agrippina, whom he had recently married only a few months after Drusilla's death and immediately following the death of her disgusting husband. I asked him then if he was determined to remain the Emperor's brother-in-law. The question displeased him, but there was no other reason for the marriage. On the night of their arrival it was my bed she came to. I told her of the question I had put to her new husband.

She laughed, then said, 'You couldn't have got it more wrong, my dear. Lepidus had not the slightest desire to marry me. He did so only at the Emperor's command. Gaius said he had got accustomed to having him in the family and didn't see why he should be allowed to escape. The poor thing was shaking with terror throughout the ceremony. I really believe he thought it was one of Gaius' nasty jokes, and that he would be led away to be beheaded immediately after, especially since Gaius had instructed him to make a will in his favour. As for me I was no more eager than he was. After all, I had heard quite enough about my new husband from Drusilla to know he was unlikely to satisfy me, or even please me. Besides, you know perfectly well that it's you I adore, and here I am to prove it.'

Her claim was a lie. Agrippina has never loved anyone but herself, with the exception of her son Nero, the child of her first marriage to Gn Domitius Ahenobarbus, himself a grandson of Mark Antony. (He was to tell me in years to come that he was well out of it, after their divorce; all the same when she discarded him he drank himself to death in only a few years.)

I always admired Agrippina's intelligence, which exceeded that of any of her brothers and sisters, being hard, cold, and masculine. I respected her determination to make the world conform to her desires. For some time indeed I desired her myself. If her face was too sharply chiselled, the nose promising that in middle-age it would resemble an eagle's beak (which indeed it does), and her lips too thin, yet her figure was seductive, being that of a young athlete, lithe, boyish, perfectly proportioned. But she could give nothing of herself. In bed she sought pleasure, had no interest in mine. She sought it indeed urgently, mewing her needs. I had doubtless been spoiled by Caesonia, so cunning in the art of love, so adroit in exciting her lover's passion, so warm in the rewards she provided. Yet I could not resist Agrippina's demands. Why not? It puzzles me still.

Her husband, who had suffered so many insults that his only remaining pride was that of family, even though he dishonoured it, did not resent my affair with Agrippina. Indeed he was relieved to be no longer required to try to satisfy her demands. Most of the time in these weeks he was silent, withdrawn, seeking only to be unobserved. That was impossible. Gaius made him another of his butts. He had taken to addressing him as 'Ganymede'. It was absurd and inappropriate. Lepidus merely bowed his head, and nursed whatever resentment he felt in his bosom.

It was Agrippina who gave me the first hint of what was afoot. One night, she said, 'There's a curse on our family. I don't know in what way we have offended the gods, but that we have is certain. I for one don't intend to be destroyed by it, as my father, mother, and brothers have been.'

'All your brothers?' I said idly.

'Certainly,' she said, 'Gaius is the most cursed of all. He destroys everything he touches. It's his madness. It can't last. What do you think? How will it end?'

I would not commit myself. I said I was no soothsayer, or prophet, or diviner, who claimed to read the future. But I smelled the direction of the wind.

There were days I caught Gaeticulus looking at me as if appraisingly; Lepidus also. Several times one or the other seemed about to broach a matter of importance, hesitated, then halted, and turned the conversation to trivialities. Once indeed Gaeticulus dared to open his heart. It was late. He had drunk deep, and was at that intermediate point between sobriety and drunkenness in which caution and prudence are relaxed, but clarity not yet lost.

His subject was decadence, the decadence and corruption of our times. I assented; he had said nothing that I had not thought myself. I was not seeking to entrap him. We were speaking in generalities

Then, 'In my youth,' he said, 'I had literary ambitions.'

'Not uncommon. I myself have written lyrics, embarked on histories, even an epic. A long time ago and all in vain.'

'And why was that?'

I sighed, reached for the bottle, and smiled.

'Lack of talent,' I said. 'The words never matched the ideas in my head.'

'I think there was another reason. There certainly is in my case. Our age is not fitted for such things. If there is any form that suits our time it is satire. And we dare not write satire, because we dare not speak our minds.'

'Perhaps,' I said.

Gaeticulus rose, awkwardly, heavy-legged, and looked out on the night.

'Full moon,' he said. 'Will the moon goddess lie with the Emperor?'

'You know of that fancy, do you?'

'Lepidus told me. The Emperor once asked him if he had seen the goddess approach his chamber. He had the wit to reply that the vision of a goddess was granted only to gods, not to mere mortals like himself. It's intolerable, isn't it?'

'A fancy,' I said again, and drank more wine.

'A fancy,' he said, 'such as no sane man would entertain. When they told old Tiberius that he was worshipped as a god in Asia, he was embarrassed. When a deputation came to him from a city in Spain seeking permission to dedicate a temple to him, he replied, "I must tell you forcibly that I am only human, carrying out tasks fit for a human, no god, and I am content to occupy only the first place among men." That was sanity speaking.'

Now I in my turn rose, so as not to have to meet his eye, and looked out on the night. Fleecy clouds scudded across the sky, sliding over the moon, and strange shadows lay across the earth. The wind blew from the north. It was cold and I shivered.

Behind me Gaeticulus spoke: 'On nights like this ghosts might walk. I was speaking of my literary ambitions. I once essayed to write the tragedy of the Liberators, those brave men who in the name of the Republic sought to make an end to tyranny, and therefore dispatched Caesar, though he had been the friend of many of them, and they recognised his virtue and his greatness.'

'Ah yes,' I said, 'the Liberators. More wine is perhaps best.' And I filled both cups. We looked at each other, and, with one accord, raised them and drank to each other.

'Men,' I said, 'worthy of admiration, and yet fools confounded by their own folly. I have heard too much of them. Gaeticulus, we were friends once. Good friends, I think. So I shall speak frankly as friendship requires one to speak. You spoke of ghosts walking, and indeed these northern forests across the river are full of ghosts who can take possession of a man's mind and deform it. But I have also campaigned in the deserts of north Africa, and there too one may be prey to delusions. Once I remember, in great heat and exhausted, I saw a grove of tender greenery rise before me, and I was not alone in seeing it, for the men saw it also and cried out in joy that there was water there. But there was no water and no greenery, it was a delusion, what they call in the native tongue spoken there, a mirage. The Republic is that greenery, that water, that mirage.'

'Yes,' he said, 'we were friends once, and indeed I loved you dearly. It would please me to think we might be so again. You may have forgotten, you may never have known that my grandfather was one of the Liberators. Decimus Brutus. A good general, though a poor thing in many ways. He too had literary ambitions, just like us. They never amounted to much, and yet he left a document, a justification, to explain why he had turned against Caesar, who had been his friend, his patron, even his idol. It's never been published of course, but I read it in my father's library when I was a youth, and I have since read it many times. He quotes Cassius, the boldest and most determined of them. I have long had the words by heart. This is what Cassius said: "If our ancestors, the men who broke Hannibal, laid Carthage waste, pursued the great king Mithridates to his doom, conquered Spain and Africa and Asia, if these men whom we revere could see us now? If they could observe our fallen State? If they could see how abject we now seem? If they could see how Caesar, a man of our own stock, a gambler, debtor, lecher, one who has broken the historic links that held the Republic together, if they could see how he lords us, dominates us, holds us as his subjects? If they saw all this, would they laugh or weep, or weeping laugh, and laughing weep?"'

'Fine rhetoric,' I said, 'worthy of Cicero himself.'

But Gaeticulus ignored me and continued, and I do not know if he was still quoting what his ancestor reported of Cassius' speech or speaking his own mind, or both.

'That is the question I put to you tonight: are you not ashamed, as I feel shame, that we have come to this abject condition? Or are you happy to bow down and worship this Caesar of ours, call him even god, regard him as a creature of a different order from us, who are of as good birth as he?'

What did I feel? Admiration? Envy? Pity? Contempt? Something of all four, and something too – I am bold enough to confess it – of fear.

Admiration, certainly, for I sensed that Gaeticulus and his friends – for there must be friends associated in such an enterprise – were preparing to risk their lives in pursuit of a dream. Envy, yes, since I knew that this dream was indeed just that, a dream, insubstantial and impossible. Pity of course, for I could not believe in the possibility of success. And contempt because they had so little understanding of realities as to suppose that the restoration of the Republic might be feasible.

And fear, very definitely, gut-stirring fear, lest by association I might myself . . .

Enough. I sought to deter Gaeticulus, to persuade him to turn aside from the path he was venturing on.

I said, 'My old friend, you yourself, as I know, were trusted by Tiberius and had a place in his councils. And I think that you had also a true affection for him. These things being so, I cannot believe that you have not heard him speak about the loveliness of the Republic and about the impossibility of restoring it. Had it been possible, he would have done so. Consider, my friend, when the Liberators you so admire slew Caesar, the Republic was still alive, in name anyway. But they could not breathe life into it. Now it has been so long buried that it is scarce a memory for many, and you propose to animate this corpse? My dear friend, I am happy to assume that this is no more than night-talk, stimulated by your excellent wine, and that things have been spoken which are best not recalled in the morning.'

'Nevertheless,' he said, as I took my leave.

Nevertheless, I thought, you will go ahead, and it is beyond me to suppose that a man who has proved as incapable as you at commanding this army of the Rhine will succeed as a conspirator. But I was troubled in my mind.

There was a night when Agrippina did not come to me, but sent word that she had a migraine. This came as a relief. I was ill-at-ease and anxious. As is my wont when the mind is troubled, I sought solace in reading, and at such times it is Thucydides to whom I turn. In his work there is no high soaring, no idealism, no sentimental pretence that men are not what they are. There is only a strong, severe, hard factuality, and a rare understanding of how men actually think and behave. A teacher of Greek rhetoric in my father's time criticised Thucydides for obscurity owing to his habit of condensation, and declared that those who can understand the whole of Thucydides are rare, and even rarer those who can do so without reference to a grammatical commentary, such as, I believe, he compiled himself. This may well be true, but in my opinion an inability to understand the great historian arises always from a certain reluctance to look reality in the face. That was now, grimly, what I had to do.

But I was interrupted by young Catullus. He brought the smell of wine with him and his face was flushed. He wore a soldier's tunic, and his long, soft, boyish legs were streaked with mud. He threw himself, uninvited, on a couch, stretched out these legs which I now saw were caked also with dried blood, and looked at me, his mouth hanging open.

He waved his hand towards the slave who had been holding and unfurling the roll I was reading from.

'I don't read myself. Not much. Get rid of him, will you?'

Then he fell silent again, and lay with his eyes fixed on me. I let him wait. Two moths fluttered around the lamp, till they were drawn to it and their wings crumbled.

'Not myself,' he said at last. 'Been drinking, you see, and got in a fight, scuffle really. Give me some wine, there's a good chap, and have some yourself.'

'You're going to have a black eye in the morning.'

'That's the least of it. Was with the Emperor, you see. Course, he was disguised. Just as well, 'cause he got clobbered. On the head. Laid out he was. But he had one of the bodyguard with him, a bloody great Illyrian I think he is. So he broke up the fight. We'd been in a couple of taverns, down by the river-port, and then a brothel. A couple of the locals took exception to some crack of the Emperor's and that was how it started.'

He took a swig of wine, holding the cup in both hands on account of his trembling.

'Is he all right?' I said.

'Oh yes, he'll be all right. Just a knock on the head, and the bloody great Illyrian slung him over his shoulder and got him out of there before all hell broke loose. That was when they turned on me.'

Again he paused and looked at me as if inviting an enquiry. I let the silence extend itself while I watched him try to regain self-control.

'There's more to it,' I said at last. 'What has frightened you so? I can't believe a tavern brawl would leave you in the state you're in.'

And indeed he was in a state, thoroughly unnerved. The trembling resumed. This time I picked up the cup and held it to his lips while he drank. His skin was moist and he smelled of fear.

'What is it?'

'It's what one of them said.'

'Go on.'

'I didn't understand him too well. I mean, their bloody language. But this was in Latin. He said, "If we finish this one off, it'll look convincing."'

'What do you think he meant?'

'How the hell should I know? It didn't mean anything then, I just knew I was in for it.'

'But later? When you started thinking about it . . .'

'It was that word, "convincing" . . . What was there to convince anyone of? It doesn't make sense.'

But it did, or at least glimmerings of sense were emerging through the mist.

'How did you happen on that brothel?' I said. 'Had you been there before?'

'What's that got to do with it?'

'Just answer.'

'Well, then, no. I've not been here long, remember.'

'So was it chance took you to that particular one?'

'Not exactly.'

'Was it the Emperor's choice?'

He shook his head.

'So?'

He swung his legs off the couch, and sat up. Then he leaned

forward, covering his face with his hands. His neck was all sweaty and when I touched it the sweat was cold. He still trembled.

'So?' I said again. 'Tell.'

I sat beside him and put my arm round his shoulders.

'Tell. It was recommended to you, is that it?'

He said nothing.

'And by whom? It was the general, wasn't it? It was Gaeticulus told you it was the best brothel in town. Is that right? He said it was the place where the Emperor would find what he wanted . . .'

He lifted his face and looked at me in gathering horror, his lips quivering and tears in his eyes.

'What am I to do?'

I stroked his cheek, caressing him for comfort, as you might a dog.

'You're not such a fool, are you? You understand, and I can't blame you for being afraid. Gaius is no fool himself, but you know that, and you're wondering when he will start to ask questions.'

'What am I to do?'

I held him close, and looked out into an imagined night. In a little while he ceased to tremble and turned his face to mine, and again mouthed his question.

'We'll have to find an answer to that,' I said. 'But I don't blame you for being afraid.'

He would have fled like a thief in the night, but I held him to the course I had outlined in my answer to his question. 'For one thing,' I said, repeatedly, to still his immediate fear and inspire in him an acknowledgement of the more terrible reality, 'there is no refuge to which you can flee, nowhere distant where you might be safe. Even if you suppose you might escape the bounds of Empire, what chance of survival among barbarians, what chance of reaching any haven? Besides,' I traced the line of his lips with my finger, 'to fly is to proclaim your guilt, to acknowledge your complicity. If we are to save you, you must do as I say.'

'But that is to betray Gaeticulus, and . . .' He wept again, and mumbled, 'He offered me his friendship.'

'Was it the act of a friend to lure you into this trap? You cannot betray him, for he has already betrayed you, and that quits you of any obligation. Believe me, dear boy, I am the only friend you have this morning, the only person who can do anything for you. When you came to me blubbering you put yourself in my hands, entrusted your life and all that is dear to you to my wits.'

So, shortly after dawn, I sent him to his quarters with instructions that he must bathe, shave, restore his appearance and return to me, all this as quickly as possible. 'For,' I said, 'the Emperor sleeps ill and will have been brooding on last night's adventure, and it is imperative we speak with him before he has taken it into his head to act on his suspicions.'

You may wonder if I felt regret at the part I had to play. Naturally I did. I am a man, and a man of honour, not a

monster. Gaeticulus was my friend. I had some sympathy too
with his hatred of Empire. I knew that as a Roman nobleman
I was in these days of Empire diminished, like all my class. I
resented that. I resent it still. But the Empire is reality, and so I
accepted it. Gaeticulus had behaved foolishly; he had tried to
draw me into his conspiracy, and might even now pretend that
I was party to it. Moreover his attempt to commit murder by
proxy was cowardly, his involvement of the innocent Catullus
dishonourable. He deserved to die.

Did I even then ask myself whether Catullus was as innocent
as he appeared? Again, being no fool, of course I did. But, if he
was not innocent, then in coming to me he had shown more
intelligence that I would have credited him with possessing,
and for that I would have to respect him. In any case he had
thrown himself on my mercy, for he could not have hoped to
deceive me about the fact of the conspiracy. His terror had
been genuine, had touched me, and I had responded to it. To
my surprise, I cared that he should be safe. I say 'to my surprise'
because I had thought such feeling for another dead in me.

Before he returned I sent word to Gaeticulus that the
Emperor had survived an attempt on his life. I added that
he would know what best to do.

The message was suitably ambiguous, but I couldn't believe
it left my old friend with a choice of appropriate action.

We found Gaius up and drinking. He shouted a greeting, leered at Catullus and touched a bump on his forehead.

'Quite a knock I got, what about you?'

'A few cuts and bruises,' Catullus stammered. He was
sweating again. The Emperor smiled.

'I patched him up,' I said. 'It's not the sort of story we want
to get about, is it?'

'That depends,' he said. 'They tried to kill me last night.
Did you know that?'

'I had arrived at that conclusion,' I said. 'But in any case

Catullus here came straight to me, to ask my opinion, because that was what he suspected and yet hardly dared to believe.'

The Emperor chewed at his thumb-nail, and at the thumb itself which was raw and had been bleeding.

'Is that so?' he said. 'And how did you get away, ducky?'

Catullus hesitated, licked his lips, sought words.

'Does that matter?' I said.

In a rush Catullus said, 'I slung a stool at one of them, caught him on the head, then I wrestled with the other who had his knife out, but I managed to get free of his grip, and ran for it.'

'So it came as a surprise to you?'

Catullus fell to his knees, crawled across the floor towards Gaius, clasped his arms round the imperial legs, and cried out, 'Caesar, by all the gods you revere, by your own divinity, I swear, I knew nothing, suspected nothing, please, you must believe me.'

' "Must" is not a word that pleases me. I shall believe you or not precisely as I choose, as the whim takes me.'

He kicked the young man away, who lay then at his feet whimpering, his long legs exposed and betraying his terror as a trickle of urine seeped under them.

The Emperor crowed with delight.

'He's pissed himself. Do you see, he's pissed himself, and when we were boys, he did everything better than me.'

He kicked out again, this time striking Catullus sharply just below the ribs, so that he yelped in pain.

'How I should like to see him whipped,' Gaius said. 'Perhaps I shall. What do you think?'

'I think,' I said, 'we should have a word together,' and I took him by the arm, as I had been wont to do, and led him to the far corner of the room, to a window that looked to the north, across the great river and towards the dark forests.

'You are in danger,' I said. 'Last night's attempt failed, but who knows what your enemies are planning now? They will already have realised that you escaped, and they themselves will now be afraid, and frightened men are dangerous.'

'That creature over there's frightened. Do you think he's dangerous?'

'Catullus is frightened because he is innocent. If he had not been innocent he would not have come to me for help. If he had not been innocent he would not be here now. And he is afraid also because of the attempt made on your life, and his, last night, which he fears may be repeated.'

He chewed his thumb again, and sucked the blood that spurted from it.

'You may be right,' he muttered, 'you may, you've been right before, and I don't know. My head's bad this morning. But I'd like to see him whipped, hear him scream, I'm sure he would scream very musically.'

'Gaius,' I said. 'Catullus is your friend, believe me, just as I am, who swore an oath to your father that I would always stand by you, as I did at the time of the mutiny.'

'You did then, didn't you? You carried me out of the camp on your shoulders, I remember. I don't know what to do.'

At that moment angry shouts rose from the camp beyond, angry shouts and the clash of weapons. He grabbed hold of my arm.

'It's started again,' he said. 'There was no moon last night, I should never have gone out on a moonless night when the goddess was sleeping and . . . now . . . now, they're going to kill me.'

'Calm yourself,' I said. 'Compose yourself,' I continued, though to tell truth I was minded to allow him to sink deeper into the pit of fear that threatened to engulf him. 'There is no mutiny. The shouts you hear are directed at the wretches who attacked you last night, and whom I sent a detachment of guards to seek out and arrest. They will be here any minute to be questioned, but first you must compose yourself, and be the Emperor, the son of the great Germanicus.'

'Yes, yes,' he said. 'I must, I must, the son of Germanicus, but I don't like that word "must", my mother used to say I must do this, must do that, till I wanted to tear her tongue out.'

He freed himself from my grasp, turned away, and stood by the window. He was breathing heavily and his shoulders rose and fell. I watched him for a minute, and then knelt by Catullus and whispered in his ear, 'It's all right, you played your part well.' I put my arm under his and helped him to his feet. His face was pale and his eyes were those of a startled colt.

There was a knock at the door. The guards brought in the wretches I had sent them to seek out. They were the most miserable specimens of broken humanity.

'Who instructed you?' I said. 'Who gave you orders for what you did last night?'

They looked sullen and said nothing.

'Are these the men?' I said to Catullus.

He nodded his head.

Gaius turned towards us. 'Their death must be painful,' he said. 'But first they must be put to the question. Tortured.' He licked his lips. 'I want to hear them scream.'

'So you shall,' I said.

One of his freedmen – Narcissus, as I remember – had followed the guards into the chamber. He now produced a letter which he handed to the Emperor.

Gaius glanced at it, and passed it over to me.

'Gaeticulus has escaped me,' he said. 'See that these men are taken to the cellar and prepared for me.'

We were left, Catullus and myself, alone. I read the letter. There was a certain dignity to it. Gaeticulus declared himself a true Roman and Republican, and expressed his hatred of Gaius and contempt for him. 'The world you command is one in which I do not choose to linger,' he wrote.

'Good in its way,' I said.

'You expected this.'

'There are not many surprises left in the world. You're still trembling,' I said. 'There's no need, not for now.'

It was when we had returned to my quarters that Catullus said, 'To be honest I couldn't swear to it that those were the men who attacked us.'

'Does it matter?' I said. 'It was necessary to produce them, to divert the Emperor. In any case, dear boy, I assure you they were notorious criminals. I made certain of that.'

Their torture produced the results that torture produces. They answered as required, confirming that the names Gaius suggested to them were indeed party to the conspiracy. Then they were crucified, and the conspirators disposed of in a manner suitable to their rank. I was sorry that Marcus Aemilius Lepidus was among them, but the Emperor had no doubt that he had been Gaeticulus' chief confederate. So he was executed. It was impossible for Gaius to believe that his own sister Agrippina was innocent of complicity. For a few days he thought of having her put to death. Then he concluded it would be more appropriate to have her sent to the island prison formerly occupied by their mother. He sent her there with, for good measure, their other sister, and put Catullus in command of their escort.

'You will be sorry to lose him,' he said to me.

'Your divinity sees everything,' I replied.

Of course Agrippina seduced the poor boy in the course of their journey, but that was a fate to be preferred to death.

In truth, despite my efforts, the Emperor was not fully convinced of his innocence and would happily have had him killed, if, at my request, Caesonia had not intervened to plead for his life. I don't know what argument she advanced. Probably it wasn't verbal. It was, I suppose, the last service she did me.

It pleased Gaius to deprive me of the boy, but in fact I was not sorry to see him depart, to lose him and give the Emperor this satisfaction. I recognised that I had been in danger of forming an attachment to Catullus, and I knew that in the world we have made, he who forms such a tie is lost. To care for another is to make yourself vulnerable. The only sure armour in the court is detachment from any affection.

XII

So Gaius survived that conspiracy. Young Catullus survived it also. Was he party to it or merely Gaeticulus' dupe? I could not be certain. But then in truth it was only the general's suicide that confirmed the reality of the plot. Some deny that reality to this day. Seneca himself has expressed his scepticism.

'Of course,' he said, 'the suicide points to its reality. Nevertheless, knowing Caligula's irrationality and vindictiveness, the fact that Gaeticulus killed himself does not offer absolute proof. If he heard of the attempt on the Emperor's life, assuming there was indeed such an attempt and that Caligula had not merely involved himself in a vulgar tavern brawl, which supposition is not, you must confess, at variance with our knowledge of his deplorable character, then it is conceivable – is it not? – that Gaeticulus, fearing he would be suspected, acted as a man of honour and departed this life on his terms, not on the monster's.'

Few could be sure of my own part in the proceedings, but much was suspected, and that not far from the truth. More has been divulged or conjectured since. In consequence I have found myself shunned by many conscious of their own virtue, and insulted and regarded with obloquy by others whose own conduct and character would not stand examination.

Those for whom I write this memoir – which daily departs further from the task Agrippina set me – may well add their reproaches to those of my contemporary critics. Though such reproaches delivered by posterity cannot affect me for good or ill, nevertheless I owe it to my own self-esteem and to my character to defend or, at any rate, explain my conduct.

It was first a matter of politics. As I have said, I did not believe that the restoration of the Republic was possible. I need not now repeat my reasons, which were however to my mind cogent, incontrovertible.

This being so, it was evident that Gaius would have a successor. But there was no obvious candidate, no one, that is, who could commend himself to both the army and the Senate, not to mention the People, who, inchoate and intemperate in judgement as they are, and indeed must be, have to be appeased, and must therefore tacitly approve the succession. The only surviving male of the family of Augustus and Livia, or indeed of Antony and Octavia – the Julio-Claudians as some call them – was Gaius' uncle, the drunken, drivelling, slobbering cripple, Claudius. He was not a credible, scarce even conceivable, Emperor.

That judgement of mine was indeed soon to be tested, and proved wise. The Senate, acting either from stupidity or malice, took it into their heads to dispatch Claudius as their emissary to congratulate the Emperor on his deliverance from this conspiracy. (I wager that some, even then, consented to this message of congratulation with bitterness in their hearts.) Claudius, having a higher opinion of his own worth and abilities than anyone else, accepted the mission as his right. He left Rome at once, accompanied by an assortment of hypocrites, flatterers, scoundrels, time-servers, and other riff-raff, including his favourite dwarf, whom he kept by him so that the creature's oddity might distract others' eyes from his own imperfections. He set out with great urgency, but travelled slowly, partly because his nightly potations were so deep that he was seldom ready or able to resume his journey before noon on the morrow, and partly because he insisted on being met with a civic reception, followed by a banquet, in every town through which he passed. But he arrived at last, and having delivered the senatorial message, which was couched in terms of revolting subservience and hyperbole, embarked on a second address of his own composition, a poem in barbarous or halting hexameters, and of the utmost emptiness and tedium.

Gaius, to be fair, attended to it with the appearance of interest for as long as it might take a man to run a mile, till, at last bored and exasperated, he called a halt, and said, 'This is intolerable fustian, dry as dust. My poor uncle, you require some refreshment. Throw him in the river for his bad verses.' (I have already remarked, I think, that Gaius had the makings of a critic.)

Naturally many in the audience, equally bored, were happy to oblige, and would of course have obeyed even if Claudius had been as mellifluous a poet as Virgil himself. So he was ducked amid general hilarity, and would probably have drowned had Gaius not taken pity on him and ordered a guardsman to 'fish the old fool out'.

Was it unreasonable, I ask you, to suppose that such a clown as Claudius could never be an acceptable Emperor?

I anticipate, and must resume the argument that is my justification.

There being no alternative, no member of what we had learned, alas, to call 'the imperial family' competent to succeed Gaius, it was obvious to me that his murder would lead to a struggle for supremacy between the commanders of the different armies quartered on the frontiers. There was no reason to suppose that the army on the Danube, for instance, would accept that the army of the Rhine had the right to choose its commander as Emperor. I foresaw a return to the internecine struggles of the late Republic, a renewal of the wars fought between Marius and Sulla, Caesar and Pompey, Antony and Octavius, who became Augustus. All that I had ever read, ever been told, ever learned, taught me the horror of such wars. Gaius might be a bad Emperor, but civil war was worse.

These were my political reasons for acting as I did, and even today I cannot find them anything but compelling.

But there were other reasons. I had sworn an oath of loyalty to Gaius, as indeed had those who planned his murder. It was not in my nature to break my oath.

Then I had, still retained, a certain affection for Gaius. I had known him as a child. I had been a favourite of his father. His grandmother Antonia, for whom I had an infinite respect, had urged me to care for him. I knew him, certainly, to be wayward, unpredictable, capricious, too given to cruelty; yet I had also been subject to his charm. I felt unwillingly tenderness for him, even sympathy. Caesonia I knew to entertain similar sentiments, and I trusted her judgement. It was not yet impossible that he should mature and, if well guided (as I believed myself capable of guiding him), prove a good or at least acceptable Emperor. Whatever he became later, he was not at this stage a monster.

Finally, and I am not ashamed to confess this, I acted in self-interest. It is true that Gaeticulus had been my friend, but my refusal to join him in the conspiracy when he sounded me out would have persuaded him that I was not to be trusted. It was unlikely I would be permitted to survive Gaius. It would have been necessary for the conspirators – these new self-appointed Liberators – to act to secure their position. There would have been proscriptions, and I did not doubt that my name would have been near the top of the list. Why so modest? I was sure it would have been first.

Lest any think this conceit, I may state here that I have since learned that my apprehension was well-founded. Some years ago, I discussed the conspiracy with Agrippina. She was frank as she always is, when she has no reason to lie. She smiled and said, 'But of course, my sweet, you are right. Lepidus was determined to be Emperor, even though that old fool Gaeticulus believed they were going to restore the Republic. You may think he was quite unsuitable, but that wasn't his opinion. He could never forget that his great-grandfather had been one of the Triumvirs after the murder of Caesar, and he believed he had been cheated of Empire by Antony and Augustus. And though he was fond of you in his weak way, and admired you certainly, he was also jealous and afraid of you. So, yes, he would have had you killed, before you had the chance to get yourself re-appointed as an army commander, and so become a rival and a candidate for Empire.'

I trust that my reasons for acting as I did at the time of the great conspiracy are now clear; and that, being clear, the course I followed is seen to be fully justified. It was realism, nothing less.

XIII

Spring arrived, and Gaius' mood was in accord with the season. The successful crushing of the conspiracy had invigorated him. He took the credit for this himself, and I did not trouble to remind him that, but for me and the part played by young Catullus, however dubious that really was, he would probably have been murdered. As it was, he felt himself superior to Julius Caesar, who had died, he said, 'like a beast in the shambles' at the hands of his enemies. He also expressed yet again his sympathy for Tiberius. 'I am only sorry,' he said, 'that I did not understand the essential loneliness of his position when I lived in his household on Capri. Had I known then what I know now, of the burdens of Empire, I would have been a comfort to him.' This was ridiculous, for Gaius could no more begin to fathom the depths of the old Emperor's mind, or indeed despair, than he could have matched the achievements of Alexander the Great. Which, however, he often spoke of doing.

There was another reason for his contentment. For the first time in his life he was satisfied in bed. Caesonia saw to that, and I could no longer resent his taking her from me, when I remarked the benefits she brought him. There was no more 'bed-wrestling', his word, with louche young men, no more escapades with other men's wives, no more frantic deflowering of virgins (who, admittedly, this being a military establishment, were rare as hen's teeth). It is true that he still had his wild moments, once, for instance, proposing to have Caesonia tortured so that he might test the depth of her love for him. But these passed. They were mere whims.

Indeed, in these weeks as the late northern spring welcomed us, and even that wild land revealed beauties, Gaius seemed as he was meant to be. That is badly expressed, for it is impossible of course to suppose that anyone is meant to be anything in particular. No philosopher that I know of has maintained that there is any such design in life, and I should despise any who did so as a mere charlatan. But let me put it like this. I remembered the zest and glee and charm of the small boy Gaius once was, in those days when I would carry him round the camp on my shoulders, and he would drill the men with gusto, and crow with happy and infectious laughter, knowing himself to be the darling of the legions. That boy had been long lost. He had lived in fear and uncertainty and, even when he succeeded Tiberius, could not quite believe that he was indeed Emperor. So he set himself to test his power and the response of others to his most outrageous acts. I do not say of course that he did this consciously, that he knew what he was doing, but this is my interpretation.

Now, in his newborn confidence he seemed as the small boy might have been if he had been permitted to grow up straight rather than twisted, if his natural exuberance and, yes, goodness of heart had not been trampled on, if he had not been schooled in hypocrisy and sought refuge from his torment in what is commonly styled vice.

You think this absurd, sentimental? It may be. I feel myself old, my judgement softening. Nevertheless this is how I remember him in these weeks.

I had thought to be appointed to Gaeticulus' command, though that is not of course why I had acted against him. But the Emperor's explanation of his refusal was flattering. He must, he said, keep me by his side; there was no one else he could trust or rely on. Besides, with him, I should have overall direction of the German campaign. My formal title would be chief of staff and second-in-command.

So it was by my advice that the executive command was

given to Servius Sulpicius Galba, who had served under me in the African war. He was an honourable man, of firm but limited intelligence, upright and austere, at least on public occasions. Like me he belonged to the old nobility; there were consuls on both sides of his family. His great-grandfather had been one of the Liberators who murdered Caesar, but his grandfather, no soldier but a historian, was a familiar of Augustus and Livia. There was a story that Augustus had once pinched him on the cheek when a small boy, and said, 'Someday, you too will taste power.' But that was the kind of teasing remark Augustus used to make to children, whose company he enjoyed. There was also a foolish prophecy that Galba himself would some day be Emperor. This came about because on one occasion when his grandfather was invoking sacrificial lightning, an eagle swooped down, seized the victim's intestines from the old man's hands and carried them off to an oak-tree. The story may be true; it was certainly widely believed. When it was relayed to Tiberius, he merely grunted, 'That's of no concern to me.' Or, indeed, I should think, to anyone.

I recommended Galba for one good reason: I knew him to be a stern disciplinarian of the old school. That was what the Rhine legions required, and it did not perturb me that I knew him to have no imagination and very little understanding of strategy. I myself could supply these. He soon set himself to restore order and efficiency. When some soldiers started clapping at a religious festival, he immediately issued an order that, on parade, 'Hands will be kept within cloaks at all times.' He believed in hard drilling and within a few weeks of his arrival the legions were certainly much smarter.

For myself, I always found him a bore. Even as a young man he had been fond of dilating on the greatness of his ancestors, and the habit had grown on him. Gaius was greatly amused, and used to offer a very exact imitation. It took Galba some times to realise that the Emperor was mocking him, but, when he did, he had the sense at least not to express his displeasure. But he scowled and looked sullen, which amused the Emperor still more. Nevertheless even Gaius admitted that Galba was doing a good job in preparing the legions for the invasion of Germany.

He wasn't popular with the troops, but was respected. The respect would have been less if they had known more about him. His wife had died some years previously, and he had shown no interest in marrying again, had indeed flatly refused several suggested brides. Women were not to his taste. Nor were handsome boys. On the contrary he shared his bed with a thickset, hairy fellow of his own age at least, a Spaniard. In this relationship it was Galba who played the wife. That's the sort of thing that soldiers, both veterans and recruits, find disgusting. They understand very well an officer who fancies a good-looking youth. Many of the veterans, accustomed to years of serving on the frontiers where the only women are common whores, share that predilection. It is so common that no one thinks of it as vice. Besides, these affairs are for the most part sentimental, even though they may often be given physical expression. But a mature man who plays the wife to another mature man disgusts them, and is regarded with contempt. Pathics are derided and insulted. Fortunately Galba's Spaniard was so ugly that no one except those close to the general suspected their intimacy, and we sensibly kept our mouths shut.

Gaius, however, knew. You couldn't keep that sort of thing from him, he had a veritable genius for knowing what was going on in that way. He wasn't disgusted, often saying that 'nothing people get up to in their bedchamber can surprise me' – which, considering his own declared couplings with Diana the Moon goddess, was itself no surprise. Indeed it amused him because it gave him a further opportunity to tease the general, and to address lewd innuendos to him (which Galba pretended not to understand). Besides, Gaius was convinced that chastity was impossible. Anyone who pretended to it was a hypocrite.

It amused him, I confess, to tease me also, saying, for example, 'When I see how happy that oafish Spaniard makes Galba, I almost feel guilty of having deprived you of the beautiful Catullus.'

'Almost, Caesar,' I would reply, reducing him to giggles.

There was serious work to be done. He was eager to press on with the invasion. I consulted with Galba, and was happy to find him of my mind, agreeing that the troops were in no condition, in consequence of Gaeticulus' slackness and indulgence, to engage in so arduous and uncertain an enterprise. It was hard to convince the Emperor of this. He had all the enthusiasm of youth and inexperience. I spoke to him of his father's campaigns, of the dangers and difficulties he had encountered. I reminded him of how Augustus' general, Varus, had been cut off in the German forests and his three legions utterly destroyed. I told him of how I had been with Germanicus when we came on the scene of Varus' disaster, and of the horrors that had met our eyes, even so many years afterwards. They were, I said, such as had given even seasoned veterans bad dreams.

'If, my lord, you wish to encounter the same fate, and be remembered as a second Varus, then by all means give the order to launch an invasion. But if it is your ambition to go down in history as a great commander, the equal of Julius Caesar or Tiberius or indeed your own father, then let us take such measures as will ensure success next year, rather than rush on catastrophe now.'

It is to Gaius' credit that he was persuaded by my argument. I am happy to record this because so many now speak of Gaius as if he was, even then, thoroughly deranged, a tyrant deaf to reason and indifferent to reality. This is a slander. When he was sober, as he mostly was in the north, and when his brain was not over-stimulated or excited, he was neither devoid of common sense nor beyond reason.

We therefore embarked on a series of training exercises, designed to transform the debauched and disorderly legions into an effective fighting force, capable of endurance and rapid movement. It was also necessary that they learn the nature of a campaign against Germans.

It was then at my suggestion that we embarked on these training exercises, and it is concerning them that so many ridiculous stories have been told.

It is widely believed for instance that Gaius, afraid of engaging in real warfare, staged an elaborate pretence. He sent some of the German auxiliaries who formed his bodyguard across the river with orders to hide themselves among the trees. Then, while he was at table, scouts ran in to tell him excitedly that the enemy were at hand. Whereupon Gaius leaped to action, collected his cavalry and an available legion and set off in search of the enemy, knowing of course that they were not the real thing. When he had rounded them up, he pretended that they were indeed dangerous barbarians, instead of his trusted bodyguard, and awarded trophies to those soldiers who had accompanied him and distinguished themselves in the pursuit.

Now, like so many ridiculous stories that achieve wide circulation and are believed and repeated, gaining in absurdity with each repetition, this one contains a kernel of truth.

Certainly members of his German bodyguard were dispatched across the Rhine, and instructed to act as if they were the vanguard of a powerful German force. They were selected for this purpose precisely because, being Germans themselves, they knew the German manner of war, and would act convincingly. It is true also that the cavalry were given the task of seeking them out, and that one legion acted in concert with the cavalry. And it is true that this was mimic war.

But that was its exact purpose, and nobody who took part

in the exercise supposed it was anything but an exercise. The fact was that the Rhine army had been inactive for so long that few of the soldiers were either accustomed to the rigours of hard marches or acquainted with the terrain or the German way of fighting. The purpose of this training exercise was to remedy that deficiency, to give them experience which would prove invaluable when we undertook the advance into Germany planned for the following summer. And I insist it was successful. The morale and efficiency of the troops were raised. Even Galba, sour and unwilling to praise anything which he had neither thought of nor originated himself, was impressed, and obliged to admit that things were going well.

'When I first saw this army,' he said, 'I did not believe it could be got ready for war in so short a time.'

The truth is, that in recent years, the sort of training which was common, even a matter of routine, in the armies of the late Republic, and in those commanded by Tiberius, Drusus and Germanicus – though the last was, as I have written, no stern disciplinarian – had been so completely neglected as to be all but forgotten. This is why when reports of what we were doing reached Rome, it was not only the malicious who misinterpreted them. There was no shortage of ignorant men ready to believe the nonsense that was talked.

I know our soldiers, none better. It is therefore no mere assertion on my part to declare that, if there had been any substance in the stories relayed by gossips at Roman dinner-parties, the soldiers would have been disgruntled, mutinous, and would have despised Gaius, even loathed him, for making them appear ridiculous. But the reverse was the case. They found these exercises both enjoyable and rewarding. They rejoiced in their regained vigour and efficiency. There is a paradox concerning soldiers, revealed only to those with long experience of the camp. On the one hand, our legionaries delight in avoiding arduous and boring duties; they are adepts at 'swinging the lead' – to use their own phrase. But on the other hand they take a real pride in belonging to the greatest army in the world and in making their unit the smartest in that army. They are great grumblers and, if their commanding officers are lax and indolent, they will themselves take their ease, lie about the camp, drink heavily and frequent taverns and brothels. Any veteran will tell you that he longs for the easy life, to laze on his bed and booze the night away. But, in truth, this way of life also disgusts him. He knows that commanders who allow him to be idle also degrade him. He welcomes slackness and also despises it. So now, the men found themselves re-invigorated and regained their self-esteem.

So effective were our training exercises that in later years this army, which under Gaeticulus' command had become a disorderly rabble, performed admirably under Galba in successive German campaigns. And I shall not pretend that I do not deserve the chief credit for this transformation.

Yet, conscious as ever that we now lived in the Empire and no longer in the days of the Republic, I was careful to ascribe all credit to the Emperor himself; and it is fair to say that Gaius enjoyed a remarkable popularity with the troops.

He was at his best when mingling with the soldiers. He spoke to them easily and frankly. They took pleasure in his bawdy jests. He relaxed in their company. He also always demanded that he be well briefed before he moved among them, so that he was able to address veterans by name and recall where they had served and any great deeds they had performed. In short, this Emperor before whom the nobility trembled seemed to the common soldiers and even the centurions a man after their own heart. It is not too much to say that they adored him. Even his odd appearance and eccentricities amused them and, when he dressed Caesonia as a legionary and paraded her before them, they cheered lustily.

I sometimes think, even now, that if Gaius had remained

with the armies, he might have lived to be a successful Emperor.

But it was not to be.

Towards midsummer he was distracted by the appearance of a British prince. His name was Adminius and he was the son of the king of that part of the island which is called Kent, a mighty province, rich in corn and with rivers where an abundance of pearls may be found. Julius Caesar had conquered it a century before, but had not been strong enough to establish a garrison there, so that it had slipped from Roman rule.

Now this prince Adminius, a handsome young man, who spoke some Latin and had a winning manner, sought the Emperor's help. He had quarrelled with his father and been banished by him. Furthermore his father, who was old and feeble, had fixed the succession on Adminius' half-brother, who, the young man said, had no love for Rome, but in the most boastful fashion declared himself the sworn enemy of our Empire. Adminius proposed that Gaius invade Britain and offered in return to make his province part of our Empire, with the provision only that he should reign there as a client-king.

The project delighted Gaius.

'It will make me greater than Julius Caesar,' he said. 'I shall achieve what even he failed to accomplish.'

He was so enamoured of this idea that it would have been vain to try to dissuade him. Even Caesonia, whom I approached with the suggestion that she should try to do so, found it beyond her. 'When he's taken an idea in his head,' she said; and left it at that.

I should have left it at that myself, knowing how little Gaius relished any advice that ran counter to his inclinations. Yet, distrusting the British prince, whose charm of manner could not disguise an instability of character, and fearing that no good could come from this enterprise, which might also disrupt plans for the next summer's German war, I urged Gaius not to press ahead with it. He replied, 'I believe you are jealous of the glory I shall win.' And it is from this day that I date the withering of the influence I formerly possessed. Certainly little would go right for the Emperor henceforward.

The British expedition was doomed from the start. It took several weeks to collect merchant vessels to transport the troops across the narrow sea; and in these weeks they lost much of the fine condition they had attained. Moreover, the conscription of the fleet provoked grumblings in Gaul. Rich men were deprived of the luxuries they looked for; there was also a shortage of certain necessities.

Then the weather defied Gaius. The wind blew unremittingly from the west, making it impossible to set sail. When at last it dropped, a thick fog covered the channel, a fog grey, damp, insidious, bitterly cold. The men began to mutter that the gods had cursed the expedition.

Gaius himself was irritable, fractious, his temper, sunny in Germany, now clouded as the sky. He ordered the execution of two centurions merely because they had been been heard to complain of their inactivity. This was stupid. While any commander knows how easily grumbling can lead to disaffection and sap morale, he also accepts that soldiers regard it as an inalienable right, none more so than old sweats and senior centurions. Galba, I should add, approved these executions; he was severe by nature, whereas the wise man's severity is occasional, and a matter of policy.

The season advanced. It became obvious to all but the Emperor, and (I suppose) the British popinjay, with whose charms he seemed every day more infatuated, that there would be no channel crossing that year. Yet, even when the equinoctial gales blew up and destroyed a good half of the merchant fleet as it lay at anchor, he would not yield his purpose. He became savage as a chained yard-dog. No one, not even Caesonia, dared to speak to him unless forced to reply to some question. There was of course one exception: the British prince, who continued to flatter him as a great conqueror and to hold out promises of the victory, glory and rewards that awaited him when the invasion was launched. But it was impossible for anyone else to believe in the invasion; and it rained day after day.

It was a relief when news came from Rome of mutterings and dissension in the Senate, which alarmed Gaius to such an extent that he determined on an immediate return to the city. It may be that he welcomed this necessity as a means of extricating himself from a situation that was becoming intolerable. He ordered the soldiers to break up camp and remove the engineers' huts. Years later in Rome a wit suggested that in his anger and contempt he had ordered them to collect sea-shells. It was a ridiculous story which could be believed only by those who have never served in the army and are ignorant that the word for shells, *musculi*, is soldiers' slang for these huts, applied to them on account of the obvious resemblance in shape. Witty remarks, good stories, often, I have observed, have their origins in such ignorance.

Before setting off for Italy, he took certain measures, partly to disguise the failure of his enterprise and partly to soothe his wounded pride.

First, although one reason for returning to Rome was the news of a financial crisis, he issued a generous donative to the legions. This at least ensured that they set off for their camp on the Rhine in good spirits. It particularly amused Gaius to find that his generosity irritated Galba, who went about muttering that he was accustomed to commanding his soldiers, not to bribing them.

Second, he gave orders for the erection of a huge lighthouse on the coast where we had awaited a clear crossing. 'It must be on the same scale as the Pharos at Alexandria,' he said, and had the plans drawn up under his immediate supervision. (I believe it was never built.)

Third, he ordered the destruction of a temple which Julius Caesar had built for the god Neptune in gratitude for the easy passage to Britain that Neptune had granted him. This childish act gave him much satisfaction.

Finally, he appointed Adminius King of All Britain, and made him promise to pay an annual tribute to Rome. So he was able to send a letter to the Senate informing them that Britain had yielded to him, and was now a client-kingdom of the Empire. Thus, he said, he had achieved something denied to Caesar and accordingly he commanded the Senate to make preparations for his triumph, adding that, for this purpose, they might consider anyone's property as being at their disposal. To make his claim to have subdued Britain more convincing, he left Adminius, of whom in any case he had quickly tired, behind. He also gave him a letter addressed to his father king Cunobelinus, in which he announced his deposition and replacement by his son. The young man, who had hoped to be made king in reality and not in make-believe, was as terrified as he was disappointed. He begged Gaius to allow him to accompany him to Rome, and wept when his request was sharply rejected. So he remained in that fishing-port in Gaul where, I believe, he was murdered a few months later by emissaries of his father to whom the contents of Gaius' letter had been leaked. He was a foolish and empty-headed fellow, who had ventured rashly beyond his capabilities.

XIV

Gaius had insulted the Senate.

'How?'

'Oh, in more ways than I can number,' Catullus said. It was after supper. He had removed his toga and lay on the couch in a short tunic. With his left hand he scratched the inside of his thigh. He bit into the peach he was holding in his right, and his tongue followed the juice that escaped, trickling down his chin.

'His demand of a triumph, for one thing,' he said. 'Everybody knows he achieved nothing. People say that most of the so-called prisoners he sent to Rome to march in it were really criminals plucked from the prisons in Gaul. Is that true? Were any Germans taken prisoner?'

'A few,' I said, 'not many. There were some deserters of course, odds and sods, enough to make a decent show.'

'But he doesn't deserve a triumph.'

'Who cares? He's the Emperor.'

'Well,' he said, 'as to that . . .'

I had dismissed the slaves some time before. I leaned across, poured wine for both of us, placed the flat of my hand on the young man's neck, and stroked it.

'As to that,' I said, 'this neck of yours, if it wasn't for me, would no longer attach your pretty head to your body. Which would have been a pity. That's what I mean when I say, "He's the Emperor."'

He took my hand and kissed it.

'I'm grateful of course, but . . . it can't go on.'

'What? This?'

'No, that. You know of course that he sent the Senate a furious letter reproaching them for enjoying banquets and parties, and frequenting theatres, brothels, and country villas, while he, their Emperor, was risking his life, exposed to all the dangers and hardships of war. Absurd, don't you think?'

'Absurd. Nevertheless, some of the time he's brave enough, dear boy, and I daresay would have acquitted himself well, if it had ever come to war . . .'

'So you admit it didn't?'

'Oh, yes.'

He shifted on the couch. The discomfort was moral, not physical.

'I know what you're thinking,' he said. 'That if Caligula's a coward, I am a worse one. You can't forget that you saw me grovelling at his feet, and pissing myself. Well, I am a coward, I admit it. I keep it hidden from the world, but I can't conceal it from you. And I'm afraid of Caligula, mortally afraid.'

'Poor boy,' I said.

'Me or Caligula?'

'Drink your wine,' I said. 'You know I love you, inasmuch as . . .'

'Is it true he's bringing Agrippina home?'

'Oh, yes, there are times when he thinks that only his sisters understand him, even if she did agree to his murder. I suppose she seduced you, didn't she? Are you afraid of her too?'

'Not of her, but of what her demands on me might mean.'

It was the hour when black night casts her cloak over the world, and our thoughts run to extremities.

Again, as if he had read my mind, he said, 'Are we wiser in the dark?'

'It's the hour of Minerva's bird.'

'Not a goddess I have much acquaintance with.'

'No?' I said. 'If we were guided by Minerva we would not be as we are. Tell me more, more of what is said.'

'That, for instance, before he left Gaul he planned to

have the veterans who long ago mutinied and besieged the headquarters of his father Germanicus put to death, because they had so frightened him as a child.'

'Not true.'

'Well that's what's believed and, moreover, that it was you who dissuaded him, but that even then he ordered the execution of every tenth man, and so had them parade without swords. But when he noticed that a number of legionaries had become suspicious and slipped away to fetch their weapons, he himself fled, leaped on his horse and headed home.'

'Grotesque.'

'If you say so, but this at least is true because I had it myself from one of those concerned: that the other night, late as it is now, he summoned three senators, commanding they be brought from their beds, and when they arrived at the palace, more than half-dead from fear, for which you can't surely blame them, they were led to a stage and music was playing and they didn't know what was expected of them till suddenly Caligula burst upon them dressed as a Syrian dancing-girl and performed before them, then had them whipped because he thought their applause insincere.'

'Well, it would be,' I said, 'he dances very badly, as you know.'

'And then,' Catullus said, 'the word is that he's going to make his horse consul at the next elections.'

'Incitatus? He's a very beautiful horse, and a well-mannered one. We have certainly had less decorative consuls, and stupider ones.'

'But we can't have a horse as consul. You're teasing me, aren't you?'

'Just a little. Dear boy, it doesn't matter, it simply doesn't matter. You know, as well as I do, that since the time of Julius Caesar, it doesn't matter who – or indeed what – is consul. The post no longer means anything. You know that. All the trappings of the Republic that we have retained belong to the theatre. They are illusion. Better, they are delusion, for they were retained by Augustus as an element in his great deception, to disguise the reality: that now there is only power. Dear boy, you're crying.'

And so he was, great body-shaking sobs. I had not thought him capable of such depth of feeling. Later I reflected that such a display of emotion was not necessarily evidence of depth. On the contrary, those most readily moved to tears are very often the most superficial. Tears come easily to them. For my part, I have not wept since I was a child.

His emotion spent itself. He did not apologise, nor look ashamed, which pleased me. I was glad to think he had that much self-respect. But he was moved to explain himself.

'What you say is no doubt true, and it horrifies me, because it is at variance with everything I have ever dreamed of. I once told you,' he said, 'that I read very little.' He blushed, charmingly, remembering the occasion as one at which he had not shown himself at his best, but which had led, nevertheless, to our present – what shall I say? – arrangements. 'What I said was true enough. I do indeed read very little. But it was different when I was a boy. Then, for the space of a couple of years, I immersed myself in books and my favourite reading was not, as you may be thinking, poetry, which to my mind is fanciful stuff, but history, and especially the histories of Livy. I know you don't admire him,' he added quickly, 'or at least I've heard you speak disparagingly of his work, but to me, at the age of twelve or thirteen, it was wonderful, especially those books which tell of the early history of the Republic, and the heroes who lived in those days. You're smiling, and I understand why. I'm not heroic. I've already confessed that I'm a coward. And in any case you have me marked down as one that lives for pleasure, haven't you?'

'And gives it. Be fair to yourself.'

'All right, I accept that, gratefully. But to get to the point, I may live what my mother calls a selfish and dissolute life –

indeed she has often reproached me for my manner of living
– but in my heart I retain fond memories of what that reading
meant to me, and of the noble aspirations it kindled in me. I
know I'm not Coriolanus or Cincinnatus, men bold enough to
be entirely themselves. But I have this ideal – I think that's the
word – of the Republic, the Republic of free men, and now
when you tell me that there's no freedom, no law, nothing but
naked power, it grieves me, all the more so because I recognise
that what you say is true. And so I ask myself how can we live
in such dishonour? How can we endure it? I must be drunk to
speak like this. I hope you're drunk too . . .'

'We're both drunk. There's truth spoken in wine.'

(So indeed there is, occasionally, and much nonsense more
often. I have been told too many lies and extravagant stories by
drunkards to give credence to that old tag 'truth, in wine'.)

'We made a Republic of free men, and now we tremble
before a tyrant.'

'Don't suppose,' I said, 'that, because I endure it, I haven't
often thought the thoughts you have so bravely spoken tonight.
Yes, it's fair to call Gaius a tyrant. But he's fortunately a tyrant
in a small way. He's got no ideals, no ambition. The real
tyrant – or shall I say, the really dangerous tyrant – is one
ready to sacrifice armies and nations to his ambition. Julius
Caesar was a worse tyrant than our poor Caligula could
ever be, worse because he was sane, and his ambition was
insatiable.'

Catullus sighed and, muttering, 'More wine is perhaps best',
filled our cups. We raised them and drank to each other.

'That's too deep for me,' he said. 'Small tyrant or big one,
all I know is that Caligula will kill us if we don't kill him first.
The trouble is, there's no understanding him.'

'There's no understanding fate,' I said.

We found ourselves both smiling. We embraced. Later,
much later, I said, 'Caligula's not the problem, you know.
The problem is, we want to live and no longer know how

to. He's merely an extreme manifestation of the disease that afflicts us all.'

Catullus said, 'All the same, there are moments when life's worth living. Even now.'

XV

But I had that night spoken truth in wine, or truth as I saw it. Gaius was unstable, unpredictable, dangerous. That was undeniable. But he was dangerous only to a few. The Empire was everything he wasn't: stable, organised, safe. The provinces were at peace. Provincial governors saw that the law was obeyed, taxes paid. Trade flourished. Towns prospered from Gaul to the fringes of the Arabian desert. Of course there were occasional small local disturbances, a recent one in Judaea for instance; but nothing that need cause serious alarm. The outbreak in Judaea had been handled competently by the procurator, a distant cousin of mine, as it happened. He was a man, this Pontius Pilate, of no great ability and indeed of only average honesty. But that was in a sense the point. The imperial system as established by Augustus and maintained, actually more efficiently, by Tiberius who, whatever his personal failings, was a highly competent administrator, worked so well that it could be run by mediocrities such as Pilate.

To my mind this was, indeed is, proof of its excellence. If you consider that it continues to function efficiently with a clown like Claudius as Emperor, that is evidence of its inherent stability. And aren't peace, stability, the rule of law, precisely what the citizens of this vast Empire most desire? Even the corruption which, in my opinion, is common to all governments, and ultimately ineradicable, has been reduced to a tolerable level. No imperial provincial governor has ever skinned those he is set over as that high-minded Republican idealist, the liberator Marcus Junius Brutus, skinned the inhabitants of Cyprus, to whom he lent money (first gathered from them in taxes) at a rate of 60 per cent interest. That sort of thing went out with the Republic. Tiberius once sent instructions to a provincial governor that his flock were to be sheared, not skinned.

Gaius himself . . . so much has been said about Caligula the monster, these stories, rumours, slanders Catullus recounted to me being but examples of how people spoke even then, and far more extravagantly since his death; so much that to hear the common talk you might suppose that is all he was, was indeed without remission. I deny nothing except what I know to be untrue; so, yes, the Emperor was vicious, cruel, wayward, dangerous to those who offended him or aroused his distrust. Yet he was not altogether neglectful of duty. I have seen him spend a morning in close examination of the Treasury accounts, or of dispatches from provincial governors. He attended assiduously to the requirements of the army, remained popular with the troops and the People, whom he delighted by the lavishness and imagination of the Games he sponsored. The senators might sneer to see the Emperor consort with gladiators, actors, dancers. But the People will always cheer anyone who puts on a good show. His care for their amusement contrasted with Tiberius' parsimony, lofty disdain and reported distaste for gladiatorial combat. Gaius was far more popular than either Augustus or Tiberius had been. I took care to gauge public opinion, and my agents reported that it was commonly said that 'He's our boy, he's on our side against Them.' Indeed the humiliations to which he subjected the senatorial class delighted the People.

As I say, he did not altogether neglect business, though his manner of conducting it was sometimes whimsical.

I have mentioned the disturbances in Judaea towards the end of Tiberius' reign. These had been efficiently suppressed, but now there arose new difficulties, concerning emigrant Jews settled in Alexandria. Or at least that is where trouble started.

The Jews are difficult. Augustus had little patience with them. Tiberius was content to let them go their peculiar way, so long as they paid their taxes, obeyed the law and did not trouble the public peace. But this is always likely on account of their absurdity.

They insist against all Reason that there is only one god. That would be no more than laughable, were it not for their claim that they – and they alone – are the Chosen People of this single god. If you ask a Jew (as I have done many times) why in that case they have no kingdom of their own, are subjects of the Empire, and are scattered across its many provinces, he can give you no satisfactory answer. Sometimes they say it is because they have neglected the commandments of their god, which may be true; at other times they will tell you – and I quote – 'the Lord chastiseth those whom he loveth'; an answer that flies in the face of common sense and experience, since we all know that the gods are indifferent to our welfare but must be appeased by worship and sacrifices. Poets may tell us of lovely girls and boys with whom various gods have fallen in love, and whom they have enjoyed; but nobody of any intellectual repute has to my knowledge been so arrogant or absurd as to suggest that the gods love mankind, or any portion of it; nobody except these strange Jews. For my part I am as indifferent to the gods as I believe them to be to me.

One thing is to be said for the Jews. Though they hate paying taxes (which is reasonable), they do pay on demand. Therefore they have been treated with considerable generosity in return. In Alexandria, for instance, they have their own Senate and their own Jewish governor, known as the ethnarch. These privileges are bitterly resented by the Greeks, who are in the majority in that great city, and who, incidentally, are skilled in the art of tax avoidance. They think the Jews unfairly favoured, and anti-Jewish riots are common. There had been one in the second year of Gaius' reign. There was some provocation. The Jewish prince Herod Agrippa, whose friendship with Gaius I have remarked, called at Alexandria on his way back to resume the government of Judaea. He had lived there some years previously and lived extravagantly, incurring huge debts to leading merchants in the Greek community. The news of his return to imperial favour encouraged his creditors to hope that he would now pay these debts. When he showed a marked disinclination to do so, for it was an axiom of his that such obligations have a time-limit set on them, the merchants stirred up feeling against the Jews and burned and looted the Jewish quarter of the city. Then, fearing retribution from the imperial power, one of their leaders, named Aristippus, thought of a way to fend this off. He persuaded the governor, Quintus Flaccus, to order that a statue of the Emperor be placed in every Jewish place of worship. (These are called synagogues in their language.)

The Jews were aghast. Their Law, which derives from a (probably mythical) legislator called Moses, forbids what they call 'idolatry' – the worship of 'graven images'. So, instead of obeying the order like sensible people – for what possible harm could a statue of poor Gaius do them? – they responded by rioting themselves, and then, more prudently, by sending a deputation to Rome to lay their case before the Emperor in person.

It was led by one Philo, a philosopher, himself a native of Alexandria. I had met and debated with him when I visited the city as a young man, and he was already middle-aged. Now, knowing that I was believed to be intimate with the Emperor and in his confidence, he asked for an audience with me before he was required to present himself at the palace. Naturally I consented.

I remembered that I had found him interesting. This was because, without abandoning his Jewish faith, he had studied the philosophy of the Greeks, and especially Plato's, and sought to reconcile it with his ancestral faith. This required him to be an intellectual gymnast.

But of course we were not to talk philosophy now, though we might both have preferred to do so.

After the normal courtesies – I say 'normal', though Jews are apt to dispense with such things owing to their eagerness to enter into a dispute – he plunged into the middle of the affair.

'The Emperor puzzles me.'

'That will please him.'

'He has recalled Flaccus, I understand. That's a point in our favour. You know, my lord . . .'

I made a deprecating gesture.

'You know, sir,' he took the point, 'that I myself have not only lived long in amity with Greek scholars, but take what many of my co-religionists deem a deplorably liberal line in most respects. Between you and me, sir, had it been left to me, I would have made no objection to the requirement that a statue of the Emperor be placed in our synagogue. I would have said, "Let it stand there, there's no requirement to worship it. Let us agree to receive it as a mark of respect." But I could scarcely say even that to my co-religionists without forfeiting such esteem as I may enjoy.'

'Your sentiments do you credit. I don't pretend to understand your religion, but I do see your difficulty. You assert, do you not, that there is only one god, and the Emperor declares he is a god?'

'Is that a declaration to be taken seriously?'

'A bold question. But the answer depends, I suppose, on your definition of the word "god".'

'That which is worshipped.'

'But is the word "worship" itself not susceptible to more than one meaning. The word is used, is it not, in love-poetry? In such poetry in your language also? Certainly, as you know, in Greek. Might you not intimate as much to your co-religionists? You see, don't you, that I am seeking a way out of this imbroglio, a form of words to which all may assent without loss of face?'

So we argued the matter, round and round, till the sun had passed its zenith; and came to no conclusion.

Then, boldly again, he said, 'What manner of man is the Emperor?'

'A man who one day thinks he is a god, and the next appears a frightened child; one who laughs as he orders an execution and weeps to see his horse gone lame; one who jokes to keep reality at a distance, and yet seeks to explore the darkest recesses of his own nature; one who hides his head beneath the bedclothes if the night is stormy and every day has the courage to invite his murder; one who loves the camp and dreads war, who indulges every spurt of lust and is disgusted by the flesh; a man whose nature is clear as sparkling water and darkly mysterious as the underworld, who is known by all and by none. Shall I go on?'

Gaius delayed before agreeing to meet the Jewish deputation. Meanwhile he had Flaccus, the governor he had recalled, put to death.

'A tiresome fellow,' he said, 'with his long camel's face. It was all right having him in Alexandria, but it would have been too much seeing him back in Rome. Besides, his death should please these Jews, and it is the duty of the Emperor to give satisfaction to his subjects. Nobody can say I don't care for their welfare, even if I don't give a fig for their good opinion. But then, that's no reason why they shouldn't have a good opinion of me, is it?'

Yet the very next day, still without seeing them, he ordered that a larger than life-size statue of himself be placed in the temple in Jerusalem.

'The idea came to me,' he explained, 'as a result of reading a letter from my old friend Herod Agrippa. He told me that the Jews weren't used to such things. Ridiculous, I thought, but if that's so, then the only thing to do is give them the chance to get used to them. I've no doubt that when they understand the blessings which my presence in their temple will bestow on them, they will think it a thoroughly good idea. Do you really think I should meet this deputation? They're sure to be bores.'

But the next day he had changed his mind.

'I talked it over with Incitatus,' he said, 'and he persuaded me it would be only polite. Horses have such good manners. They're nicer than people. No doubt that's why.'

But when the deputation was presented to him, he turned his back on them. They were disconcerted. Nobody dared move or speak. Then, he made a sweeping overarm gesture and hurried from the room. Philo looked at me. I gestured to him, indicating that they should follow. We found him in a gallery. He was standing before a statue of Diana, stroking the marble cheek.

'She's a particular friend of mine,' he said, 'a special friend, you understand. She comes to me on nights when there's a full moon, to my bed. What do you think of that, eh?'

He hurried off again without waiting for a reply. Again we followed. In the next room Caesonia sat on a couch with their little daughter on the floor by her feet. Gaius picked up the child, and threw her high in the air. She squealed with delight, and he caught her and held her to his chest.

'You see, she trusts me,' he said. 'It's so nice that some-body does.'

He handed her back to Caesonia and, leaning forward, fondled his wife's breasts.

'Do your wives have as good ones?' he said. 'Wait for me here. Make conversation to them, my dear.'

When he returned he had divested himself of his toga and wore a plum-coloured blouse and plum-coloured loose-fitting trousers such as Gallic noblemen are accustomed to dress themselves in on festal occasions.

'We'll talk in the garden,' he said. 'I was cold. That's why

I have changed. You can see I'm relaxed, so our conversation can be quite informal and pleasant. You'll like that.'

He led us to an arbour and stretched himself out on a wooden rustic bench under a climbing pink rose.

'You can sit on the ground,' he said, 'as if I was a philosopher and you were my pupils. Don't worry, however, I'm not in the teaching vein. I want to learn. You must never suppose your Emperor is not interested in what his subjects think or in the different ways they have of understanding the world. I know that's the sort of thing people say about me, but it's not true. It's slanderous. I don't like it when people say such things. It's sad but I have been required to have a good many noble Romans put to death, simply for speaking slanders. One of them was your old governor, Flaccus. He said the most awful things. So I had him killed. I've no doubt you approve. But wait: as I say, I want to listen to you and engage in a proper philosophical discussion – a symposium. That's the right word, isn't it?' – he looked at me inquiringly. 'Good, but we can't have a symposium without wine.'

He clapped his hands and a slave approached with a tray on which stood several jugs of wine and goblets.

'My guests first,' the Emperor said, smiling. 'Don't look so anxious, I assure you it's not poisoned. Though it could be, of course. Which of us'll drink first to find out? You? Me? All of us together? That's perhaps best. Your good health, gentlemen.'

We drank. Nobody fell, poisoned, to the ground.

'Good,' he said, 'though it might be a slow-acting poison. We shan't know for some hours. So at least we have time for our symposium. Fill the cups again, boy.'

The slave did as asked, and when he gave the Emperor wine, Gaius clasped him by the thigh, digging his nails into the flesh. (It wouldn't have been painful; he bit them so short.)

'I've not had you,' he said, 'have I? Come back when this is over.'

He smiled on the delegation.

'I've never seen so many well-dressed Jews. And clean ones.'

He pointed to Philo.

'You're the leader, I think. The spokesman, eh? My friend here,' he gestured towards me, 'tells me you're a philosopher. There are days when I am interested in philosophy. You're in luck that this is one of them. I'm told you worship only one god. Explain, please.'

'He is the god of our fathers, the god of Israel,' Philo said.

'He delivered us from the land of bondage, which is Egypt,' said another, a dark, swarthy little fellow with bandy legs. It's a thing I've noticed about Jews. They will never yield even to their appointed spokesman, but must always be interrupting and pushing themselves forward.

'Did he now?' Gaius said. 'But you come from Alexandria, so you must have returned to this land of bondage. What does your god say to that? It sounds to me as if you are guilty of disobedience, or at least ingratitude. Explain yourselves.'

'That deliverance was many generations ago,' Philo said. 'Long before Egypt was a Roman province. Now that it is so, it is naturally no longer a land of bondage, but one where the Law is respected.'

'That's good.'

'Speaking for myself,' the bandy-legged fellow interrupted again, 'I don't reside in Egypt. In any case I'm a Roman citizen. Saul of Tarsus, sir, at your service.'

'Naturally you're at my service,' Gaius said. 'I don't need you to tell me that. I've only to give the word and your throat would be cut. Don't forget that. But, as I said, you're in luck. I'm not in that mood today. I've heard that your god is a jealous god and commands you to have no other gods. Is that true?'

'Such indeed is his command,' Philo said with, understandably, a note of hesitation in his voice.

'That doesn't surprise me. I daresay all gods feel like that sometimes. I know I do. We're a jealous lot. Not always, of course. Jupiter himself wanted to take up residence with me here in the palace. But I told him it wouldn't do, I can't remember why, my memory's usually excellent, but just occasionally a bit cloudy.'

He smiled again.

'I'm enjoying this,' he said, 'a real intellectual discussion. We should put it on in the theatre, for the enlightenment of the People. I understand your god's feelings. But there are other gods, you know, and they have feelings to be considered too. What do you have to say to that? Come on, I want an answer.'

The bandy-legged one, who called himself Saul, rushed in while his colleagues hesitated.

'It is the teaching of our religion, sir, that all other so-called and pretended gods are false, not true gods at all, but impostors, created by men's vanity.'

'I'm not sure I like the sound of that,' Gaius said. 'But I'm not going to get angry, I can conduct this conversation in a level tone and friendly manner. Now, if I understand you rightly – and, pray, even though I am your Emperor, correct me if I have got it wrong – you maintain that all other gods are false, and yet that your god is exclusively the god of the Jews who are his – what's your phrase – Chosen People. Is that so? Have I understood you?'

Philo would have spoken, but again the little man Saul prevented him. I thought, 'This chap is a bit of a fanatic, he should take more care, any moment now he's going to overstep the line.'

'That is what we believe,' he said. 'For such is the word of the lord our god, as delivered to our forefather, Moses.'

Gaius thrust his hand into the loose waistband of his Gallic trousers, and scratched himself. He frowned, then gave a crow of laughter.

'That's rich, that's really rich. It's like the old joke about the mother who watched her son on her first parade and said in a satisfied tone, as the legion marched past her, "Do you see, they're all out of step but our Marcus." My dear chap, I respect your opinions and your faith, but you must see it makes no sense at all. I'm the Emperor and I know. Think of it, there are dozens of nations within my Empire, to say nothing of those beyond it, who include some that are not really barbarians, but tolerably civilised, the Parthians for example. And they all have gods whom they've inherited from their ancestors, just as you have inherited yours. Do you really expect me to believe, or accept, that you Jews, who have never conquered an Empire – I know my History do you see – worship the one true god and that no other gods exist but yours? My dear good people, I'm delighted you have come to me this morning. You've made my day. It's positively the best joke I have heard in years, and my friend there could tell you that I'm a connoisseur of jokes. Later, when we've concluded our philosophical discussion, I'll tell you some, really filthy ones, you'll enjoy them.'

Philo now turned to the little man and told him to be silent. At least that's what I supposed him to say. We had all been speaking Greek, of course, but he snapped out his command in their native tongue. Then he set himself to retrieve the situation which, he may have thought, was slipping out of control. He did so in terms of Greek philosophy. This was intelligent. He was taking the Emperor at his word. So he spoke of *Logos* and *Sophia*, and of how the Divine spirit was the mover of all things, the fount from which ran the stream of life. He spoke of how different peoples made for themselves gods which were even at their best shadowy representations of the Divine Reality. In short, while appearing to elucidate and describe the Jewish faith, he actually sought to obscure the immediate issue and blur the difference between the Jewish understanding of the world and what I may call the Graeco-Roman one. He did Gaius the credit of supposing that he was sufficiently intelligent to follow his argument, even to engage in dialogue, which indeed he was. At the same time I perceived that he was confident that the Emperor was not sufficiently versed in philosophy to realise that his argument conceded nothing to his own point of view.

But Gaius was pleased. He glowed. His body relaxed. This was flattery such as had been too often denied him. And, strange as it may sound, he was happy to find that Philo was in no way afraid.

'You are an admirable man,' he said. 'I should keep you by me. We might read together. Though I am Emperor, I am yet prepared to confess that there are gaps in my education, dark places where I stumble and lack understanding. It may be that you, sir, are the man I have been seeking, to enlighten me.'

He called for more wine, and again took hold of the slave, and this time muttered in his ear.

Then he said, 'I remember my friend Herod Agrippa speaking to me of some madman who had declared himself to be king of your people, come to deliver you from our rule, and prepare, if I have got it right, what he called the Kingdom of Heaven. I believe he was hanged. Or perhaps crucified. Very properly, I've no doubt.'

The little bandy-legged fellow, who had, to my amusement, experienced great difficulty in restraining himself while Philo spoke, frequently shaking his head, muttering in an undertone, and shifting position, now broke out: 'He was an impostor, a low-born fellow, a carpenter it's said, who set himself up to be the Messiah, a rod out of the stem of Jesse that shall be the saviour of his people Israel.'

'Really,' Gaius said. 'I can't think him of much interest or importance. Sounds like a bore. Anyway, he's dead, you say. Understand: I don't want any more talk of such matters. You've given me a lot to think about, but I'm getting bored. So we'll bring this to an end. The statue I'm having placed in your temple will be a peculiarly fine one. I've no doubt at all that you will then appreciate the honour I have done you. You may tell your people that I have ordered it to be installed as a sign of my particular fondness for you Jews. I can't say fairer than that, can I? Now go away, before I am thoroughly tired of you.'

They looked disappointed, even sullen. I couldn't blame them for they had achieved nothing, except I suppose the temporary favour of the Emperor.

He held me back.

'What do you think?' he said. 'I liked your philosopher. Tell him he's not to leave Rome. I would speak with him again. The little man looks like a troublemaker. I wonder if I should have him hanged. He wouldn't make any sort of show in the arena, I'm afraid. Well, it's of no matter. All the same I must ask you to explain to them that people who refuse to accept me as a god are criminals. That's all there is to it. See that they understand. You can go now. But send that slave-boy to me. He's got quite fetching legs. And his mouth was promising.'

The boy smiled when I gave the order. What else could the poor wretch do?

Philo didn't smile.

He said: 'I'm an old man, old enough to be past the fear of death. So I shall speak frankly. On the one hand, I felt pity for your Emperor, and he was, as you suggested, more intelligent than his reputation promised. On the other, I must tell you that if I ever saw a man who was possessed of the Devil, it is he. That's why I pity him, of course.'

XVI

In recent years, since it has been safe to add to them, the catalogue of Gaius' crimes has lengthened. I have before me as I write a scurrilous pamphlet which lists them.

For example, the author writes: 'The following instances will illustrate his crazy and debauched thirst for blood: once, having collected wild beasts for a show, he concluded that butcher's meat was too expensive to feed to them, therefore ordered that they be fed with criminals. He paid no attention to the crimes that the accused were charged with, and held no trial, but merely had them lined up before him in a colonnade, stood in the middle and said, "Kill every man between this baldhead and that one."'

Example: 'He learned that a certain knight had sworn to fight in the arena if Gaius recovered from an illness. So Gaius compelled him to fulfil this oath, and refused to release him till he was near exhaustion and half-mad with terror.'

Example: 'He heard that a certain senator on the same occasion had said he would kill himself if Gaius was restored to health. Finding that he was still alive, the Emperor ordered him to be crowned with a wreath and whipped through the streets by slaves, who kept reminding him, between blows, of his promise, till they reached the Tiber where they flung him into the water and watched him drown.'

Example, according to the author of this pamphlet (and again I quote): 'Many men of decent family were branded at his command, and sent down the mines or put to work on the roads, or thrown to the lions and tigers. Others were confined in narrow cages, where they were forced to crouch on all fours, like animals. Others were condemned to be sawn in half, and not, as you might think, for major offences or any crime, but merely for criticising one of his shows, or for failing to swear by his genius.'

Example: 'He once invited a man to dinner on the same day that he had had his son executed, and showed himself in high spirits, overflowing with an appearance of good fellowship, forcing him to laugh at his filthy jokes and even to join him in singing bawdy songs.'

Enough. The catalogue grows wearisome. It is also absurd. You will have noticed that its author, who chooses to remain anonymous, has himself named no names. Anonymity is the refuge of the scoundrel.

I am not suggesting that Gaius was innocent of cruelty, or that he committed no crimes. But so many of the allegations are grotesque. Is it possible that posterity, which we may assume to be not entirely bereft of common sense, will believe that being, as our pamphleteer asserts, on one occasion anxious that 'a certain senator' be torn to pieces, he persuaded a number of the Conscript Fathers to name him as a public enemy in the House, stab him with their pens and hand him over to be lynched by the mob; or that he was not satisfied till the wretched man's limbs and guts had been dragged through the dust and piled up at his feet?

Will posterity believe that even the most degraded of senators could have collaborated in this manner in so foul a murder?

Remember that I was close to Gaius, was called by him his right-hand man, sometimes his rock, and saw none of this, knew nothing of such despicable outrages.

I am not ashamed. It was possible that by practising discretion one might exercise an influence for moderation and good sense. We must accommodate ourselves to the times we live in. I admire the past, but I acquiesce in the present. I pray for good Emperors, but I endure whatever we get. I am proud that if any should ask me what I did in the reign of Caligula, I can answer, 'I survived.' It is easy to be virtuous when the times are virtuous.

Gaius knew this himself, in his more stable moments. He once said to me, 'I suppose that if the Empire had never been made, I might be a good man.' This was, as I recall, when he was examining, not for the first time, Tiberius' private papers, which he had first intended to burn, then decided to preserve. It became his habit to read over and over again the account of the evidence offered against his mother and brothers. It fascinated him. He knew it had been fabricated. And yet, as he said repeatedly, 'It is impossible that Tiberius should not have believed it.' The thought obsessed him. He knew he was surrounded by liars and dissimulators. Many of these accusers had offered him the most fulsome and obsequious praise; and yet they had destroyed his family by their lies.

He had early resolved that he would not listen to informers. Yet he could not fail to do so. He did not believe their allegations, and yet he could not dismiss them. He often declared that he could trust nobody but Caesonia and myself, not even his favourite slaves and freedmen; 'and often,' he added, 'I am uncertain of the pair of you. I am the loneliest man alive. Even my sisters have plotted my murder.' Yet, to assuage this loneliness, he had brought them back from the prison to which he had consigned them, and I have seen him embrace Agrippina, kissing her hard on the lips, thrusting his tongue into her mouth, then draw back and mutter, 'But should I have you killed, sister, before you kill me?'

People think that, because Gaius ended as he did, it was inevitable that he should. If you believe in the inexorable working of fate, this is doubtless correct. But if, like me, you are a sceptic, then things look very different. The truth is that, to understand historical reality, it is necessary not to know the end of the story. Even historians themselves often seem to forget that events now securely in the past were once in the uncertain and shifting future.

For instance, Gaius had not abandoned his intention to lead his army in the German campaign the next summer. Accordingly I spent much of that winter engaged in preparation for that, in the sort of business that many who write about war ignore: the organisation of stores of equipment, the provisioning of depots, the building of barges by which supplies might be transported up the Rhine. Gaius himself, when sober and calm of mind, was himself fascinated by this work. It will amaze many to learn that he loved detail and was capable of hours of unremitting industry. He worked harder at the business of preparing the army for an arduous campaign than his father had ever done. One elderly knight, who had served for many years in the Department of Supplies, even remarked to me that the young man (as he called him) had a capacity for hard work comparable to that of Tiberius. This was high praise, and may have been merited. At any rate it was the evidence the Emperor gave that winter of his attentiveness to the business of government and warmaking which enabled me to hold to the hope that he might yet outgrow his youthful waywardness, prove himself a competent Emperor, and win the renown for which he so ardently – and, as it now seems, pathetically – longed.

In other respects too he seemed to my partial eye to be maturing. Caesonia exerted a good influence on him. She assured me that their marriage was strong and – her word – 'loving'. He showed himself a tender father to their little daughter, in whom indeed he took an inordinate pride. 'She's the first person ever,' he said to me once, 'who trusts me entirely and who loves me only for what I am.' His sex-life remained less turbulent, even now that he was back in

Rome, with all its temptations. He no longer roved the alleys of the Suburra by night, picking up whores and rent-boys. Though that incident with the young slave on the occasion he met the Jewish deputation was no doubt repeated with others from time to time – and why not, you may say – he was often faithful to Caesonia for days, even weeks, on end.

No more himself a slave to excess – there were nights when he drank only water fetched from the springs of Foggia – his health and stability of mind showed signs of improvement. He still suffered frequently from disabling headaches, which made his intermittent attention to business the more commendable; and his temper remained unreliable, perhaps in consequence. Likewise he continued to complain of insomnia, and would roam the sleeping palace in the hours before cock-crow. 'I plan building projects then,' he said to me once. 'My great-grandfather boasted that he found Rome of brick and left it of marble, but I intend to surpass his achievement'; and, saying this, he would show me exquisite plans, which he assured me he had drawn with his own hand. He may have been speaking the truth; he didn't lack gifts in that direction. Some of this building had already been started, then abandoned by Tiberius, who thought it an extravagant waste of money. So, for instance, he saw to the completion of the Temple of Augustus and to the renovation of Pompey's theatre. He was especially proud of his projected aqueduct which would supply the proletarian district of Trastevere with a reliable supply of fresh drinking water, which it has never had; it certainly added to his popularity with the People, who contrasted his tender care for their welfare with the neglect they believed themselves to have suffered in previous reigns. And he took great delight in the amphitheatre he designed, also for Trastevere, which would be able to hold more spectators than any in the world, and enable the most gorgeous Games to be held.

Nor were his projects confined to the city itself. So, for example, he ordered the rebuilding of the ancient walls and temples of Syracuse, the restoration of Polycrates' palace at Samos, the completion of the temple of Didymaean Apollo at Ephesus, and even planned the building of a marvellous city high up in the Alps. Less glorious but far more useful was his project of cutting a canal through the Isthmus of Corinth to spare sailors the time and danger of a voyage round the Peloponnesus.

Those who would have posterity think of Gaius only as a half-crazy and tyrannical playboy make no mention of these undertakings, some beautiful, others useful. Yet they occupied much of his attention, and their purpose was not only his glory; they were for the use and elevation of the people over whom he ruled. Call him monster if you like, but admit that he was also, often, a practical man, and even a benign ruler. The People recognised this, even if the Senate and nobility did not.

After three years as Emperor Gaius' relations with the Senate were very bad. You will remember that on his accession he spoke of his intention to work closely 'in Harmony' with that august assembly. Nowadays nobody thinks this sincere, any more than they give credit to the same aspiration pronounced by Tiberius. Yet in both cases I believe the original intention was sincere. When Tiberius became Emperor, he continued for some years to attend the Senate, where he urged that he be treated as an ordinary member. He begged the Senate to resume responsibility for a number of matters that Augustus had formed the habit of reserving to himself. It was all in vain. The Senate would carp and criticise but shunned responsibility. Many of its members disgusted him by their sycophancy. That's why he came to mutter, 'O generation fit only for slavery.'

Gaius had had no experience of the Senate before he became Emperor. He was too young and had in any case been kept away from Rome by Tiberius. But he had an idealistic view of the body; it came from his devoted reading of Livy, that enthusiasm which, as a boy, he had shared with Catullus. He was all the more disgusted when the Senate behaved to him exactly as it had to Tiberius: now grumbling feebly, now grovelling repulsively. His hope was extinguished. His admiration turned swiftly to contempt. Before long he had transferred elections back from the Senate to the Popular Assembly and, after the involvement of a number of senators in Gaeticulus' conspiracy, he removed command of the legions in Africa from the proconsul appointed by the Senate and gave it to an imperial legate of his own choice. Africa had been the last province with a military establishment which Augustus had left to the ordering of the Senate. Now all the military provinces and all the legions were the Emperor's.

The senators were offended too by his quick temper. Once when the consuls crossed him, he summarily deprived them of office and smashed their *fasces*. He no longer deigned to honour the Augustan pretence that the Senate were the Emperor's partners in government. 'I stand for autocracy,' he told me; and when I warned him that he was stirring up hatred, replied, 'Let them hate, provided they fear. I am not afraid of their hatred. I welcome it, I tell you. No, they cannot make me afraid.'

This was a lie, or self-deception. On days which followed a sleepless night, his nerves were a-jangle. He alternated between wild exuberance, when he was full of jokes – some of them making no sense – and periods of acute depression. That spring he had many long talks with Philo (the Jewish philosopher), to whom I had given lodging in my own house on the Aventine. He fascinated Philo, who, years later, wrote to me shortly before his death. (I omit those parts of his letter which are full of expressions of gratitude to me and admiration for my person and parts):

I remember with pleasure those nights during which we talked at length of philosophy, and of the art and purpose of government; when, also, with what would in other circumstances have been rashness and daring, had we not been each sufficiently virtuous to repose absolute trust in the other, we dissected the character of the Emperor.

Poor Gaius! I apply the epithet in all sincerity. I have read deeply in the history of my own race and other peoples, and have come upon no personage so perplexing.

I do not think he was by nature cruel. On the contrary he was born to be tender-hearted. No one who saw him playing with his little daughter, or stroking his horse's neck, or – as I did once – enticing a sparrow to perch on his finger and then gently touching it with the outstretched fingers of his other hand, could surely question that.

Again, in the conversation of a tranquil afternoon, this being a privilege which he accorded me on at least three occasions, I found him to be quiet, not at all boastful, eager to learn. Once, I remember, he said to me, 'There are so many different peoples in my Empire. It's important that I learn about their history and different ways of living.' 'I like simple people about me,' he said. 'That's because my earliest memories are of the camp.' There was a certain naivety about him. When I told him the story of our great Jewish hero David, he wept as I described how David in old age was betrayed by his son and his senior general. 'I'm afraid that will be my fate too,' he said. 'It's a wicked world where even those you trust most may betray you. I feel for David. He was lonely as I am lonely. It can't be otherwise when you have the supreme power. It's so hard to find anyone who will speak the truth to you. But I won't live to be old. Someone is sure to murder me first, like Julius Caesar, you know.'

That was one side of him, and I liked it. Of course I was flattered. A poor scholar is always flattered when a man of power condescends to speak frankly to him. But I think it was some relief to the Emperor to be able to do so.

Of course the other side was different and, I can say now, disgusting to me: heavy drinking and shameless gluttony, that insatiable appetite I recall you mentioning which had him stuffing himself even when his stomach was swollen, then his habit of taking emetics to enable him to eat and drink more . . .

I can't understand such behaviour, or the indecent practices with boys and women in which he indulged. It was as if he welcomed all the vices which destroy body and soul simultaneously.

You said once he wanted to escape from himself. But, in my opinion, the faster he ran, the more he found himself alone with the self he was trying to flee from. It followed him like the very hounds of Hell.

Poor man, for that is all, ultimately, that he was, a poor naked man, ignorant of the Divine and so deluded as to think himself a god – he who had no mastery even over his own mind.

I quote this letter from the wisest scholar and most intelligent man with whom I have ever conversed, to show that I am not alone in having found Gaius so much more remarkable than the monster his enemies have painted – a crazy monster at that.

XVII

Despite the long days spent in preparation, despite the Emperor's often expressed ardour, when summer came the German campaign was again postponed. Gaius spoke of it longingly, yet would not stir. His health was poor, the headaches from which he suffered now more frequent, more disabling. Once he even had to leave the Games, which he adored and which gave him a more innocent pleasure than anything else, and retire to lie in a dark room with bandages soaked in icy water pressed to his temples. At other times he cried out with the pain, or was reduced to sobbing like a frightened child. His insomnia was worse too, and when he did contrive to sleep, would (Caesonia told me) wake shrieking with terror on account of his evil dreams.

In vain I urged that what he needed was the life of the camp. I reminded him how he had been invigorated and how much better his health had been in our months on the Rhine frontier. He nodded dumbly, but would not move.

Then, one day, he said, 'I dare not. My astrologer has assured me that I shall be safe as long as I remain in the city or its neighbourhood. It is not in my stars that I conquer Germany this summer. Therefore I must wait. Don't bore me by urging this course on me again. Besides, I must root out the traitors from the Senate before I dare leave Italy. And many are cunning as serpents, hiding their evil intentions behind flattering smiles and assurances of loyalty. But I shall seek them out and destroy them. This morning I had an idea how best to do so. Don't you want to know what it was?'

'Of course I do,' I replied. What else could I say?

'I intend to put the eldest son of every senator under arrest, and then announce that all those will be executed whose fathers do not confess their treason. Don't you think that's clever?'

'It's certainly ingenious,' I said.

'I can see you have an objection to it.'

'Only a small one, Caesar.'

'Well, out with it. I'm a reasonable man and if it's a reasonable objection you shan't be punished for disagreeing with me.'

Still I hesitated.

'I'm becoming impatient,' he said. 'You should know better than to keep your Emperor waiting.'

'Very well,' I said. 'You will agree that those senators who are contemplating, or even plotting, treason, are bad men.'

'That's self-evident.'

'And bad men are not swayed by natural affections?'

'Not at all.'

'And it's natural that a man should wish to spare his son even at risk of danger or death to himself.'

'Yes, that would seem to be natural.'

'But the treasonous senators, being bad and indifferent to natural affections, will rather see their sons killed than confess their treason and expose themselves to whatever punishment you think fit. Isn't that likely?'

'I follow your argument. Very well, I must think of some other way of dealing with them.'

It was what they call a close shave. When I recounted the conversation to Catullus, he said, 'Surely even you must concede that the man's mad, and has become a public danger.'

'He's wild,' I said, 'certainly, but as you can see, still susceptible to reason.'

'Aren't you afraid yourself? One day, when you offer him your – what did you call it? – your reasoned objection, isn't it, to some lunatic proposal, he's going to have you killed.'

'The thought has occurred to me,' I said.

I didn't add, even to Catullus: but I am so closely associated with him that any conspiring to kill Gaius will surely kill me also, not leave me alive to play Antony to their Brutus and Cassius.

In high summer, with the city intolerably hot and fever raging, Gaius yielded to Caesonia's entreaties and retired to his villa overlooking Lake Nemi. I myself, relieved to be for the time being free of him, removed to the villa where I now write this account and spent some happy weeks, delighting in the beauty of the landscape, the play of sunlight on the azure waters, and reading Virgil and Horace, poets of a happier time and a ripe wisdom. Or so I told myself, choosing for the moment to forget that both had lived through the Civil Wars, Horace indeed running away from the Battle of Philippi; and that they had come to their wisdom laboriously. What horrors did the poet have to recognise before on his Sabine farm he learned 'to hide this anxious life under sweet forgetfulness' and ask 'what is the true nature of good and what its essence?'

Do not think that in these summer weeks I did not put such questions to myself. Do not think I do not pose them still.

But my solitude was interrupted by a succession of visitors. First, uninvited, came the Emperor's uncle, Claudius. I looked on him with surprise. He was evidently nervous, probably because he knew I regarded him with contempt. No doubt he couldn't forget that I had last seen him being ducked in the Rhine. He huffed and puffed in his pompous, stammering manner, and it was not till I had fed him a good dinner at which he gorged himself, though, as was my habit in the country, I ate nothing but a few anchovies, some pecorino cheese, good bread and a couple of apples, and till he had engulfed a litre and a half of my wine, which he drank neat and I well-mixed with water, that he was ready to explain why he had come.

Which, after all, proved to be no great matter. He had

embarked, he explained – I shall not try to give his words verbatim, for that would be wearisome – on composing a history or memoir of his brother Germanicus. I nearly laughed, for no one could be less suitable for the task than this stuttering book-worm who had passed his whole life away from the camp. But then, with an unexpected humility, he explained that this was why he had come to me. I could supply, from my memory and experience, the deficiencies he recognised in himself. 'They would not let me be a soldier,' he said, several times, dribbling drunkenly at the mouth. 'Do you understand what it is to be denied, partly by nature and partly by the scorn that my own family, especially my grandmother Livia, felt for me, denied what at heart you most desired, military glory?'

My contempt for him abated. I had not realised how deeply his incapacity and others' judgement of it had wounded him, soured his life. So I spoke at length of Germanicus, and then, since it was evident that he would be in no condition to remember what I had told him, promised that I would send him a note of my memories, which . . . But that is not to the point.

He continued to drink – another litre gone – then wept.

'I loved my brother. I worshipped him. I was not even jealous, though I might have been. And I loved his children and would have cared for them after their father's death, as an uncle should, if that bitch his wife had not kept me from them, and my own mother, another bitch, had not concurred. And what's the result? Little Gaius, who was a charming child, as you have said, was allowed to grow up ignorant and boastful, callous and fearful. It's my belief that that old monster, my uncle Tiberius, of whom, I don't mind confessing to you, now that we're friends, I was mightily afraid, taught him all sorts of repulsive perversions and so twisted his character. And what's the result? What has become of us all? I have a dream sometimes: that Germanicus lived and restored the Republic and Rome regained its honour and dignity . . .'

I have condensed what he said, but the last sentence is

as he spoke it, though it emerged slow, hesitant, slurred. Whereupon he belched, began to sweat and, lurching forward, spewed copiously.

Grotesque, yes, but beyond or behind the grotesquery sounded a note of regret, a sense of what life – even Claudius' life – might have been, even should perhaps have been.

He lay snoring on the couch, a fat, ugly buffoon; and as I watched him I could not feel superior and I pictured the Emperor himself on the terrace of his villa at Nemi, unable to sleep, gazing at the straw-coloured summer moon, and crying his fear, his anger, his frustration, his self-loathing.

This is Rome, this the imperial family.

If there are gods, how they must laugh!

My second visitor was Agrippina. She came, unannounced, at night, with only a small train of attendants and her private guards. Her manner was agitated. As soon as we were alone, she flung herself on me, embracing me with a passion not perhaps entirely simulated. At any rate she insisted we go to bed at once. She had, she explained, been chaste for weeks. She accused me of neglecting her. What could I say? Nothing. So I yielded. She wrapped her legs round me and howled her need. She had no interest in my body, but, for the time being, I satisfied her. She lay damply in my arms and sighed, once more, that truly she adored me, she had never adored another. It would have been pleasant to have believed her. Then I found she was trembling.

'I was brought up to be brave,' she said. 'My mother used to tell us girls that the lioness was more to be feared than the lion. But now I'm afraid.'

She had come from Nemi. That afternoon her little boy, Nero, had been playing with his baby cousin, 'whom he truly loves, he's so tender with her'. Then, as he carried her about the garden, he tripped on a root, and fell to the ground, the baby girl tumbling from his arms.

'Naturally she started crying, bawling her head off.'

The cries attracted Gaius. He picked his daughter up to comfort her, and then 'accused Nero of trying to murder the little fool – a boy of six, imagine, the sweetest child that ever lived, as if he would, the pet, and anyway as I said he adores her, he loves babies, I can't think why, except that he has such a soft charming nature. But Gaius looked black as thunder and swore terribly, and shouted for his guards to put little Nero in chains. "It's treason," he shrieked, "it's treason." Can you imagine? Have you ever heard the like?'

'What then?' I said, raising myself to lie propped against my elbow so that I could look her in the face.

'What do you think? I flew at him and scratched his face, as I used to when we were children, tore it open with my nails so that the blood ran, and I yelled that he was mad, crazy, dangerous, shouldn't be allowed out loose, I don't know what.'

'And Gaius?'

'Well, he was frightened, he's such a coward, I've always known that and been able to dominate him, just as Drusilla used to. So he turned and ran away, and I picked up Nero and held him to me. Later I sought out Caesonia, because, whore though she is, maybe because she's such a whore – yes, I know she was married to you and I daresay you are fond of her, but all the same you can't deny she's a whore – anyway, she's the only person who has any control over him, for which I must say I'm grateful. But she said she's never known him so angry, that he kept muttering that Nero had thrown his daughter to the ground, deliberately, to try to smash her head in. Caesonia said she'd told him this was nonsense, and that this silenced him, but she left him chewing his nails and swearing what he said was true, and made Caesonia promise that she would never let the little girl be alone with Nero again. Then Caesonia said it might be a good idea if we made ourselves scarce – "just till he recovers his balance", she said. But when will he?

So that's why I'm here, because if she's the only person who can control my maniac brother, you're the only other one who has any influence over him. He listens to you, doesn't he?'

'Less and less, I fear.'

'But you can protect me. You must.'

She wept and shivered in my arms. Then she said, 'I was cold as death when I came here. Warm me, make me live again.'

She wrapped her legs round me again and nipped my neck, and gasped as we made the beast with two backs, till at last she was satisfied, and relaxed, and slept in my arms. The moon played on her face, and even in her sleep, a nerve twitched in her cheek.

My third visitor was Seneca. He came at Agrippina's invitation, indeed her insistence. He wasn't comfortable. The little eyes in the big fleshy face betrayed his wariness. Or so I told myself. The philosopher was being drawn towards action, and he wasn't sure of his ability to conduct himself in a manner worthy of respect.

Agrippina had decided that her brother must go. It was the only way she knew to protect her son. Twice, waking in that first night together, she had said, 'This time perhaps Gaius will forget his intention, Caesonia will smooth it away, set his mind at rest as much as it can be put at rest. But he will watch Nero grow and he will see him as a threat, just as Tiberius was persuaded my other brothers were a threat, as he believed my father to be a threat, and so all were murdered. I can't forget that Gaius himself murdered that other Tiberius, little Tiberius Gemellus, a harmless boy with a nice nature, I'm told, simply because he was who he was.' She went on in this way, again and again, round and round. I have tried to make what she said coherent.

Seneca's task was to suggest a method. I expressed my surprise.

'I hadn't,' I said, 'realised that the philosopher was an expert at disposals.'

'He's the wisest man I know,' she said. 'Who better to turn to?'

'And are you sure that you want me to hear this? Are you so sure you can trust me?'

'If you betray me,' she said, and left it at that, looking, I must say, exactly like her late alarming mother.

Seneca was of course flattered. Perhaps, in his heavy way, he was a little in love with Agrippina. He was certainly in awe of her. Indeed he was so much in awe that for the first part of our conversation, though his sentences became ever more rotund and packed with subordinate clauses, by the time he arrived at what should have been the decisive verb, it seemed that all meaning had evaporated.

'We have,' he said at last, 'no satisfactory precedents.'

'Oh, come,' I said, 'there is surely no lack of precedents for murder. Think of the Gracchi, of Julius himself.'

'We are not talking about murder,' Agrippina said. 'Murder is the last resort. Besides, despite, everything, he is my little brother. We come from the same womb.'

There was no answer to that. I waited, in silence.

Seneca said, 'Theoretically there is no office of Emperor. Therefore it is difficult to find a means of dismissing someone from an office that does not technically exist. Even the title of Princeps or First Citizen, by which the Divine Augustus preferred to be known, is or was merely honorary. So we must enquire into the legal foundations of what we have come to recognise as the imperial power.'

'The power,' I said, 'came first. Its legal foundations, as you call them, subsequently.'

'Be that as it may,' Seneca was now settling to his task, speaking as if to eager students in the Lyceum, 'be that as it may, Augustus rested his authority on two planks: the first was the tribuniciary power which rendered his person inviolable.'

At this Agrippina looked puzzled. No wonder: the words were a distant, ever-fainter echo of the Republic. I should explain (for the benefit of my grandchildren, who may read this) that the tribunes were Republican magistrates elected to safeguard the interests of the plebeians (or lower classes), and that it was not only illegal but accounted sacrilege to harm a tribune while he held office. They were, I may add, very often, obstructive and ignorant demagogues. Augustus, being a patrician, was not eligible to be elected a tribune, but – how I can't remember – he had persuaded the Assembly of the People to vote him the powers, and therefore the inviolability, of a tribune. Seneca now explained all this to Agrippina at much greater and decidedly tedious length.

'Secondly,' he said at last, 'he was granted proconsular authority in all the provinces committed to his charge which were also those where there was a military establishment; and he had the soldiers take an oath of allegiance to him personally as well as to the Senate and the Roman People. Because this proconsular authority lapsed when he entered Italy, the Senate also voted him what was called *Maius imperium*, an overriding authority. As you will know,' he continued, almost certainly aware that Agrippina knew no such thing, 'he declared in his *Res gestae*, the record of his achievements, and I quote: "In my sixth and seventh consulates, after having extinguished the Civil Wars, and having by the consent of all attained supreme power, I transferred the State from my own power to the control of the Roman People. For this service of mine I received the title of Augustus by decree of the Senate and the doorposts of my house were publicly decked with laurels, the civic crown was set up over my doorway, and a golden shield set up in the Julian Senate House, which, as the inscription on it bears witness, the Roman People gave me in recognition of my valour, clemency, justice and devotion. After that time, though I excelled all in authority, I had no more power than those who were my colleagues in any magistracy." What do you think of that?' Seneca sat back and smiled.

I thought it was an impressive feat of memory, and said so. He beamed more broadly.

'It's a different world,' Agrippina said. 'Did he really suppose he was only chief magistrate, excelling others in authority but not in power?'

'It is what he wanted others to believe,' I said, 'and perhaps what he liked to believe. But he knew really it was all pretence.'

'Nevertheless . . .' Seneca tapped his stylus on the table. 'Nevertheless, that was the position – legally – of Augustus, and by my reading of history, which I assure you is accurate, that was the position inherited by Tiberius and subsequently by our present Emperor Gaius. Their authority and legal power derived ultimately from the vote of the Senate and the Assembly of the People. What the Senate and the Assembly have given, the Senate and the Assembly can take away. I see no legal obstacle to what I may call the deposition of the Emperor, none at all. It can be done smoothly.'

'Come,' I said, 'which word, Seneca, did you use to describe Gaius? Wasn't it Emperor – the title Augustus chose not to assume? And doesn't the mere fact that you yourself, in the course of your learned disquisition, find it natural to use the word, prove that everything has changed? That we are living, as Agrippina correctly says, in a different world? And in this world, our world, do you really imagine that anyone will be bold enough – I might say stupid enough – to rise in the Senate and propose that Gaius be deprived of his powers? My dear Seneca, everything you say is no doubt true. But everything that you say is also nonsense. There may indeed, as you suggest, be a legal means of depriving an Emperor of his powers, but believe me, that legal means is not practical. I know. I have seen too much not to know.'

I looked at Agrippina and her eyes would not meet mine, and I saw that she was convinced.

The visitor I had looked for and did not receive was Catullus. He wrote from Capri excusing his absence. There was a boy, he said, with the mouth of Ganymede, the legs of Apollo and a bottom like a peach, a slender youth 'to be courted on roses in some pleasant cave', who had not yet yielded to his entreaties, but whose hour was approaching, and so, alas, he made his excuses and could not come to visit. I would understand.

XVIII

A few days later Gaius summoned me to Nemi. I obeyed, though reluctant to leave my country home where I was free, in the poet's words, 'to bury this anxious life under sweet forgetfulness'. So I set off that very day, with the last lines of another Ode running in my head, those about 'our fathers' time, worse than that of our ancestors, the time which brought forth our own generation, steeped in vice, and soon to give birth – alas – to still viler offspring'.

For that was the thought which I could not, after my talk with Claudius, Agrippina and Seneca, rid myself of: after Gaius, what? Civil war? Insurrection? Murders and anarchy?

Caesonia met me. She had lost weight. Her cheeks, formerly round, were hollow. She carried herself like an old woman. We embraced.

'Agrippina ran to you?' she said. 'Yes?'

'She came.'

'She left in terror.'

'She arrived afraid.'

'I've never known him so agitated.'

She paused before that last word, as if she knew it was inadequate. Then she continued, 'Our little girl's the only person he has ever truly loved. You have to understand that. He had said to me in the past that he was incapable of love. It has surprised him to find he isn't. And, oddly, this has frightened him too.'

'I know only Agrippina's version,' I said.

'Oh, this time,' she said, 'I think she was speaking the truth.

Of course wee Nero's not the angel she says he is, but I'm sure he meant little Julia no harm. But Gaius won't believe it. I can usually in the end persuade him to come round to my way of thinking, but not this time. He's adamant. He keeps muttering, "An emperor must be absolute for death." I don't know what it means.'

I found Gaius stretched out on a couch on a terrace overlooking the lake. Two tall yellow-bearded German guards were in attendance, standing within a few yards of the Emperor, their swords drawn.

'They don't speak Latin,' he said. 'I can no longer have guards who speak our language and may repeat whatever I say to my enemies. That's the only security I now have. So my sister is planning my murder, is she? Did she send you here to kill me?'

'Caesar,' I said. 'I am here at your request. Agrippina has no such intention. She's devoted to you. But she fears for her little boy. That's all.'

'All? The child's a monster. He tried to kill my daughter.'

He continued in this vein for some time, growing ever more impassioned. His face turned purple. For a moment I thought he was about to have a fit. Then he got to his feet, swayed, and collapsed on the couch, pressing hands to his temples.

'I am not well,' he moaned. 'That woman has cast a spell on me. I'm bewitched. There are laws against witchcraft, aren't there?'

In a little while he was asleep. I stood over him. I glanced at the Germans. They kept their eyes fixed on me, their hands on their sword-hilts.

I thought: 'What earthly reason have they to watch over him?'

Later, towards evening, Gaius roused himself. He was now pale but calm, like the sea after a storm. 'Come with me,' he said and, escorted by his German guards, we descended the hillside to the edge of the lake. A boat was waiting there and we stepped into it, and took our places in the bow, while the Germans rowed. It was a soft evening, the blue fading from the sky, and the air heavy with the scent of thyme and oregano. The water of the lake was still and dark except where streaks of dying sunlight fell on it. Gaius was silent as the surrounding honey-coloured evening, broken only by the plash of the oars and then, beautifully, by the nightingale's song from the woods beyond.

We came to the further shore. One of the guards stretched out his hands towards it to draw the boat in and tie it to a metal ring sunk in a stone on the rude landing-stage. We disembarked, and Gaius led us along a twisting path that ran first by the water's edge and then made its way through the trees. The moon had risen and threw long sharp shadows before us.

Then it lit up a clearing. Gaius thrust out a hand, palm downwards, and bade us stop. I stood by his shoulder and would have spoken, but he put his finger to his lips. We waited. The nightingale fell silent, and the shadows danced as a little breeze stirred the uppermost branches of the oak-trees.

Ahead of us, at the far side of the clearing I could see a rude altar bedecked with flowers. A thin spiral of smoke rose from a dish set on its table. Then a man appeared from the woods behind.

He was dressed in a tunic that stopped short of his knees, and he moved warily, stiffly, like one on the watch. He turned towards us and the moonlight glinted on the drawn sword which he carried in his left hand. I could not see his face. The hair on his head was short. I felt Gaius tremble. The man we were watching approached the altar, circled it twice, moving against the direction the sun takes in its course. A sound reached us, as if he was muttering an incantation. He held his right hand over the smoking dish, and must have dropped something from it, for a flame flared. Then he stood very still, his head bowed.

He jerked upright, as if he had heard a sound inaudible to us. He waited, as I have seen dogs quiver before a bush in which some movement has attracted their attention. A shout came from the other side of the clearing. Another man emerged from the trees at a run. He too carried a sword. He halted. The first man, who had been waiting at the altar, now seemed – I swear it – to relax. He lifted his chin as if in challenge. But it was the second man who was the challenger; I knew that. He now advanced light-footed, with a movement which suggested he was younger than the other, who now spoke, but I could not catch what he said, though I recognised the tone; it was that of a sentry.

The second man approached, his sword at the ready. His adversary did not move, or raise his sword, but I knew that he was looking the other up and down, assessing him. Then, as if wearily, yet with assurance, he assumed the on guard position, holding his ground, waiting.

I heard the sharp intake of Gaius' breath.

The swords clashed, once, twice, thrice. Then both men stepped back a pace, and they began to circle each other, the first ever moving to his right and keeping his sword-point raised. His enemy lunged. He parried the blow, and continued to move away, his steps now as precise as those of a dancing-master. The challenger paused. Then he rushed forward swinging his blade in a great circular sweep. It met only air, and he stumbled, losing his balance. But the first man waited; perhaps it had been a feint, a trap. He was speaking now. The words came to us in a low mutter. It was my imagination that they sounded menacing. Again the swords clashed. This time the challenger bore the other's sword down, and with a backhand flick wounded him in the neck. Gaius stiffened.

For the first time the wounded man attacked. He lunged at the other's face. The sword was raised to parry a weapon that was no longer there. Before he was through the lunge, the defender – the champion as I now thought of him – pulled back and then, quick as the darting of a snake's tongue, drove at the belly, and drove home. The other fell to the ground. He lay screaming. Blood bubbled from his mouth – or did I imagine that? It was darkening, I could not see well. But for a moment what I saw was as if carved in marble, or on a frieze: the dying gladiator, agony, knowing death, gazing as if at his departing soul. Then the first man placed his foot on his fallen foe, pulled the sword out of the body, drew a dagger from his belt, and, kneeling, cut the other's throat. He rose, and his voice rose with him in a cry of triumph and, face lifted to the moon, he chanted the goddess's praise.

I felt Gaius relax.

He sighed: 'All will be well. Again, all is well.'

He gave gold to one of the Germans, told him to take it to the victor, 'Though he has no use for it, it's my custom'; then turned and led the way back to the boat.

He spoke only once as we crossed the lake.

'Great is Diana, my love, my protectress.'

That evening at supper he was in genial form, lucid and coherent. He told jokes. Some of them were new, and some of them were even amusing. He gave an imitation of Tiberius refusing a petitioner; the accuracy was uncanny. You caught the satisfaction the old Emperor experienced at being able to say 'no', a satisfaction all the more intense for being concealed and for following on a rigorous examination of the suppliant's case. Then Gaius imitated his uncle Claudius addressing the Senate, and getting lost in a pedantic parenthesis. It would have been cruel if there had not been a note of indulgence, even affection, in the Emperor's voice. He called for his daughter, and bounced her on his knee, and fed her tit-bits from his plate. He demanded admiration for her beauty and cleverness. All through the meal he drank only well-watered wine. Caesonia too relaxed, smiled, shedding years as she did so.

When the women left us alone he talked seriously: about the army, the imperial finances, the problem of the Jews, 'to which,' he said, 'I see no final or absolute solution.'

Then he said, 'You understood what we witnessed tonight?'

'I think so.'

'You remember that I once told you how I had discovered that the priest who guards Diana's temple and the Golden Bough had not been challenged for many years. I determined to put this right. And I have done so. I have arranged for slaves to escape and directed them to Nemi. At first I did this, I admit, in a spirit of mischief, simply because it amused me. That was foolish on my part. I know better now. I see that each successful defence of his position by the priest is a sort of omen. If he is defeated and slain, I myself shall not be safe. Do you understand this? It's why Tiberius survived so long. Because no one challenged that priest.'

'But, Caesar . . .'

'I dislike that word "but".'

'Nevertheless, Caesar, would it not be wiser, now that you know this, not to arrange challenges to the priest?'

'Wiser? I don't know.'

'I mean that one day he may indeed be defeated . . .'

Gaius poured himself a glass of wine, without watering it, and drank it at one gulp.

'Of course you are right,' he said. 'I know that perfectly well. At the same time you don't understand. You don't even begin to understand. It's become a compulsion. I never feel more alive, more surely myself, than when I watch these contests as we did this evening. The excitement of the arena is nothing to it. It's my life that's at stake, you see. So tonight I know that all is well. Even if you had come here determined to kill me, I would have no cause for anxiety. It's a question of my destiny.'

He stretched himself on the couch as one might lie in the sun.

'Do you know who is closest to me now?' he said. 'Old Tiberius. When I think how I hated him, and feared him, it's strange. But now he often comes to me in dreams, and takes my hand and speaks soothingly to me, as he never did in life. He understands, you see, as nobody else can, what it means to bear the burdens of Empire. If you think sometimes that I'm capricious, that's because you don't realise what it means to be able to do exactly as you please, whatever you please.'

He sighed.

'At moments like this,' he said, 'I'm almost happy, almost at ease. Poor Tiberius, he came to hate himself, to hate what he had been compelled to make of himself. Do you suppose we Emperors like having to sentence people to death? Not at all, not even when they've thoroughly deserved it. Tiberius wept for Sejanus, you know. How could he fail to? He'd been his closest friend, his only friend, and then he betrayed him. It was as if you were to betray me. So he had no choice but to have him killed, just as I would have no choice if you . . .'

'Unlike Sejanus,' I said, 'I have no ambition.'

That was true, but I added, prudently, 'No ambition except to serve you, Caesar, to the best of my ability.' And did not add, 'and to survive you'.

'When they kill me,' he said, 'the Empire will be delivered to anarchy. You know that, don't you?'

'Then we must see to it that they don't kill you, Caesar.'

'Of course,' he said, 'it's the greatest of all temptations – to loose anarchy on the world. I know it. I have felt it, felt the rapturous power of the destroyer. It's ecstasy, nothing less. The joy of the creator is nothing to the joy one knows when unleashing the power of the destroyer, the ruthless joy of the logic that crushes out human lives, extinguishes them like this candle. But painfully, yes painfully. I haven't experienced it to the full . . . yet.'

XVIX

I returned to the city in October; it was a fine autumn, my favourite season in Rome. The skies were blue, the sun warm but not oppressive, windless days leading to clear, sharp nights. But that autumn was uneasy. Catullus told me that at least half the Senate's members had found reason to remain on their country estates.

'Some are sick, others find pressing business that keeps them there. All are afraid.'

He laughed: 'As if Caligula can't kill them equally well out of the city,' he added.

'That's what they're afraid of?'

'My dear,' he said, 'it's difficult to know whether fear, or hatred, or resentment is uppermost in their minds. But the word is that the Emperor is planning a purge of the Senate. There's even talk of proscriptions.'

That word sounds horribly in our historical memory. It's associated with Sulla and Marius, and, more recently, with the Second Triumvirate of Augustus, Antony and Lepidus, who met together on an island in the River Po to draw up the list of their enemies whose property was to be confiscated and whose lives were forfeit.

'As far as I know,' I said, 'Gaius has no such intention.'

'No?' he said. 'Perhaps because he doesn't know the word. But I assure you, that's what many believe is coming.'

'Do you believe it?'

'I don't know what to believe. I do know I'm afraid.'

I told him of Agrippina's visit and of her fears.

'Is she ready to have her brother killed?'

'Perhaps not. She recruited Seneca to try to persuade me it was possible to depose him, or force him to abdicate. These are new words in Rome. The idea's absurd, of course. Sulla surrendered the dictatorship, but only after he had destroyed all his enemies. And he was an old man, fond of luxury, happy to withdraw from public life. You will remember that Caesar thought this extraordinary. He said it proved the dictator didn't know his ABC.'

'So,' he said, 'you too are coming round to the idea of assassination?'

'You are brave to speak the word.'

'Not at all. I do so only to you, and only because I am more afraid of Caligula living than Caligula dead. All I want, my dear fellow, is safety and the leisure to enjoy life or, as my mother would have it, indulge my vices.'

'Ah, your vices,' I said. 'And did they flourish as you hoped?'

'The boy was a darling. But dull unfortunately. I soon tired of him. Now, shall we get drunk?'

'Why not?'

Why not indeed? Liquor offered oblivion, freedom for the moment from care, anxiety and, in Catullus' case, fear. But fear returned in the morning. A detachment of the Guard marching in the street below made him tremble.

Fear ran through the city. The common people were of course immune. They still, for the most part, adored the Emperor who provided them with splendid entertainments. If he killed a few senators – some half-dozen that October found themselves charged with treason and executed – what was it to them? The aristocracy and the knights might grumble at the taxes which the imperial extremities caused to be levied, but this was of no matter to the plebs.

Few people gave dinners that autumn. They kept to themselves, lest in their cups they might speak unwarily and word of their disaffection be brought to Gaius. Everywhere, it was believed, he had spies. No one felt secure. There were many mutterings concerning ominous signs and prophecies, too silly, most of them, to repeat. Everyone was eager to learn the Emperor's mood, but no one dared to interpret it. Did smiles and jokes indicate that he was planning some new atrocity? Who could tell? If he frowned, was that proof that he was brooding on something or someone who had aroused his displeasure? No one dared hazard an opinion. Since no one could envisage the future, all were compelled to exist only in an anxious present. Catullus told me he frequented a brothel every night; it was only there that he felt himself truly alive.

'And I get drunk to blot out reality for a few hours,' he said.

Seneca continued, despite the arguments I had put to him in the summer, to believe that a change of regime could be effected without violence and, in his words, 'a sensible political system put in place'. Agrippina sent him to me to urge this course yet again. Catullus also attended the meeting. As Seneca spoke, I saw a mocking smile on his face. The absurdity of the philosopher's argument made him look younger, restored for a moment his natural high spirits.

Seneca did not notice. He was puffed up, carried away, by the beauty of his own rhetoric.

'What we require,' he said, 'is to engineer a situation in which it will become apparent to the Emperor that the foundation of his power has crumbled. I have thought deeply,' he said to me, 'about what you remarked when we last discussed this, regarding the pusillanimity of the Senate. It grieves me to have arrived at the conclusion that you may have judged wisely, grieves me, I say, because I am reluctant to think ill of that noble body. Nevertheless, I concede that your doubts as to the willingness of its members to speak their minds openly may be justified. Therefore we must pursue another course.'

'What have you in mind?'

'The army and the army commanders are the key that will unlock the gate.'

'What do you mean?'

'But it is obvious,' he said.

'Not to me.'

'Nor to me,' Catullus said.

'Very well, let me explain. I have drafted, after consultation with the Lady Agrippina, a letter to be sent to all the army commanders in which the need for a change of regime is argued, and, if I may say so myself, cogently argued. I believe it will convince them to withdraw support from Gaius and to establish again the Republic. Then they will inform Gaius that they no longer owe him obedience or allegiance. His life will be spared, but he must retire. It may be necessary for a time to confine him to to an island, or some such place where his movements can be restricted.'

'What a beautiful scheme,' Catullus said.

'I am pleased that you approve it. I thought you would.'

'Approve it? It is the most perfect idiocy. Why not approve it?'

'When I was a child,' I said, 'my nurse told me the fable of the mice and the cat. Do you remember it? No? Very well, then. The cat had been doing great execution among the mice. So the survivors met to consider a remedy. One came up with an idea. They should tie a bell round the cat's neck, so that they would have warning of his approach. It seemed to them all an admirable suggestion. So they approved it, and all were happy, till one old grey mouse put the question: "And which of you will be bold enough to bell the cat?" There were no volunteers. The Emperor is the cat, and I have little doubt, Seneca, that a number of the generals would be happy to have, as it were, a bell tied round his neck. But which of them will move first?'

'They have all sworn an oath of allegiance to Caligula,' Catullus said. 'It probably means something to some of them.

I remember one of my uncles once telling me, "Roman generals don't mutiny." I admit that my reading of history does not entirely support this claim. Nevertheless . . . Besides, it's my opinion, and I suspect that Lucius here agrees with me, that the ordinary legionaries are loyal to Gaius.'

'Probably,' I said. 'He's not only Germanicus' son, which still counts for something, but he has been notably generous to them. For the first time in my recollection, the soldiers are paid on time, discharged on time when their term of service is complete, and granted land to settle on. You all make the mistake of thinking Gaius a fool. He isn't. He knows very well that ultimately the imperial power rests with the armies. The day is approaching, I've no doubt, when they will realise this themselves, and will learn how to make and unmake Emperors. But that day isn't today.'

'Your scheme's brilliant, but it's not on,' Catullus said.

'Seneca,' I said, 'if you send that letter, you might as well cut your throat. It will save you from a more painful death. But I don't suppose you are ready to die?'

The philosopher made no reply.

XX

Three weeks later an attempt was made on Gaius' life. A young man of noble family, a distant cousin of mine and a descendant on his mother's side of that Metellus Cimber who had been one of the Liberators who murdered Julius Caesar, approached the Emperor as he was on his way to conduct a sacrifice at the Temple of Jupiter. His manner was calm, apparently friendly; and indeed he had often been a guest of the Emperor and even one of his favourites. So he was not regarded with suspicion. But for some reason he hesitated for a few seconds after drawing his dagger before plunging it in the Emperor's breast, and in that instant, the German bodyguards acted. One slashed at the hand holding the dagger and severed it at the wrist. Two others hurled themselves on the young man and would have killed him on the spot, if Gaius had not called 'Halt.'

'There should be no easy death for traitors,' he said.

I have no doubt his intention was to have the young man tortured in order that he might reveal the names of his confederates, for it was unlikely he had acted alone, of his own initiative. But in that moment someone in the crowd swirling round the Emperor cried out 'Treason' and some of the lower orders, believing that their beloved Caligula was still in danger, brushed the German guards aside, seized the would-be assassin, and tore him limb from limb.

Some said afterwards that there had been no conspiracy: Gaius had seduced the young man's wife, and the attempted murder was an act of private revenge. But others said that the man who had called out 'Treason' and incited the mob to avenge it was one Trebonius, a close friend of the deluded young man and his accomplice in the conspiracy, who had sacrificed his friend to prevent him from naming names. I do not know. The matter remained obscure. But this Trebonius has since flourished and is now proconsul in Further Spain.

That evening I found Gaius in unusually solemn mood.

'I have been playing it over in my mind,' he said, 'and when I do so, when I go through it all again, I conclude from my wondrous salvation that nothing bad is going to happen to me, that I am being preserved by the gods for some great purpose. Evidently this must be the conquest of Germany, the subjugation of the German tribes, and their incorporation into our great Empire. Was not Aeneas promised limitless Empire? And is it not for me to secure that? Fate could have taken a different turn. You might be shedding tears over my corpse tonight. Think of that.' His tone softened. 'For my part, if my life had indeed been ended by the assassin's dagger, I can say it would have been a sort of liberation, from anxiety, sleepless nights and severe nervous strain. In a mere fraction of a second I would have been at peace. The thought is not unwelcome. There are long nights when sleep is denied me when I ache to be at rest. But the Fates have determined otherwise. We have wasted this summer, but now you must set to work so that, with the first breath of spring, we may to the north and launch the last great expansion of the Empire.'

'Indeed, Caesar,' I said.

Then he smiled.

'But why the last?' he said. 'What am I saying? Alexander sighed because there were no more worlds to conquer. I am not yet Alexander, but that is what the Fates have in store for me. I am certain. Am I not the child of the camp, the darling of Fortune?'

'How did you find him?' Caesonia asked.

'First calm, then elated.'

'Tomorrow,' she said, 'his suspicions will return. Tomorrow he will be certain that the Senate is a nest of vipers determined to destroy him. Why do I say tomorrow? He is as changeable as . . . as I don't know what. Tell me something that changes with every breath of wind, and I shall show you poor Gaius.'

'I believe,' I said, 'you have come to love him.'

'Love? I don't know. Pity, unquestionably. The other night he did sleep for a little and when he woke, or perhaps still in a light sleep, muttered, "Why can't I be good? Why can't I be the good Emperor I longed to be?"'

The next day twenty-three senators were arrested. Six were freed after examination. Ten were sent into exile or required to live on their country estates. Four were held in prison. Three were put to death.

To celebrate his deliverance Gaius held special Games. They were intended to be of an unparalleled splendour. This was impossible to achieve. He had given the promoters only a few days' preparation. Some of the gladiators were under-trained, some of the contests sadly ill-matched. The crowd which had come eager to applaud started to jeer. Gaius withdrew to the darkness at the back of his box to sulk. His dissatisfaction was such that he made two unpopular decisions, sparing one gladiator who had displayed cowardice because (he said subsequently) 'it pleased me to do so and I thought he showed admirable good sense', and then giving the thumbs down to a popular swordsman who had had the misfortune to slip in a pool of blood. ('Careless idiot, needs to be taught a lesson. Besides, he got a louder cheer when he entered the arena than I did.')

The failure of these Games encouraged his enemies. For the first time, they said, Caligula has lost favour with the People. They had lost favour with him too. I think it was after these Games that he spoke of wishing that the Roman People had a single neck, to be severed with one blow. Of course this was an example of his quilpish humour.

The end of the year saw him sink into despondency. There were days when he refused to talk, even to Caesonia. Only the company of his little daughter could enliven him, and that only briefly. Other days he talked incessantly, a monologue in which he spoke of his wretched life, his childhood fears, even the evil course which the Fates had set him on. 'But,' he said, 'I shan't give my enemies the satisfaction of seeing me kill myself. Let them do that for me. If they dare. Let them show their face and cut me down themselves, if they have the courage.'

I had no doubt that the Emperor's enemies were seeking a sword; equally that, till they found one, Gaius was safe. I knew also that I was viewed with distrust. Those who wanted to kill Gaius did not know what part I was ready to play. Some of them dropped hints to me, suggestions that if I spoke the word then they would divulge all to me, even allot me a leading part in the reconstruction of the State. But I gave no sign of understanding, for I had no wish to engage in that comedy.

Now, in retrospect, I find it difficult to remember just what I thought then, just what my sentiments were.

I think I knew Gaius' time was up. He had so many enemies it was barely conceivable that he could long survive. And it was at least arguable that he deserved to die and that Rome and the Empire would be the better for his disappearance. There was a case for saying that he should be dispatched with no more hesitation than one would display in ridding the world of a mad dog. Whatever succeeded him could not be worse. Catullus certainly was convinced of that, and strove to persuade me.

Yet something in me rebelled. What was it? The fear that I would be killed with him? No. Loyalty? Yes indeed I felt that, but loyalty in my observation is a weak emotion. Affection? That too, extraordinary as it may seem, as indeed it seems to me myself now. Yet, I cannot deny it, I could not dislike

Gaius. I could not deny that I was fond of him. I might deplore, condemn, most of what he did. Nevertheless . . .

Then there was obstinacy, pride if you prefer. I had been for Gaius against the Senate. Was I to admit that I was wrong?

It was Catullus who showed me my pride. He rebuked me for it.

He said, 'Because you are the only man in Rome who is not afraid of Caligula, you think there is no need to kill him. Furthermore it is your infernal pride that keeps you from joining yourself to those senators who see the necessity of removing him, keeps you from them because you despise them. You know I love you, but . . .'

'No,' I said, 'I know you do not love me. How could you, since I do not love myself?'

He thought I was joking, and I did not disillusion him. But he was right to identify the contempt I felt for Gaius' enemies. They were men who had crawled before him as they had crawled before Tiberius. If they were now screwing their courage to the point at which they were ready at least to contemplate action, it was only because of their terror. If that is a paradox – that terror can inspire men with courage – so be it. It was how I saw them.

In these days of waiting, some words of the Emperor's ran in my head like an irritating tune: 'men are not happy, and then they die', he had once said, frowning as if the thought perplexed him. Men are not happy, and then they die. It's a fair summation of life.

Did I value Gaius because he showed me this truth, which he was brave enough to confront?

There was a young poet who was in love with the Emperor. (I shall not write his name; it would embarrass him, for he is no longer a poet, but an officer in the army which our present gracious Emperor has charged with the conquest of Britain.) When I say he was in love with the Emperor, I don't mean that he had any vulgar desire to share his bed, or have Gaius cover his face with slobbering kisses. His love was pure, ideal; he was in love with the idea of the Emperor's solitude, his superiority – 'superiority,' as he said, 'to all that has hitherto been thought and done. He has gone beyond good and evil. In his world there are no moral facts. I find this perfectly beautiful. Moral judgements are so easy, the refuge of weak men. I find Gaius the first Free Spirit in the history of the world.'

He spoke much in this vein, being greatly confused. And yet, in the midst of his confusion, a light shone in the darkness. He recognised in the Emperor the incarnation of the strongest instinct in man: the will to power. 'Everything else,' he said, 'is an illusion, everything else a lie devised to comfort the weak.'

Of course what he said was nonsense. Gaius was weak himself. I knew that. Nevertheless this young poet had a glimmering of a great truth: the will to power is indeed the marching-song of the world. It is the music to which Rome has marched, the tune of our Empire.

In Gaius Rome attained perfection. He was what we had made ourselves. When the giddy-headed young poet saw in him the incarnation of the strongest instinct, I could only assent.

Making our Empire we had destroyed everything that was once good in the Republic. We had reduced all relations between men to a question of power: who does what to whom?

If the proper image of Rome was now the bloodstained arena, the slaughterhouse that delighted us, was it not proper that the Emperor Gaius should be in his chair, pronouncing the verdict: death or life? Why remove so perfect a summation of what we had made of ourselves, of the world we had shaped?

XXI

There was a colonel of the Guard named Cassius Chaerea for whom Gaius had developed an intense dislike. It was difficult to know why. Certainly he was an unattractive fellow, but not so remarkable as to make the Emperor's repugnance understandable. Sometimes Gaius said he couldn't bear seeing him about, with his shifty eyes and pursed-up mouth. Other times he insisted on his attendance, so that he could give himself the pleasure of teasing him. This Cassius Chaerea had once suffered a wound in the groin; it was perhaps in consequence of it that, in middle-age, his gait was decidedly effeminate, mincing. The Emperor fastened on this and always spoke of him as an invert. When he extended his hand for Chaerea to kiss, he would thrust out his middle finger and waggle it in a suggestive manner.

One day he said, 'It amuses me, my dear Cassius, to see that you always choose as your escort guardsmen with peculiarly big cocks. I like a man who's not ashamed of his taste.'

Chaerea flushed and scowled, but did not dare to protest. From that day on, I believe, he hated the Emperor.

He had other reasons for doing so. He had been a protégé of Macro, Sejanus' betrayer and successor as Praetorian Prefect. Indeed Macro had made him his deputy. Since there were other officers senior to him, men also who had been more often decorated for valour in battle, this promotion was resented, and gave rise to all sorts of scurrilous rumours concerning the relationship of the Prefect and his new deputy. It may be that Chaerea's reputation for effeminacy dated from this promotion; it was not, after all, only Gaius who thought him an invert. Of course there may have been nothing in it. People were ready to believe anything of Macro.

Cassius Chaerea was lucky to survive his patron's disgrace and execution. It was said that he himself had laid information against him. Be that as it may, he found himself demoted – another reason for his growing detestation of the Emperor. In truth he was eaten up by resentment.

I confess that I thought little of him. I thought so little of him it never occurred to me that he might be dangerous.

It was alleged that he had been connected with that Trebonius suspected by some of being a party to the attempt on the Emperor's life by that idealistic young nobleman, the descendant of Metellus Cimber. Report of this connection was carried to Gaius. It amused him greatly.

'I know you do not love me,' he said to Chaerea, and giggled as the wretched man protested his utter loyalty and devotion.

There was another colonel of the Guard called Cornelius Sabinus who had long been a rival of Chaerea's. It amused Gaius to arrange that they were on duty together, since he had been told that their dislike for each other was so intense that they were not on speaking terms. The story was credible: Sabinus had been a favourite of Sejanus, and fortunate not to be killed when Tiberius turned against him.

But all that was some time ago. Now, thrown together by the Emperor's caprice, they set aside their dislike for each other, and were united in their hatred of Gaius. Sabinus declared that he felt no personal animosity towards the Emperor. He opposed him because he was a bad Emperor and because he himself hoped for the restoration of the Republic. But the circumstances in which he made this declaration were not such as to persuade anyone to believe him. He was undoubtedly a hypocrite.

Coming together, talking together, this ill-matched pair resolved to rid Rome of the Emperor.

That at least is what we are supposed to believe.

For my part I think it incredible.

However, as you will learn, it was difficult for me to determine the truth, to discover what was planned by whom, and what counter-plots were devised.

On the surface what happened was clear enough. I shall therefore report first the official version of events.

But I shall not trouble myself to report the various omens of Gaius' approaching murder which were subsequently invented and believed. To do so would insult the intelligence of my readers. It's enough to say that there will always be such omens, even if nobody remarked them before the event they are supposed to have heralded.

It was a clear bright day in January. Just after noon, Gaius left the theatre where he had been watching his lover, or rather his former lover, Mnester, in rehearsal. He felt swimpish, the result of heavy drinking the night before. He couldn't decide whether to go to lunch. Leaving the theatre, he stopped in a colonnade of the palace to watch some boys practising the Trojan war dance for a performance they were due to give that evening. He applauded vigorously, and engaged them in conversation, all the while caressing their leader. Pleased to have pleased the Emperor, and delighted to find him in so genial a mood, they offered to perform again.

Caesonia, carrying little Julia Drusilla, now approached to enquire whether he was coming to eat. He suggested they first watch this second performance, and told her it would be to her taste. All were relaxed and happy; even his German bodyguard stood at ease, some distance away. Some senators joined the Emperor and, it is said, expressed their approval of the performance also.

At that moment Cassius Chaerea and Cornelius Sabinus, followed by a number of the Praetorians, marched up as if to enquire whether the Emperor had any orders for them.

Gaius made an impatient gesture, and told them to await his pleasure.

'Today, my lord, it is our pleasure,' Chaerea said and, as the Emperor turned his head surprised by this insolence, struck him in the throat with his short legionary's sword. Gaius fell to the ground, twitching, his jaw-bone split. 'I am still alive,' he cried out. They were his last words. One of the guardsmen, or perhaps Chaerea himself, thrust his blade through the Emperor's genitals. Another stabbed Caesonia, and one brute seized little Julia Drusilla, Gaius' adored daughter, and dashed her brains out against a wall. Then they turned and ran. Alarmed by the cries, the German bodyguard at last moved. The murderers had escaped, but they killed a few senators who stood about, open-mouthed and either aghast or delighted, nobody knows.

Well, that is what happened, and my narrative is probably accurate enough. I say 'probably' because I was not there.

Why wasn't I there? You may well wonder. Many did. Some believed or affected to believe that my absence proved that I was privy to the plot. Of those who thought this, a number later offered me their thanks and congratulations. I merely smiled. There is no point in correcting favourable opinions, however erroneous and unfounded they may be.

But of course I had no part in it. I might have misgivings about Gaius but, as Catullus had said, Roman generals don't mutiny. He was speaking ironically, but he spoke also what was in my mind. I couldn't bring myself to consent to Gaius' murder, or even to his deposition.

The night before he was killed, I attended a dinner-party given by the young poet, whose name I have withheld, in his apartment near the theatre of Pompey. We sat long, drank deep. It was late when I stepped out into the street, a night of frost, moonless. As I did so I was seized from behind by two ruffians whom I took for thieves. Then, a hand was pressed over my mouth to prevent me from calling out, and I knew no more.

When I came to I was lying on a bed in an unfamiliar room. My head ached. The room was dark and I did not know if it was day or night. I tried to get to my feet, and discovered that my wrists and ankles were bound and I was tied to the bed. I cried out, and there was no answer.

Later – how much later I could not tell, for I may have slept again – an old woman entered with a candle in her hand. She set it on a stool beside the bed and took a wet towel and mopped my forehead.

'That's a fair dunt they've given you,' she said.

Naturally I questioned her but she refused to answer.

'I just do what I'm told,' she said.

She dressed the wound on my head, and said she would fetch me some broth.

'At least,' I thought, 'they don't intend to kill me, whoever they are.'

She brought the broth, fed it to me with a horn spoon, then left me in darkness again.

The second time she came I tried to bribe her to release me, but she merely smiled. The third time I threatened her, and she smiled again. If she knew who I was, her indifference to my threats told me that she had a powerful protector.

I have always cultivated detachment. I had need of that now that my world was confined to this narrow room, this hard couch, this darkness. I did not know how long I had been there.

I woke to find the room awash with sunlight, the shutters thrown open, and for a moment could not see, being dazzled. My bonds had been cut. I felt that. Then I heard a familiar voice, my vision cleared, and I saw Catullus standing over me.

'Hope you haven't been too uncomfortable,' he said.

I tried to rise, felt dizzy and weak, fell back.

'Sorry,' he said, 'but it seemed the best thing.'

He called for the old woman to bring wine.

'You mustn't hold it against her,' he said. 'She's my old nurse, devoted to me, she is.'

XXII

I was weak as a new-born kitten till I had drunk some wine. Catullus smiled at me, even fondly.

'You'll think I've behaved disgracefully,' he said.

'I don't think anything,' I said.

'But I hope when I've explained you'll understand. Please take my word for it I have acted for the best, for your best interest. But you were too loyal to Gaius, we all agreed on that.'

'Were?'

'Yes, indeed, we have a new Emperor.'

'A new Emperor?'

'The divine Claudius. Let me explain.'

He was enjoying himself, which irritated me. Yet he was also nervous.

'Claudius? You're mad. And Gaius?'

'Dead. Murdered. Not by me, must make that clear. Though I won't say I didn't have foreknowledge of it. Listen.'

They hadn't, he said, arrived at a decision as to how to deal with Gaius. My arguments had impressed them. So they were still doubtful, still procrastinating. It was at this point that Catullus himself had been approached by a group of senators who first swore him to secrecy, and then revealed their plans. They were determined to restore the Republic.

'Well,' he said, 'you had convinced me that was impossible, but I didn't say so. I kept quiet.'

They told him of the disaffection of the two Praetorian colonels, Chaerea and Sabinus. They had agreed, for a con-sideration – 'a considerable consideration, I must say' – to act as the necessary swords. They had access to Gaius and were sure they could 'dispatch' him. As they did, 'no trouble at all'.

As soon as the news of his death was brought to them, these senators acquainted the consuls, and summoned a meeting of the Senate where they announced the end of imperial rule and the restoration of the Republic.

'They had reckoned without me,' Catullus said. 'I hadn't of course kept my word. As soon as they told me of their plans I went to Agrippina. Naturally she considered warning her brother, but Seneca who was there argued that the opportunity was too good to be lost. "If these people don't kill him tomorrow," he said, "then somebody else will do so soon." Agrippina agreed. She was ready to sacrifice her brother for, as she said, "the good of the Empire", by which she meant her family. "But," she said, "we must have a candidate for Emperor." I suggested you, I hope you don't mind. But she wasn't having that. It must be one of the imperial family. Well, there's only poor uncle Claudius. If you want my opinion, by the way, I would say that she regards him as a figurehead, a stop-gap till her own boy Nero is old enough to inherit. Not that she's said so. Mine is what you might call an intelligent guess. More wine?'

Catullus had been assigned the task of recruiting a number of loyal Praetorians who would secure the person of the Emperor-designate and make sure that he came to no harm.

'And where do I come in?' I said.

'You saved my life at the time of Gaeticulus' conspiracy,' he replied. 'Now it was my turn. The two colonels had instructions to kill you, along with Gaius. Perhaps you don't know just how unpopular your loyalty to him has made you with our class. I'm sorry to say that Agrippina was quite ready to let them do so. It took all my powers of persuasion to change her mind. Eventually she did so, but only after I argued that you might very well prevent her brother's murder by coming to his aid. So I promised I would get you out of the way – as I did.'

'Should I thank you?'

'Depends on how attached you are to life. It's a matter of indifference to me. The colonels incidentally have been arrested and dealt with. Not before they had been persuaded to name the senators who instigated the murder.'

'And Claudius is now Emperor. Truly?'

'I'm afraid so.'

'Grotesque.'

'You don't know how grotesque, my dear. It was all nearly bungled. Nobody had told him, you see. Well, naturally. Agrippina couldn't trust him not to blab.'

So, he said, there had been a rare comedy. When Claudius heard of his nephew's murder, he was terrified and hid behind a curtain in the palace. A guardsman who was passing by with his sword drawn, himself doubtless afraid and not knowing just what was going on, saw his feet sticking out below the curtain and pulled it aside. Claudius, convinced that he was about to be killed, fell to the ground and grabbed the soldier round the knees and begged him to spare his life. Then some other members of the Guard came up and recognised him and hustled him off to their camp, carrying him through the streets in a litter, and shutting their ears to his pitiful wails.

'Meanwhile,' Catullus said, 'we didn't know what had become of him and Agrippina was afraid that he might indeed have been killed. There were several to say that this was the case. The senators of course never thought of him. They were far too busy securing the Forum and the Capitol with the support of the city cohorts. For a little it did indeed seem as if our plans had miscarried. I tell you, it was a relief to get the news that the old fool was in the Praetorians' camp. All the same it was chancy, and I hurried there to see him and get him to promise each of the loyal Praetorians 150 gold pieces. Shameful, isn't it? Meanwhile Agrippina had organised support for him, getting some of her freedman – and that one of Gaius's called Narcissus, whom she had previously suborned – to infiltrate the crowd that was surging round the Senate-house and get them to demand that the brother of the hero Germanicus be named as Emperor. It won't surprise you to know that our brave Conscript Fathers panicked and gave way. So we have a new Emperor – Clau-Clau Claudius . . . What do you think of that?'

What could I say? That it was absurd?

'I congratulate you,' I said. 'What of Caesonia? Is she safe?'

Catullus sighed. 'I'm afraid not. The men who murdered Gaius killed her, and their little daughter. I'm sorry. That wasn't intended. She was in the wrong place at the wrong time, I'm afraid. But it wasn't intended.'

'No,' I said. 'I suppose not.'

Envoi

I mourned Caesonia and her poor infant. Perhaps she was the only woman I came close to loving truly. For years she came to me in dreams. My last wife, the mother of my children, left me when she heard me call out 'Caesonia', and mutter endearments to her.

Gaius? Perhaps I mourned him too, up to a point. I couldn't forget the enthusiasm with which he had spoken of his good intentions in the first weeks of his reign. I couldn't forget the little boy I had carried on my shoulders through the camp, and how he had crowed with glee.

Agrippina made a show of mourning her brother. His murderers had thrown his body into a ditch in the Lamian gardens. She saw to its proper cremation and the placing of an urn containing his ashes in a magnificent tomb. It wasn't, perhaps, entirely hypocritical. She denied her acquiesence in his murder, assured me, unprompted, that Catullus had lied. I did not believe her, said nothing in reply. Now I think that when in a letter, years later, she spoke of it as 'cruel necessity', she was not insincere. Gaius, she said, had to go, for the good of the Empire and the family. (She cannot, by the way, distinguish between them.) 'Our poor accursed family', she wrote. I would not disagree.

The people mourned Gaius. They had enjoyed his reign. They said, 'He was the one as cared for us.' In the poorest quarters of the city, they continued to celebrate his birthday. Why not? He did them no harm, presented them with magnificent spectacles.

For years it was said that his ghost haunted the Lamian

gardens. On starry nights his perturbed spirit could be heard howling to the moon goddess.

A curiosity: on the morning Gaius was murdered, a runaway slave challenged the priest of Diana at Nemi, and killed him.

Agrippina was determined from the first to dominate her uncle Claudius, both for her own satisfaction and to ensure the succession of her son Nero. She did not immediately dare to propose marriage which the law would have deemed incestuous. Instead she supplied the old slobbering pedant with a lively young wife, a girl of fifteen called Messalina, whom she was sure she could control. Naturally the poor girl soon tired of her elderly husband and took lovers, first secretly, then openly. One of them, I was amused to learn, was Gaius Caligula's old paramour, the actor Mnester. Another was my friend Catullus. He said she was 'remarkable', and enjoyed her, before concluding that the position of lover of the Emperor's wife was somewhat dangerous, and removing to Athens 'to study philosophy'. 'You know,' he told me, 'I was always a coward.'

Agrippina may well have encouraged Messalina's infidelities. Why not? They gave her power over her. She was less pleased when Messalina bore a son, whose paternity Claudius acknowledged. He named the boy Britannicus in honour of the conquest of part of the island of Britain. It was obvious to Agrippina that this little boy might be preferred to her son Nero as the next Emperor – if Claudius lived long enough.

Then Messalina embarked on an affair with a nobleman called Gaius Silius, who was then consul-designate. That was too much. Silius could not be thought of as politically insignificant. The regime was in danger, or so it seemed. So Agrippina saw to it that the guilty pair were denounced, and Claudius, though still doting on his darling young wife, was persuaded or compelled to agree that she was guilty of treason. So she was killed, as were her lover and another half-dozen young nobles who were accused of having shared the Empress's bed. When I heard the news I could only reflect that Catullus was wise to have run away to study philosophy.

This time Agrippina took no chances. Incest might be against the law, but if the only way she could be sure of controlling the Emperor and securing the succession for young Nero was by breaking that law, she would do so. Before he had emerged from the drinking bout into which he had plunged on being told that Messalina had betrayed him, Claudius' fate was determined. Bleary-eyed and trembling, he married his niece, and found himself subject to her rigorous, almost masculine, despotism.

I observed all this from a distance.

A few days after Claudius' accession, I had received this letter from him.

> While appreciative of the loyalty you have displayed to our family over thirty years, it is our wish and our command that you remove yourself from Rome, and indeed from Italy. You are in the view of ourself and our advisers too closely connected in the public eye with the iniquities of our nephew, the late Emperor. It is for your own safety as well as for the common weal of the Republic that we issue you with this our command, our sentence of exile.

It was Catullus who delivered the letter to me.

I said, 'Agrippina dictated this. The bitch.'

'In a manner, yes. But it's not as you think. The fact is, our new Emperor hates you. He's been jealous of you for years. He can't forget how his adored brother Germanicus used to sing your praises at a time when the poor thing would have given his eye-teeth for a single word of praise from the same quarter. And since then, in his view, you have never failed to humiliate him. The truth is, you are everything he would have wished to be, and in his heart knows he isn't. Actually, if he had had his way, this would have been a sentence of death, not exile. It was all we could do, Agrippina and myself, to talk him out of it. Mostly Agrippina, I have to admit. I don't have much influence myself. I'm sorry, I'll miss you.'

The next day I had a second letter, this from Seneca, writing, as he informed me, on instructions from the Divine Claudius. (How he must have relished ascribing the fool a divinity in which he didn't for a moment believe.) My place of exile, he explained, was appointed as Tomi on the shores of the Euxine.

> For myself [he added in a personal note attached], while regretting the necessity of your departure, I cannot but find some consolation in the reflection that your place of exile is that appointed for the poet Ovid, where he wrote his *Tristia*. I have no doubt we may look for some comparable work from your pen, but one less redolent of self-pity and expressing a more robust philosophy. Yet even this will be poor recompense for the loss I shall suffer in being deprived of your company and conversation. Meanwhile, be assured that I, in concert with your other friends, shall be unremitting in efforts to persuade the Divine Claudius to rescind this sentence of banishment.

Unremitting or not, it was three years before that happy day arrived, years in which, like Ovid, I endured that miserable climate and the tedium of uncivilised neighbours, often sighing, like the greater poet Virgil, 'O Jupiter, give me back the time I have lost.'

In the end it was, I suppose, Agrippina who made my return possible, though with the proviso that I was barred from public life.

That was no hardship. I had seen too much.

And now she requires this memoir of poor Gaius?

Can I contrive a sanitised version?

One that presents her in a wholly admirable role, an entirely favourable light?

Let us see.

Poor Gaius . . . how he would have resented and despised that peculiar act of meanness on Claudius' part – the order, in the first days of his reign, that the poor horse Incitatus be killed. And why?

Because Gaius said once: 'You are quite right. It was a mistake to make my poor uncle a consul. Incitatus would certainly have been a better choice.'